DEVIL'S ROPE

Reader Comments On McCathern Books

Recently, I purchased your book Horns, at a visit to Canyon. You were kind enough to autograph it for me, and I must say, I have enjoyed it as much as anything I have ever read! --Tim Zimmerman

The first book (Horns) I thoroughly enjoyed, the second (Dry Bones) I couldn't put down. I can't wait for the third one! -- Richard Opperud

I purchased all three of your novels, Horns, Dry Bones, and Quarantine in Palo Duro Canyon, and I must say that I haven't enjoyed reading this much in a very long time. I usually spend my lunch breaks watching TV but since I started reading your books, that is all I have been interested in. --

Both my husband and I enjoyed your book Horns. We can't wait to receive the other books. -- Darla Criswell

I recently purchased your book Horns for my husband. He has never enjoyed a book as much as this one. Thanks. -- Cheryl Shepherd Grothe

I hope you are working on another book after Devil's Rope. I have never been so interested in reading as I have since I purchased your books. -- Kathy Rhea

Author!! Author!! Author!! Just this moment finished Dry Bones. Had to sit down and let you know how much I enjoyed this book. It is every bit as enjoyable as Horns and maybe more so. Thank you! -- Earl J. Gorel, Houston

I have enjoyed both your exciting books, Horns and Dry Bones. Very interesting! -- Jason Connel, Oklahoma

I have just finished reading Horns, and enjoyed every minute of it. It touched every part of me so much that I haven't picked up Dry Bones for fear my red eyes will never disappear! -- Katherine Tinney, New York

I recently purchased your book, Quarantine. I must say, as a Robin Cook fan, that it is as good as any he has ever written. -- Rodney Thompson, Florida

Devil's Rope

This is a work of fiction, based on actual historical events and characters.

ISBN No. 0-9656946-5-8
First Printing June, 2001
Second Printing, 2003

Published by Outlaw Books
419 Centre Street
Hereford, TX 79045

Phone 806-364-2838
FAX 806-364-5522
Web Page outlawbooks.net
e-mail gmccath@wtrt.net

Acknowledgements

Thanks to all those writers of history who have preserved the events and the lives of the people of the old west for our education and enjoyment--especially writers such as J. Evetts Haley (*Charles Goodnight, Cowman and Plainsman*); C.L. Douglas (*Cattle Kings of Texas*); J. Frank Dobie (*The Longhorns*); Pauline Durrett Robertson and R.L. Robertson (*Panhandle Pilgrimage*); Fredric R. Young, (*Dodge City*); Sallie Harris (Hidetown); Glenn Shirley (Temple Houston, Lawyer With a Gun): J.Evetts Haley (The XIT Ranch of Texas); Dulcie Sullivan (The LS Brand).

I highly recommend these books to readers who are interested in western history.

I also wish to thank the Panhandle Plains Historical Museum in Canyon, Texas, whose archives are full of authenticated historical documents of the old west, which were invaluable in telling the story of *Devil's Rope*.

And to Delbert Trew, curator of the Devil's Rope Museum, my thanks for information on the history of barbed wire.

A special thanks to my editor, Virginia Lee, for smoothing the rough spots of *Devil's Rope*, to Leon Murray for the cover art, and to Cathleen Baldauf for her excellent work in designing the cover.

And a special thanks to all of my reader friends who urged me to continue the story of Cole and Armstrong, their fictional ranch, Ceebara, and their association with all of the noted historical figures who were involved in the settling of the *Llano Estacado*.

Gerald McCathern

Dedicated to Mary Kate Tripp -- a dear personal friend, and friend of many struggling authors, without whose help we would have remained unknown. Her encouragement and book reviews in the Amarillo Sunday News-Globe have given us courage to continue our writings.

DEVIL'S ROPE

an Outlaw Books Publication

Commentary

Enclosing the vast prairie grasslands with barbed wire did not come without provocation. Some saw only the injury to livestock saying it was the work of the Devil and called it " The Devil's Rope." Those who had grazed the ranges for years without paying compensation could foresee the end of their way of life. Travelers and trail drivers found the prickly barrier blocking their journeys and unscrupulous land owners often fenced in more than their rightful share of the bountiful prairies.

The significance of barbed wire can best be described with the word "change." From chaos, disorder, and a nomadic way of living, barbed wire became the great equalizer allowing each man, no matter how big or how small, to mark his spot and valiantly defend it to the death. These simple barriers eventually created a pride of ownership of land unequaled throughout the rest of the world.

But in the end, with all prejudice put aside, barbed wire is just a simple tool to be used at its owner's whim, and that is all it can be. *Delbert Trew -- Devil's Rope Museum -McLean, Texas.*

* * *

The Devil's Rope Museum, located on historic Route 66 in McLean, Texas, is the largest barbed wire historical museum in the world, established in 1990.

For additional information on the history of barbed wire, log on to // barbwiremuseum.com

Devil's Rope Principal Characters

Historical Characters

Charles Goodnight
Temple Houston
Deacon Bates
Cap Arrington
Billy the Kid
Quanah Parker
Billy Dixon
Casimiro Romero
Tom Bugbee
Mark Husleby
Jack Ryan
Tom Harris
Henry Kimball
Bat Masterson
W.M.D. Lee
George Littlefield
Outlaw Bill Moore

Fictional Characters

Ned Armstrong
Kate Armstrong
Cole Armstong
Belle Cole
Jim Bold Eagle
Smokey Brown
Manuel Garcia
Sonny McArdle
Bart, Concho, Red
Vince Abercrombie

Foreword

The Red River Indian wars have been fought, the Indian tribes have been defeated and pushed from the *Llano Estacado* and relegated to the reservations in Oklahoma Indian Territory. The huge buffalo herds have been slaughtered, and hundreds of thousands of longhorn cattle have been trailed in to take their place.

Huge ranches have been established by the Texas cattle barons along the Canadian and Red Rivers -- Goodnight's JA, Bugbee's Quarter Circle T, Cole and Armstrong's C Bar A, Littlefield's LIT, Lee's LS, Reynold's LE, Bates and Beal's LX, and Creswell's Bar CC.

Two of the wildest towns in the west have taken root, Mobeetie and Tascosa, and in this forty thousand square mile area of free grazing, prairie land, the only law is the law of the Colt revolver and the Winchester rifle. With the ranchers and cowboys have come the gamblers, gun slingers, outlaws, cattle rustlers, prostitutes -- and the boot hill cemeteries.

There has never been a survey of the Texas Panhandle, and even though maps show twenty-six counties, no one knows where one county begins and the other ends. Wheeler County, finally organized in 1876, with Mobeetie designated the County Seat, has the remaining twenty-five counties attached for legal purposes. By the beginning of the year 1880, there is only one Sheriff, one Judge, and one District Attorney to uphold the law in this wild, forty thousand square mile area.

It is in this environment that Colonel Jim Cole and his young side-kick, Ned Armstrong are struggling to build their ranching empire, the million acre Ceebara Ranch. They had been the first cattlemen to put down roots in the area after the Civil War, and had made friends with Quanah Parker and the Comanches before the buffalo hunters began to slaughter the huge herds.

Now, the Indians and most of the buffalo are gone -- and another war is being waged -- who will control the free grazing lands of the *Llano Estacado.*

Colonel Cole, killed in a gun battle on the streets of Dodge City, has been brought back to the ranch on Red Deer Creek for burial. Friends, including Quanah Parker and Charles Goodnight, have traveled by buckboard and horseback for hundreds of miles to attend the funeral and pay their last respects.

This is the story of Ned's, Belle's and Kate's struggle to hold the ranch together, the coming of age of Ned's son, Cole -- and just a few of the activities of the historical characters who were involved in changing the last frontier in the State of Texas into the greatest cattle grazing country in the world.

1

The sound of the first shovels of dirt echoed hollowly as they fell on the pine box which held the body of Colonel Jim Cole, one armed patriarch of the Ceebara Ranch. The colonel had been gunned down by outlaws on the streets of Dodge City, when he, Ned, Bat Masterson and Billy Dixon had attempted to arrest them for rustling Ceebara cattle. Cowboys continued the sad work until a neat mound of yellow earth covered the remains of their beloved leader in the small, family cemetery just a short distance from the ranch house and overlooking the valley of the Red Deer Creek.

Neighbors and friends walked dejectedly away from the grave, climbed into buggies and wagons and started their long journeys back to surrounding ranches which were located along the Canadian and Red Rivers in the sparsely settled Texas Panhandle.

Those who had traveled great distances to show their respect to the colonel and his family, would remain another night before starting their journey homeward. Bat Masterson,

Billy Dixon, and Vince Abercrombie would accompany the Honor Guard from Fort Dodge back to Dodge City. General Mackenzie, his aids and Quanah Parker would travel together back to Fort Sill. Jim Bold Eagle, Quanah's son, would remain at the ranch for an extended visit with young Cole, the Colonel's grandson.

Belle, Kate, Ned and Cole were the last to leave the grave site, each silently saying their last goodbyes to their beloved "Colonel." Although he tried hard, Cole could not hold back the tears, and his fourteen year old body shook uncontrollably as he sought comfort in his mother's arms.

Kate held him tightly as she said, "We're all going to miss your grandad, son, but I know he would want you to be strong during this time. Remember all of the good times you had together, and remember the things he taught you. Your Pa is going to have to step into Grandad's boots now and that means that you are going to have to take your Pa's place in keeping the ranch going. It's going to be hard but I know you can do it."

"I'll try my best," Cole said through his sobs.

They turned and walked arm in arm back to the ranch house.

* * * * * * * *

The Kid, watching from the cliff above, turned and sadly mounted his steel dust dun. The only two people of influence who had ever treated him like he was worth something, Colonel Cole and Mr. Tunstall, had both been killed by the gun, and now he was wanted by the law for shooting Mr. Tunstall's killer. He would have liked to have ridden down to the ranch house and joined Ned and the family during this time of sorrow, but with so many people around, he knew that it would only bring trouble to them. He turned the dun towards Tascosa and kicked him into a ground-eating trot.

Reaching the lawless frontier town as the stage from Fort Elliot was unloading, he watched as another load of painted ladies from Mobeetie disembarked. Since the organization of Wheeler County and the election of a judge and sheriff, a small semblance of law and order had been established in Mobeetie and many of the town's five hundred prostitutes and gamblers were looking for greener pastures. Tascosa seemed like an ideal place to set up shop.

To call them whores or prostitutes could result in one staring into the double barreled chamber of a small derringer pistol or having a whiskey bottle broken over one's head. They considered themselves entertainers, consequently, the cowboys and buffalo hunters preferred to refer to them as painted ladies -- and the girls voiced no objection.

The town was bustling with activity, for only an hour before arrival of the stage, another group had arrived. A state surveyor by the name of Munson, along with a large group of workmen and five Texas Rangers, was on his way to Buffalo Springs on the northernmost border of the Texas Panhandle. From the Springs, they planned to travel due west until they located the stake designating the corner of the Oklahoma Strip, New Mexico Territory and Texas. The stake had been set by John Clark when he made a survey of the Oklahoma

Strip in 1858. From that point, they intended to start their survey, south and east, of the twenty six counties which would make up the area of the unorganized Texas Panhandle. The survey would be the first nail driven into the coffin which would carry the wild Texas Panhandle into the Boot Hill Cemetery of the lawless past. The land and its people, however, would not bow to this passage peacefully.

The Kid joined the members of the surveying party as they crowded into the Equity Bar, adobe saloon of Jack Ryan, not realizing that five members of the party were Texas Rangers. He listened as Munson explained their mission, to make the survey in order that the twenty six counties could eventually be organized. The cowboys, gathered around the bar, realized that once organization took place, law and order would come, putting a damper on the wild entertainment that Tascosa had to offer -- and with it, the end of free grazing on State lands.

They were not too overwhelmed with agreement as they began to discuss the possibilities among themselves.

"First thing you know," one of them voiced, "we'll have a sheriff and judge and they'll be wanting to close down the Equity and make it illegal for us to even have the gals in town. Since Mobeetie now has a sheriff, no one can have any fun there anymore without worryin' about getting arrested for disturbing the peace."

"Outlaw" Bill Moore, foreman of the LX, added his disappointment. "Once the counties have been surveyed, the next thing that's going to happen is the Governor's going to say all this grass that's feeding our 'horns belongs to the State and that'll be the end of the LX, LS, LE, C Bar A, and JA and we'll all be out of work."

Deacon Bates, owner of the LX, standing next to Moore, looked around and in a voice loud enough to be heard in the entire room, said, "Now listen, men. This country belongs to us that first set claim to it. If the state comes in and tries to take it from us, they'll have a war on their hands."

Cowboys crowding the room, thundered their agreement.

Munson, seeing that his crew was in danger of being tarred and feathered and run out of town, tried to smooth over the reasons for the survey, although he, himself, had requested that the rangers accompany him on the venture for protection from hot heads such as these. "You boys got it all wrong," he said. "The state ain't going to take the grass from you -- what could they do with it, seven hundred miles from Austin. You'll still have your ranches and maybe it'll be a little easier to tell where one ranch begins and the other ends."

As one of the men, standing next to the Kid, turned to him to offer a comment, his rangers badge flashed in the dim light. "Say," he spoke, "Ain't I met you somewhere before?"

"Probably not," the Kid said, looking him square in the eye, "unless you been spending some time over in New Mexico Territory."

"That's it!" the ranger said, "I seen a poster with your face on it over in Fort Sumner when I was trying to find a half-breed that had killed a nester family down by the Yellow Houses."

The Kid's hand released the glass of beer and slid slowly downward towards his holstered Colt.

"Now wait a minute, friend," the ranger said as he saw the movement. "We got plenty of troubles over here in Texas just trying to take care of our own law. I ain't seen no posters saying you're wanted in Texas -- and New Mexico can take care of their own problems. Besides, if I tried to arrest everyone in Tascosa who might have done something illegal, I'd have to arrest the whole damned town."

The Kid relaxed, smiled and said, "Now that's right neighborly, friend. How about me buying you a drink?"

"Arrington," the ranger said, shoving his hand forward, "Cap Arrington. You buy it, I'll drink it."

The Kid took the hand in a friendly handshake, "Bonney," he replied, "Billy Bonney. But most folks just call me Kid."

* * * * * * * *

Munson had not been totally honest with the men in the saloon, whether knowingly or unknowingly. Politicians in Austin had been eying the Panhandle for a couple of years as the answer to one of their major problems. The Civil War had left the state destitute and the treasury had been drained dry. A new state capitol building was in dire need, the old one being a "fire-trap," as one Senator had so aptly described it. But, alas, there were no funds to construct a new building.

The Republic of Texas became a state in 1845. It was the only state allowed to reserve all of the public land as State land, rather than Federal land. A smart move on the part of the founding fathers of the largest state in the Union, since most of the land had never been purchased or filed upon by settlers.

Texas was land rich and dollar poor!

In April of 1879, the state legislature had passed legislation designating three million acres of ranch land in far northwest Texas to be reserved for barter in the construction of a new state capitol building. The reservation, stretching for two hundred miles along the New Mexico Territory border, had an average east-west depth of twenty seven miles. Beginning at the northwest corner of the Texas Panhandle and lying south , it would entail most of nine counties and a small part of the tenth -- and would include many of the new ranches which had been established along the New Mexico border.

The legislators could care less if the reservation would cause hardship on the established ranches. They needed a new state house, and this was land owned by the state.

The purpose of the Munson survey at this time was to officially map the twenty six counties of the Panhandle, in order that the Capitol Reservation Land could be described and designated, and bids could be advertised for the swapping of the land for the new state capitol building.

So much for the free grazing. The cowboys had good reason to be wary of the surveying party.

With the ranch owners and cowboys unaware of the long range plans, the Munson party embarked from Tascosa, less any tar and feathers, and proceeded to Buffalo Springs to begin the tremendous surveying job.

* * * * * * *

"I'm taking the boys to Hide Town for a load of supplies," Ned announced to Kate, as he buckled his gun belt around his waist. He continued to call the settlement next to Fort Elliot by it's original name instead of the new name of Mobeetie, changed to satisfy the postal authorities.

"Now you be careful, Ned, and keep those two young'uns away from them wild women and them cussing hunters and gamblers," Kate responded. She hated to see Cole and Bold Eagle even close to Hide Town because of its reputation as being the wildest and bloodiest town in the west. She realized, however, that the boys were getting old enough that she couldn't always protect them from the sins of the world -- and it *was* the nearest place they had of getting supplies for the ranch.

The boys were already at the horse corral catching their horses and laughing at the prospect of a new adventure.

"Chief," Cole said as he threw his lariat accurately over the head of his favorite horse, *Comanche*. "You ain't going to believe it, but there's more pretty girls in Hide Town than there is cowboys, soldiers and buffalo hunters altogether."

Cole had tacked the name of *Chief* onto Jim Bold Eagle when they were no more than eight years old because of his Indian blood, besides, it was just easier to say. Actually, Chief's father, Quanah Parker had named him after Cole's grandfather, Jim Cole. The two boys had spent a lot of time together, riding their ponies up and down Red Deer Creek, hunting small game with bows and arrows and exploring the hills and canyons which surrounded the ranch. They had been on cattle drives to Dodge City together even before they were teenagers. Now they were fourteen years old and believed that they were men.

When a band of renegade Indians had bolted the reservation, slipped into Ceebara headquarters at night and had stolen meat and kidnapped Cole, Chief had helped his father, Quanah, rescue him. When his mother, Morning Star had been killed in the raid, Chief had remained on the ranch for a year, learning the ways of the white man, and he and Cole had become as close as brothers.

In response to Cole's statement about the pretty girls, Chief smiled awkwardly, and asked, "Maybe they be as pretty as the Indian girls on the reservation?"

"Prettier!" Cole emphasized, rolling his eyes the way he had seen some of the cowboys look when they were talking about their escapades with the painted ladies.

They changed the subject quickly when Ned appeared, uncoiling his rope to catch the pack mule.

* * * * * * * *

The ride from the ranch headquarters to Mobeetie was made below the caprock along rolling hills which were covered with thick mats of gramma and buffalo grass. Now and again they would top one of the hills to surprise small herds of grazing buffalo, which lowered their heads and in their awkward gate, disappeared over the next hill.

Sunlight bounced off the face of the caprock, turning the white sandstone to a deep golden color. Red and gray clays below the sandstone blended with the deep green of the grass and scattered cedar trees, to add to the beauty of the scene.

"Boys," Ned said, "ain't this about the prettiest country you ever did see?"

The boys were far more interested in the buffalo and antelope than they were in the topography of the country they were traveling through. "Sure, Pa," Cole replied as he winked at Chief.

Gunfire could be heard long before they topped the last rise at the outskirts of Mobeetie. That wasn't unusual, because Mobeetie had the reputation of harboring some of the toughest gunfighters in the west -- and they were quick to kill for the hand of a woman or a turn of the cards.

Holding his hand up, Ned motioned for the boys to stop. Listening, there would be three or four shots, then a short period of silence before another group of shots could be heard.

"Don't sound like a gun battle or some drunk cowboys whooping it up. Beats me what's going on. You boys stay back behind and we'll ride in slow like. No need in us getting caught in the middle of something we can't get out of," he instructed.

As they reached the top of the rise, they could see down Main Street, which was filled on both sides with onlookers as two men stood in the middle of the street, pistols drawn -- and shooting at tin cans which were being tossed into the air by a third man!

Mobeetie, like most frontier towns of the time, consisted of one main street of businesses -- a hotel, blacksmith, mercantile, and thirteen saloons. On either side of Main Street, homes of assorted sizes and shapes had sprung up -- from rock structures, adobe, picket, tents and occasional buffalo hide lean-to.

Ned and the two boys rode slowly into town, stopped in front of the J.J. Long General Merchandise store, dismounted and tied their horses to the hitching rail. Joining the crowd, they watched as Mark Huselby, owner of the hotel, tossed a tin can into the air as one of the shooters quickly drew his pistol and fired four shots, hitting the flying can four times before it fell to the street.

The crowd applauded and shouted their support. "Way to go, Temple!" -- "At-a-boy, Temple, you showed him that time."

The gunman who was receiving the accolades, removed his Stetson, and bowed as if performing on a stage. Dressed immaculately in black frock coat, white shirt, black string tie, and black trousers which were tucked into high topped boots. Twirling a pearl handled Colt revolver on his finger, in one motion, he slipped it easily back into its holster.

"Good shooting, Houston," his opponent said. "I guess the drinks are on me, ain't no way I can best you on that one."

The shooting contest was the result of a good natured argument which had taken place in the Lady Gay Saloon between those who believed that Houston was the better marksman and those who believed that Curley was the best.

Temple placed his arm around the shoulders of his opponent as they turned and walked towards the swinging doors of the saloon. Smiling, he said, "Well Curley, I'll say one thing -- you danged sure made me earn it. You're the best shot

I've been up against in many a day."

As Temple and Curley approached, Ned turned to Cole and said, "Take this list down to the mercantile and tell Tom to start filling it, and maybe add a couple of chunks of licorice for you and the Chief."

"Aw, Pa, we'd druther go with you into the Lady Gay and talk to Mr. Houston," Cole said. And licorice! He and Chief had been experimenting with chewing tobacco, he was fourteen and almost grown, and he wished his pa would tell him to ask Mr. Tom for some chewing tobacco.

"You know what your Ma said, Son. She'd hang and quarter me if she found out I took you into one of these sin holes," Ned said, smiling as Temple walked up.

"Well, howdy Ned. Didn't see you come into town. Guess you saw the little shooting match me and Curley just had. He owes me a drink, come on in and join us." Spying Cole and Chief, he shook their hands and said, "How's my two favorite cowpokes?"

"We're doing just fine, Mr. Houston, but we'd be doing some better if Pa'd take us inside with you and the rest of the men."

Temple laughed. He could see himself in this young cowboy, no more than seven years ago, when he decided to make a name for himself.

* * * * * * * *

Old Sam's boy! That was what they called him. It was never by his real name. Old Sam, his father had died when he was only five years old, but he could remember the tales Sam Houston had told him about his adventures on the frontier after he left home at the age of fourteen, lived with the Cherokees as the adopted son of Chief Oolooteka, learning the Cherokee language and receiving the Cherokee name of *Raven*.

As Old Sam lay dying in Huntsville, he took pride in his youngest son, Temple, who sat by his bedside and listened enthralled to his tales about his escapades.

"Tell me again about the General, Papa," he would say. And Old Sam would relate how he had joined General Andy Jackson's frontier army after leaving his Cherokee family. He told about moving up in the ranks from private to lieutenant in less than six months, how he was wounded three times in the battle against the Creeks during the Indian wars, how he was wounded in the Battle of New Orleans when the General and his small rag-tag army had defeated the British in 1812, how the General, himself, had decorated him for his bravery and had taken him to his plantation, *The Hermitage*, in Tennessee and nursed him back to health.

Even at five years old, Temple was interested in Old Sam's tales of his entry into Tennessee politics. "Books! That's the key, boy," his father would say. "I learned to read at an early age, and I'd read anything I could get my hands on, from Greek and Roman history to the Holy Bible. And while I was healing from my wounds at the Hermitage, I was able to study the law and received my law degree in less than six months. I'm not going to be around to help you, son, so always remember, if you want to be a leader, you've got to have two things -- book learning and horse sense!"

Even on his death bed, the hard drinking old politician instructed young Temple to pour him another drink from the bottle of bourbon which was sitting on the table next to his bed.

Continuing, he said, "It was the law that did it for me in politics. The folks in Tennessee elected me to Congress for two terms, and when the General was elected President of the United States, they elected me as Governor of the state. Me and the General were as close as two peas in a pod in those days."

Young Temple was more interested in Sam's association with the Cherokees and his reasons for leaving Tennessee and coming to Texas than he was in the story of his Washington, D.C. adventures. "Tell me about going back to live with the Indians, Papa," he would say.

"Well, Son," the old man would say, "When the folks in Tennessee couldn't see my side of an affair with a young lady, I resigned my position as Governor and returned to my Cherokee father, Chief Oolooteka. That was when the government was trying to push the Cherokees out of their home land and onto reservations in Arkansas Territory. The Cherokee Nation appointed me as ambassador to the U.S., and I spent a lot of time in Washington representing my adopted people."

Chuckling as he reminisced, Old Sam added. "Those high and mighty folks in Washington City were downright embarrassed when I'd show up at their shindigs dressed in my Cherokee regalia. But one thing for damned sure, they could always pick me out of the crowd. Remember that, boy. In politics, you got to be different from the crowd if you want to be remembered."

As they talked in the sick room, surrounded by memorabilia of the dying father's unbelievable life, the young boy would look at each of the artifacts -- his medals from his army career, pistols and rifles which he had carried in war and peace, flags of the United States and the Republic of Texas, Indian headdresses, his buckskin jacket with the flying raven embroidered on the back, the sword which he had worn into battle at San Jacinto when he and his rag-tag army of Texas patriots defeated General Santa Anna and his Mexican army, and the silver adorned saddle that the Mexican General had ridden when he overran the Alamo and killed Travis, Bowie, Crockett and hundreds of brave Texans.

"Tell me again, Papa, about the sword, and the saddle, and how you became the first President of the Republic of Texas, and Governor and Senator of the State of Texas," the excited youngster would ask as he picked up the huge sword which rested on a chair next to the dying hero's bed and climbed onto the Mexican saddle which was mounted on a wooden pedestal in the corner of the room.

Old Sam, weak from so much story telling, closed his eyes and softly replied, "No more stories tonight, son, we'll talk some more tomorrow."

But tomorrow never came, for the Father of Texas -- General, President, Governor, Senator -- died quietly in his sleep before the sun rose above the pine trees which surrounded his East Texas home at Huntsville.

For nine years after his father's death, Temple was

known as *Old Sam's boy*. Politicians, neighbors and friends when they came to visit were quick to refer to him as *Old Sam's boy*. Even though he was very proud of his father, he resented the name they had tacked on him. *He was Temple Houston! And he intended to walk in his own boots, not those of his father!*

Determined to someday make a name for himself as did his father, when he was barely fourteen years old, he packed a few necessities in his saddle bags, buckled his father's pearl handled revolver to his waist, shoved a nearly new repeating Winchester rifle into the saddle boot, mounted his favorite horse and headed west. Remembering Old Sam's advice, he packed a couple of books, Blackstone's Law Guide and the Holy Bible, in his bags before leaving. In the next two years, he would spend many lonely hours pouring over those two books, usually from the light of a campfire surrounded by a few cowboys who would beg him to read a few more chapters.

Unlike many of the poor and hungry East Texas boys who left their fathers' cotton patches to become cowboys in West Texas, Temple was well fed, well dressed, well mounted and well armed -- but he had that hunger for excitement and adventure that most fourteen-year-olds of the time possessed.

Tall for his age and an excellent horseman, he had no problem finding a job with a rancher who was putting together a herd of longhorns to drive to Montana. Most of the trail hands who became the nucleus of this new industry were just rawboned kids like Temple. A quick learner, he soon became the favorite of his new boss, pulling any duty he was asked to perform without complaint, whether it was riding point or bringing up drag in the dust. And he was a favorite of the other cowboys, keeping them entertained around the campfire with tales of his father's exploits or quoting passages from some of the classics which he had read. He expected no favoritism because he was the son of the great Sam Houston, and was quick with his fists if anyone insinuated that he might be less than a man. No one called him *Old Sam's Boy*, anymore -- in his own right he became Temple Houston, cowboy extraordinary!

He continually practiced with a lariat as he rode the fringes of the herd, becoming adept at snagging the horns of the cattle which tried to wander away. When he wasn't twirling the lariat, he was practicing fast drawing the pearl handled revolver strapped to his waist which he nicknamed "Old Betsy." Any time he was far enough away from the herd that there was no danger of scaring them into a stampede, he would quickly pull "Old Betsy" from its holster and shoot a running jack rabbit or coyote -- or clip a cactus or mesquite limb if there was no unlucky animal to practice on. He became an excellent shot before the herd arrived in Montana, three months, and hundreds of adventures, later.

Drawing his pay in Montana, his lust for adventure prevailed and he headed east on his horse, riding to the Missouri River where he sold horse and saddle and boarded a river boat which was headed downstream. The Missouri joined the Mississippi and thirty days later, Temple arrived in New Orleans. He spent his time on this leisurely journey learning to gamble with the river boat gamblers and perfecting his ability with Old Betsy by entertaining passengers, shooting turtles off of logs and birds out of the air.

Before he reached his fifteenth birthday, he arrived in New Orleans and looked up an old friend of his father's who was serving as Congressman from Louisiana. Using his influence, the Congressman secured an appointment for him as a Page in the U.S. Congress in Washington City. He loved to listen to the debates on the floor of Congress between some of the greatest speakers of the times. He studied and was determined to someday debate as well.

After two years of this educational process, he returned to Texas and enrolled in the newly opened Texas Agricultural and Mechanical College. After only one year, he transferred to Baylor University to study law, and after only nine months, was able to take and pass the law exam.

Applying for his certificate to practice law, he learned that Texas law required a person to be twenty-one years of age in order to be eligible. Undaunted, he used the influence of his dead father to secure the aid of several of the men on the board and suggested that since most of the men applying for their certificate at that time were well over the age of twenty one, by averaging the age of the entire group, they would exceed the required age -- and for the first and only time in the history of Texas law, the entire group of applicants were approved on the basis of their *average age*. Temple Houston became a practicing attorney at the age of eighteen!

It did not take him long to make a name for himself, setting up a private practice in San Felipe, near the San Jacinto battle site, and when a District Attorney was needed in the new Wheeler County District in the Texas Panhandle, he received the blessing of the head of the Supreme Court and the Governor of Texas to fill that position. Before he was twenty one years of age, Temple Houston rode into the wild and tough town of Mobeetie to start his political career as district attorney over the entire twenty-six unsettled counties in the Texas Panhandle.

* * * * * * *

After sharing a drink with Temple and Curley in the Lady Gay Saloon, Ned told Temple that he needed to visit with him in private. Smiling, Temple said, "Most of my business begins at that table in the corner."

Motioning for Ned to follow, he pushed through the crowd and took a seat at a table which was isolated from the others in a dark corner of the saloon. "What's on your mind?" he asked as Ned took a chair next to him.

Pushing his hat to the back of his head, Ned wiped the dust and sweat from his brow and said. "Rustling! It's got completely out of hand, Temple. We ranchers have put together an association to try to stamp it out, but the area is just too large and there's too many cowboy's putting their brands on other people's cattle for us to have much success. We've run a bunch of them out of the country, but for everyone that leaves, there's half a dozen to take their place. With over two hundred thousand cattle running loose across these plains, and herds getting mixed and no way to keep them counted, rustlers could be taking as many as ten thousand head a year."

Temple whistled. "That many, huh? How do they get rid of them?"

"We've trailed some of them into New Mexico Territory, some have been driven to Dodge City and sold to eastern buyers," then, shaking his head, Ned added, "and I hate to say it, but it looks like some of the missing cattle are being rustled by one or more of the established ranchers."

"That's a pretty strong accusation, Ned. Have you got any proof?"

"We've found some cows that looks like they've had their brands changed with a running iron. But I've kept it quiet -- an open accusation against one of our own members could erupt in a range war that could spread across the whole Texas Panhandle."

"Care to tell me who's brand?" Temple asked.

"I'd rather not at this point, Temple. Soon as I get some hard evidence, I'll let you know."

"Well, Ned, the governor sent me up here to prosecute the criminals, and I don't care who they are, if they're guilty, I'll damn sure prosecute 'em if you'll figure a way to catch 'em," the young lawyer replied. "I doubt Sheriff Fleming will have any time to be chasing rustlers all over the country, there's enough crime going on here in Mobeetie to keep ten sheriffs busy. What we need is a company of Texas Rangers but I don't expect Austin is going to see fit to spend any money north of Fort Worth!"

"Problem is, Temple, there's a strong push for a vigilante committee to take care of the problem -- and you know what that means, once the vigilantes take over, a hemp rope and a strong limb on a cottonwood tree will do the prosecuting. That won't leave much prosecuting for you to do!"

Temple removed his hat and brushed his long black hair back with his hand, nodded his head in agreement before replying. "I'm kinder new at the job, Ned, but the way I understand the law, those vigilantes would be breaking the law same as the rustlers and if we catch them in the act, I'd have to prosecute them for hanging folks without a proper trial."

Ned smiled at that statement. "You might have a harder time finding the vigilantes than finding the rustlers," he said.

Their conversation was interrupted by shouting coming from the street. They rushed outside and pushed their way through the crowd to where four of the towns local tough kids were warily circling Cole and Chief. The two young Ceebara cowboys, chaps flapping and spurs shining, stood back to back, fists balled and eying the circling toughs.

"He ain't nothing but a dirty injun," the leader of the group, a kid nick-named Snake because of his slender build, shouted, "Step aside, Armstrong, we intend to take his scalp."

Cole, undaunted, raised his fists a little higher, and replied, "You'll have to take mine first, Snake."

Temple started to step in and put a stop to the confrontation when Ned touched his arm. "Let's wait a mite, Temple. I think the boys can take care of themselves."

Snake moved in and swung a looping right towards Cole's chin. Cole ducked and countered with an upper-cut that landed solidly on Snake's nose and sent him sprawling into the dusty street. The nose began to gush blood.

The other three made a lunge for the two boys who still

stood back to back. Chief, head tucked between his shoulders, caught the first with a quick left jab to the eye, then brought his right around in a blur which landed on the tough's chin with a crack. The kid fell in a heap and didn't move.

Now it was one on one and Cole and Chief moved in, fists flying to belly and face. They made short work of the remaining two, who turned tail and ran for the nearest alley.

Looking at Snake, who still lay on the ground trying to stop the blood from flowing from his nose, Cole said, with his fists still clenched. "Chief's my friend, Snake, and I don't ever want to hear you or your bunch of hooligans calling him names. Sure, he's an Indian -- but he's the son of a chief, and the best danged cowboy that ever mounted a horse. He can out ride, out rope, and out fight any of you bar flies in Hide Town. So just remember, the next time, I may just let him take a few of your scalps to hang on his saddle horn!"

The crowd yelled and clapped their approval as Cole and Chief returned to their job of loading the packhorse with the recently purchased supplies.

Ned and Temple, smiling, slipped quietly to the back of the crowd and stepped back into the dimly lit saloon to finish their drinks.

"I'd like to ride back to the ranch with you, Ned," Temple said, after they had finished their drinks, "and if you've got the time, maybe we could make a sashay over into that country where you say the rustling is the heaviest. Might give me a feel of what we're facing."

"Be glad to have you, Temple," Ned replied.

As they topped the last ridge before dropping into the valley of the Red Deer Creek, and almost in sight of the ranch house, they heard the loud boom of a Sharp's fifty caliber rifle.

"Sounds like someone is poaching on our buffalo herd," Ned shouted as he kicked the buckskin into a run. Temple and the boys followed as another shot shattered the quiet of the prairie.

As they rode over the ridge, they could see the hunter, lying prone in a small buffalo wallow, two buffalo cows lying dead a couple hundred yards in front of his stand, and watched as smoke curled from the end of his rifle barrel before they heard the sound of the next shot. Another bull fell to the accuracy of the big gun.

The small herd of buffalo scattered as Ned pulled up in a cloud of dust, dismounted on the run and kicked the rifle from the hunter's hand before he even knew there was anyone close by.

The hunter jumped up cursing, "What in hell do you mean, spoiling my stand," he shouted as he reached for the Colt strapped to his leg.

Ned had his pistol in his hand and slapped the hunter across the jaw with the barrel before he ever broke leather.

"This is Ceebara country, and these are Ceebara buffalo, the last of the great herds, and the word has been put out from Dodge City to Fort Concho that no one is allowed to kill them. Now, you've got about three minutes to get mounted up and off this ranch before I use that Sharp's to put a hole in you!"

Temple and the boys rode up about the same time that three men in a wagon, pulled by a team of mules appeared over the ridge. They each held a Winchester in their hands as they stopped next to Ned and the hunter.

"What's going on, Scratch?" one of them said as he climbed down from the wagon.

"These fellers say these buffaler belongs to them," Scratch replied. "Ever hear tell of such a story? Buffaler don't belong to nobody, what few of them that's left."

"I'd take this man's word as gospel, if I were you," Temple interjected, standing ten yards to Ned's right and to the left of the wagon. "This is his ranch and he has the blessing of the State of Texas to preserve this herd."

"And just who the hell are you to be telling me what to do?" the hunter asked, with a snarl, the huge scar on his cheek showing through the mat of black whiskers that covered his face.

"I happen to be the district attorney for this part of the state, and I can assure you that I will prosecute you to the fullest extent of the law for poaching, if you don't do what Mr. Armstrong has ordered."

"Hear that, boys? This gent says he's the district attorney for the whole goldanged State of Texas and he ain't even wet behind the ears yet. You going to believe that?" the hunter said, as he turned towards Temple and his hand began to drop towards the Colt which was strapped to his waist.

Temple smiled, looked the hunter square in the eye and said, "Mister, you are just about two seconds away from shaking hands with the devil if you go for that gun. Ned, why don't you keep your eyes on them gents in the wagon, it seems me and this poacher has a problem to settle."

"Mr. Temple, you don't need to worry about them men in the wagon," a voice from behind him said. "Me and the Chief have been shooting eyeballs out of rabbits since we was eight years old, and we've got them covered with our saddle guns."

No one had really paid much attention to the two boys who sat their horses a few paces behind Temple. When the wagon stopped next to Ned, they had quietly pulled their Winchesters from their saddle boots and had them pointed towards the three men in the wagon.

"O.K., I 'spect you fellers had best just lay them rifles in the floor of the wagon," Ned said," while the D.A. and your boss decide which one is the best shot."

The three sweating skinners decided they wanted no part in a gun battle and lay their rifles down. The hunter was not as smart, as his hand dropped for his Colt. Temple's hand was a blur as he palmed *Old Betsy* and fired, hitting the hunter's wrist before he could get his pistol up. Blood covered his hand and the pistol slipped back into the leather holster.

Screaming, the hunter fell to one knee, clutching his broken wrist with his other hand.

"You're about the luckiest sidewinder I ever did see," Ned said, "the D.A. could have put that lead right between your eyes if'n he'd had a mind to. Now why don't you climb into that wagon, git back to your camp, load up your poke and git off my ranch!"

The hunter whimpered, as he held his wrist, "I'm going, but this ain't over yet. You'll be sorry."

Ned smiled and replied, "Any time you feel like you want to continue this argument, I'll be waiting."

2

The sun was still an hour away from setting and was casting shadows on the multicolored cliffs which rose from the sandy course of the Canadian River. A buck mule deer bounded from its hiding place in the middle of a plum thicket and quickly disappeared around a bend in the river. A covey of Bob White quail, flushed by the deer, rose in a blur of wings from the thicket as Ned, Temple, Manuel, Cole and Chief pulled their horses to a stop next to the river. A small herd of longhorns raised their heads from the lush grass and watched as the cowboys approached. The LX brand of the Bates and Beal ranch could be seen burned into their hides.

After the run-in with the buffalo hunters, Ned, Temple and the boys had spent the night at headquarters and had left the following morning to show Temple the area where most of the rustling was taking place. They were searching for remains of branding fires or tracks of cattle being driven away from the area. Reaching a clear deep pool of water in a bend of the river, Ned pulled his buckskin to a stop.

"Be sundown soon, guess we might as well make camp here and see if we can't get a fire going to cook some grub," he said as he prepared to dismount.

"Pa!" Cole shouted, " Look yonder, hanging from that big cottonwood. Them's men, ain't it?"

Ned looked upstream about two hundred yards where Cole was pointing. "Danged if I don't believe you're right," he answered as he turned his buckskin and rode towards the tree.

There were three of them, slowly swinging in the slight breeze. The ropes were thrown over a limb about fifteen feet from the ground, one end tied around the trunk of the cotton-wood and the other around the neck of the men. It wasn't a professional hangman's knot, just a regular loop on a cow-boy's catch rope, probably ropes which belonged to the men dangling in the air. They were swung above the ground about the same height as a good saddle horse.

A hangman's noose is designed to break the neck of the person being hung, thus killing him instantly. These men had died from strangulation, as the ropes tightened from their weight when their horses were led from under them. Their faces were blue and their tongues lolled out between swollen lips. Their deaths had been painful.

Pinned to each shirt was a crudely written note on a sheet of Big Chief tablet paper. "Caught burning the wrong brand on other people's cattle. Rustlers take note!" It was signed, "Panhandle Vigilantes." A couple of running irons lay on the ground below them.

"Well, it's started, Temple," Ned said. "Looks like the ranchers have run out of patience with the law, and have taken the law into their own hands."

Bold Eagle, young son of Comanche Chief Quanah, gritted his teeth and stared at the swinging bodies of the three rustlers. A Comanche brave was taught from infancy to never show emotion, but a shiver went over the young boy and he nervously fingered the stock of the Winchester which protruded from the boot of his saddle holster.

The scene was too much for Cole to bear. He turned his head away from the three men dangling from the tree before he spoke. "What we going to do, Pa,?" he asked.

In answer, Jim drew the Bowie knife from his belt, rode up to the hanging men and cut them down, one by one. "Get the shovels from the pack horse, Manuel," he said. "We got a burying to do."

They dug one grave and dumped all three bodies in, after first going through their pockets and retrieving any identification they could find. Two of the men had letters addressed to them in their pockets, the third had no identification at all. They all looked as if they were down-and-out cowboys.

Temple took the letters and shoved them into his pocket as he said, "I'll write their families, Ned, and tell them what has happened."

The sun was setting by the time they finished their grisly job, but Ned decided to ride about a mile upstream, following the trail of the vigilantes, before stopping to make camp. He didn't want the two young boys to have to think about the dead men being too close to their bedrolls when they went to sleep. After witnessing the grisly scene, no one seemed to be too hungry. They chewed on some dried jerky and drank some coffee before pulling their blankets up.

"Pa," Cole said, after they had pulled the tarps over their bed rolls, "Why do you suppose the vigilantes hung them men instead of bringing them into Hide Town?"

"Well, son," Ned responded, "You know the ranchers formed an association and appointed me to head up a ranger force to try to keep cattle rustling down, and we caught several rustlers. But we had no sheriff and no jail -- not even a court where we could try them. Most of them we just ran out of the country, warning them not to come back, but many of them -- maybe these three -- came back and continued to rustle our livestock. Like I said, I guess the ranchers lost faith in justice being done and just ran out of patience."

"What we going to do now, Pa? Looks like these hombres we cut down had it coming," Cole said.

"I hope they had it coming, son, and weren't just innocent cowboys riding through the country. We'll follow the trail of the vigilantes tomorrow. Maybe find them and see who's heading up the group -- see if we can't talk some sense into them. I guess I'd have to say they got the right but the fact is, they're breaking the law same as the rustlers who have been stealing their cattle. You heard what Temple said, it's his duty to prosecute anyone who's caught breaking the law, and I 'spect he'll stand by his word."

* * * * * * * *

Next morning they broke camp and were on the trail by good daylight. There was no doubt where the vigilantes were heading -- Tascosa. Tracks indicated there were ten of them, and they were in no hurry nor were they trying to cover their trail.

"I have a court date, first thing tomorrow morning, Ned," Temple said. "I'd like to go on with you, but guess I'd best head back to Mobeetie, it's a long ride. I'd appreciate it if you'd let me know what you find."

"I'll do that Temple. I guess you can see now what I was talking about -- the ranchers have taken the law into their own hands."

Nodding his agreement, Temple said, "Adios," waving, as he turned his horse back to the east and rode away.

"Adios, Mr. Temple," Cole shouted, as the lawyer disappeared behind a stand of willows.

"Looks like they are heading to Tascosa to celebrate, Senor Ned," Manuel said, as they followed the trail to the west.

"I think you're right, Manuel. Not only to celebrate but to spread the word that the first rustlers have been hung and all others better git out of the country," Ned responded.

It was near mid-afternoon when Ned, Manuel and the two boys rode into the small frontier town nestled on the banks of the Canadian River. Although small, the town was a beehive of activity. Freight wagons from Dodge City had just arrived and supplies were being unloaded at several of the businesses. Hitching posts along Main Street were crowded with horses which stood with heads lowered, lazily switching flies with their tails. Now and then, one of the horses would stomp a foot to put a bloodsucking deer fly to flight. A thin haze of dust rose from the dry dirt street.

Two of the wagons were carrying live freight -- a covey of pretty dance hall girls who had heard that Tascosa was a wide open town, and had left Dodge City for greener pastures. A group of men -- cowboys, hunters, gamblers and merchants -- had gathered around the two wagons, eyeballing the new ladies and shouting terms of endearment to them.

Ned pulled up in front of the Equity Bar, where several horses, still wet with sweat were tied. He walked slowly a-round the horses, feeling of their wet hair and eying the brand of each. There were five LX's, one of them, a large bla-ze-faced sorrel which Ned recognized as being that of LX owner, Deacon Bates. Another, a long-legged steel-gray grulla, was one he had seen Outlaw Bill riding. Outlaw Bill, Bates' foreman, was known to have little respect for the law and a person Ned had suspected of stealing a few cows himself. The moniker, *Outlaw*, had been tacked onto him because he had killed his brother-in-law in California and his black coachman in Wyoming and was a fugitive from the law in both states.

Cole and Chief followed Manuel and Ned into the Equity, since Ned hadn't specifically given orders for the two boys to remain outside. They watched as Ned shoved his way through the crowd and approached Deacon.

Seeing Ned, Deacon smiled and shouted, "Well, howdy Ned." He nodded to Manuel. "Me and the boys was enjoying some of Ryan's good whiskey. Step up and have one on me."

The other cowboys, lined up along the bar, were laughing and enjoying their drinks and talking about catching the rustlers red-handed. Ned heard one remark that he bet half the town would be heading for New Mexico Territory when they heard that vigilantes had started hanging cattle thieves.

"Thanks, Deacon," Ned replied, "make mine beer." Looking back at Cole and Chief, he added, "Better give these boys a couple of sarsaparillas, they're just as dry as we are."

"Beer's fine for me," Manuel said, speaking to Jack Cooper, the bartender.

"What brings you up this way, Ned?" Deacon asked after Cooper had poured the drinks.

"Me and the boys was riding our west pasture along the river and shoving strays back towards the ranch when we come upon three cowboys who seemed to have got the worst end of a necktie party. Tracks were pretty plain, so we thought we'd follow them and see who might have been giving the party," Ned answered, taking a sip from his beer.

Outlaw Bill laughed, winking at Deacon, he said, "I'll bet them's the same three hombres we saw hanging from that cottonwood, Boss. The ones with the notes pinned to their shirts saying they was rustlers."

The other cowboys laughed at the statement.

"I hope whoever done it knows that we've got law and courts in the Panhandle now," Ned said. "I was talking to District Attorney Temple Houston last week in Mobeetie and he said he'd prosecute anybody caught rustling. District Judge Willis has promised to sentence anyone convicted in his court to the fullest extent of the law."

"Looks to me like those vigilantes just saved the state the expense of a trial and a hanging," Deacon responded.

"I guess you're right, Deacon, but they were breaking the law same as the rustlers they hung. The law says they have a right to a fair trial in a duly appointed court of law," Ned argued.

"I'll bet they got a fair trial, Ned, if they was caught redhanded burning their brand on somebody else's steer," Outlaw Bill interjected.

"I'm not arguing they wasn't guilty, and I'm not arguing they didn't deserve to hang for their crime. I'm just telling you that Houston says he'll prosecute anyone who is caught breaking the law, and hanging folks without a fair trial is breaking the law. I don't doubt that Houston will stand good to his word."

"Well, Ned, until someone starts bringing them rustlers in for trial in Judge Willis' court over in Mobeetie, I 'spect them vigilantes will probably keep conducting court ''neath the spreading limbs of a cottonwood tree," Deacon said, smiling.

The other cowboys in the saloon loudly agreed.

Ned took a sip of his beer, before he responded. "Deacon, maybe you ought to consider what could happen. Them men that was hung for rustling have probably got friends, maybe right here in the Equity, and they might just decide to take revenge on those who did the hanging. First thing you know, we might have a war on our hands."

* * * * * * * *

Ned, Manuel and the two boys left the saloon, mounted their horses and rode east down Main Street, past Hogtown to the Casimiro Romero residence. They tied their horses and were met at the door by the stately old Mexican.

"*Buenas Dias*, my friends," he said. "Welcome to my *casa*."

Shaking his hand, Ned said, "Thank you, Senor Romero. We couldn't come to town without dropping by and saying howdy."

"Please, Ned -- we have been friends for a long time -- call me Casimiro."

Turning, he shouted towards the kitchen, "Piedad! Bring our friends some coffee."

Soon, the beautiful Piedad, Casimiro's daughter, appeared with a steaming pot of coffee and poured five cups. Cole and Chief beamed, to be offered coffee along with the grown-ups. "Thank you, ma'am," Cole said.

Manuel stood up and bowed slightly, smiling at Piedad. She nodded and returned the smile. She and Manuel had been courting since they first met over a year ago. As she turned to return to the kitchen, Manuel followed. Her father looked at Ned, smiled and winked.

"Piedad has been pining for Manuel to pay a visit. I am glad that you brought him, Ned," Casimiro said.

Piedad and Manuel blushed.

Ned smiled, then proceeded to tell Casimiro about the hanging and the formation of the vigilantes. "I'm afraid that this is just the beginning, Casimiro. It's understandable that the cattlemen are upset. We've been losing hundreds, maybe thousands, of cattle each year to rustlers, but taking the law into our own hands will only add fuel to the fire. And eventually, an innocent person is going to be the victim of the rope. I tried to reason with Deacon Bates, who seems to be heading up the group, but he refused to listen."

"Bates?" Casimiro said. "I can understand your concern, Ned. Bates and his cowboys have murdered two of my sheep herders for no reason at all. They bragged about it at the cantina and said that was the only way they were ever going to rid the country of these 'Chili Bellies'. They don't seem to realize that we were in this country with our sheep long before they came in with their cattle."

"I'm sorry to hear that, Casimiro. You know that Ceebara is not involved. The colonel and I have always respected your right to run your sheep. And since his death, I have not changed my thinking, whatsoever."

"I know, Ned. You are a good man and a good friend. Let us hope that these vigilantes do not decide to deal with us Mexicans the same way they deal with the rustlers."

Ned nodded as he took a sip of the coffee.

* * * * * * * *

The three cowboys rode along the rim of the Palo Duro, looking down into the depths of the canyon. It was plain to see that they were up to no good.

"Ain't no way we could git a herd out of there without being seen, Bart," the young one with red hair said as they pulled their horses to a stop. "And they say that old coot Goodnight would just as soon shoot you and ask question's later."

"I 'spect you're right," Bart replied. "But maybe we don't have to git them out of the canyon. See that," he pointed to fresh cattle droppings in the grass in front of his horse, "looks like they got cattle running up here on top. Let's spread out and ride west and see if we cain't find 'em. If there's some up here, it'll be easy to drive them up the Tierra Blanca and into New Mexico Territory before Goodnight's men ever miss them."

Red rode the south flank, Concho rode the north flank and Bart took the lead in the middle. They rode no more than two miles before coming upon a small playa lake which was about a quarter mile across and had a couple of feet of water which had been caught during recent rains. Fifteen brown, tan and white antelope bounded out of the lake and disappeared over the ridge to the north.

There were more than a hundred head of longhorns standing up to their bellies in the shallow water! They raised their heads and water dripped from their mouths as they watched the riders approach.

The three rustlers converged on the herd, pushed them out of the water and headed them west. At first the cattle ran, in an effort to outdistance the cowboys, but soon became tired and slowed to a brisk walk. Reaching the Tierra Blanca Creek, a tributary of the Prairie Dog Town Fork of the Red River which flowed through the Palo Duro Canyon, the rustlers pushed the herd slowly to the west.

By nightfall, they had put more than twenty miles behind

them, circled the small herd and made camp. Sitting around a small fire of buffalo chips, they joked and laughed at their good fortune.

"They ought to bring at least twenty-five hundred at Fort Sumner," Bart said.

Red laughed, and said, "That's about eight hundred apiece, Bart. I'm going to spend the first hundred on me a bottle and one of them pretty Mexican senoritas."

"Won't take no hundred dollars for that, Red," Concho interrupted. "I'll bet a ten dollar gold piece will buy all the whiskey and women you can take care of!"

Bart laughed.

His laugh was short-lived, however, when a voice from the dark said, "You boys just reach for the stars, slow like, if you don't want this Winchester to punch a few holes in your ornery hides."

There was nothing they could do but follow orders, the fire had them silhouetted and the voice was hidden in the dark. They raised their hands and stood up.

Nine men, each holding a Winchester pointed at their chests, appeared out of the darkness. A huge bewhiskered man,Charles Goodnight, stepped forward, disarmed them, and said, "Looks like you boy's luck just ran out. We was out looking for strays and came on your trail about midday. Wasn't no problem in following it. Looks like you might have been heading to New Mexico with some of my cows."

"No, sir," Bart stammered. "We thought we'd round 'em up and push 'em back into the canyon for you. Figured you'd be right pleased and give us a reward."

Goodnight laughed, "Guess you must have gotten lost, you been going the wrong way all day. The canyon's back east."

When Bart started to make more excuses, Goodnight slapped him and told him to shut up. "It's bad enough you tried to steal some of my cows, you're just going to make it worse by lying about it!"

Turning to one of his men he said, "Bring up the wagon, we'll camp here for the night and in the morning we're going to hold court!"

The three rustlers were tied to the wagon, and Goodnight gave orders for a night watch to keep an eye on them until dawn. After a quick supper of bacon and beans, Goodnight and his men rolled out their blankets and with their saddles as pillows, were soon snoring loudly.

The sun, rising in a cloudless sky, found them gathered around the Goodnight chuck wagon, eating steak and beans. One hand of each of the rustlers was untied and they were allowed to share in the breakfast. When breakfast was over, Goodnight said to his cowboys, "Jess, I'm appointing you to defend these skunks -- Pete, I want you to prosecute 'em. O.K. -- the rest of you boys are appointed as a jury, and I'm setting as judge. Slim, you're foreman of the jury. Pete, get started!"

"Dang, Mr. Goodnight, I ain't no lawyer," Pete said. "I wouldn't know the first thing in hell about prosecuting nobody."

"Nothing to it, Pete. Just tell the jury why you think these coyotes is guilty of rustling my cattle."

Pete stood, looked at the jury then at the three rustlers, and said, "Well, men, from what I saw yesterday, these owlhoots came across them cows out there by the creek and decided they would just drive them over to New Mexico way and sell 'em. It just so happened them are JA cows -- got the JA brand on their hides, plain as hell, anybody can see that."

Pete was beginning to warm to the idea that he was a prosecuting attorney, and tried to act the part, although he had only seen one trial in his life -- that was when he and some of the trail hands on a cattle drive to Dodge City had gotten arrested by Marshall Masterson for being drunk and disorderly. They were found guilty and each had to pay a five dollar fine.

He walked back and forth before the breakfast fire, pulled a plug of tobacco out of his pocket and took a bite before continuing. He spit on the fire and listened to it sizzle.

"Git on with it, Pete," one of the jury cowboys said, "we ain't got all day."

"Now these three skunks says they were just herding Mr. Goodnight's cows back to the canyon, but all day long they was driving 'em west, and we all know that the canyon is back east. We all heard what they said last night when we was slipping into their camp -- that the herd ought to bring twenty-five hundred in Fort Sumner, and the young'un saying he was going to spend his first hundred dollars on a bottle of whiskey and a pretty senorita. I says these men are guilty of stealing cows, and I 'spect you boys feel the same," Pete said.

Goodnight spoke up, "O.K., Pete, that's enough. Jess, you got anything to say in defense of these three thieves?"

Jess, not to let Pete outdo him, set down his coffee cup, and stood before the jury, who were all squatted on the backside of the fire. "Well, sir, I admit it looks kinda bad, these boys driving these cows in the wrong direction. But you know as well as I do that sometimes a man can get turned a- round out here on these plains, what with no land marks of any kind. They say they was intending to push these cows back to the canyon, and you can see they ain't used no run- ning iron on them -- they's still carrying Mr. Goodnight's brand. About all I can see that they're guilty of is getting lost and heading in the wrong direction. It could happen to any of us."

Jess walked over to the fire and poured himself a cup of coffee.

"Alright, men," Goodnight said to the jury, "You've heard both sides of the story, now it's up to you to say whether they are guilty of rustling my cows or not."

The six cowboys looked at each other, no one saying a thing. Finally, Slim said, "Is there anyone here that thinks these owlhoots is not guilty?"

Still, no one spoke.

"Well," Slim asked, "Do you all say they're guilty?"

Each one of them nodded their heads in the affirmative.

"Mr. Goodnight -- Judge," Slim said, "Looks as how we all think these men are guilty as hell of cattle rustling."

Goodnight looked at the three men who were still tied to the wagon. "You men know what the punishment is for steal- ing horses, cows or molesting women. Wouldn't make no difference if you was being tried in the Court House at Fort Worth or out here on the prairie. A jury of your peers has found you guilty of cattle rustling and as Judge, I sentence you to hang until dead. Boys raise that wagon tongue up with three ropes swung over the double-tree."

The three rustlers started pleading for mercy. "Please, Mr. Goodnight, just let us go and we promise to never set foot on your ranch again."

The red-headed kid began to cry.

The JA cowboys continued to erect the hanging gallows with the wagon tongue and double-tree. Goodnight directed the cook to bring three tubs from the side of the wagon and placed them under each rope which was dangling from the upraised wagon tongue.

The three rustlers were forced to step up on the tubs and the ropes were looped around their necks.

"Have you got any last words before we hang you?" Goodnight asked.

Tears streamed down their cheeks as they continued to ask for mercy.

Goodnight instructed three of his men to pull the tubs out when he gave the order. Even his own men believed that the rustlers had only a few minutes before they would be dangling and kicking and breathing their last breaths at the end of the ropes.

But Goodnight had other plans. He let them beg for awhile before interrupting, "Tell you what I'm going to do, boys. I'm going to let you go free under one condition. I want the whole territory to understand that anyone caught messing with JA cattle will be strung up for the thieves they are. I want you to promise me you will go to Mobeetie and Tascosa and tell everyone that has a hankering to steal someone else's cows just how close you came to getting your necks stretched. And tell them that I don't intend to show any mercy on the next thieves that lays a hand or a hot iron on my herd!"

The red-headed rustler began to sway back and forth, his eyes turned glassy and his knees started to buckle. Jess grabbed him before he fainted, and Slim removed the rope from around his neck. They lay him on the ground, next to the fire.

The ropes were removed from the other two cowboys, and the one named Bart, unable to control himself, began to wet his pants.

"Thank you! Thank you, Mr. Goodnight," Bart said. "We'll head straight for Tascosa and tell everyone what you said, sir. And you don't need to worry none about us, we ain't never going to be seen in this part of the country again. We'll be heading for Arizona Territory."

3

The sun had just about reached the western horizon when Shep began to bark at the approaching rider. He was riding a sweat stained bay, and sitting in an army issue cavalry saddle. His bed roll was tied behind the cantle, a canteen was swung from the leather straps on the front, and a repeating Winchester rifle was stuffed into a boot on the right side, under his leg.

The uniform of a cavalry soldier was dust covered, the yellow stripe down the legs and the sergeant's stripes on his coat were barely visible through the grime. His hat was weather worn and faded.

His skin was black, not from the dirt or the sun -- but from his ancestry.

He rode through the gate at the Ceebara Ranch compound and dismounted at the rail in front of the headquarters. Dismounting, he removed his hat and stood awkwardly, waiting for someone to step from the house.

Belle opened the door and walked out onto the veranda with a smile on her face. "Howdy," she said, "looks like you got here just in time for supper."

"No, ma'am," the stranger said, " I didn't come for no supper, I come looking for a job."

"My name's Belle. What's yours?"

"Archiball Brown, Miss Belle -- but most folks jes call me Smokey."

"Well, Smokey," Bell said, "Looks like you might already have a job in the U.S. Cavalry."

"No, ma'am, I ain't," Smokey replied, pulling a paper from his shirt pocket. "I got me a discharge from the army jest this morning over at the Fort, and I thought maybe Mr. Ned might could use a good hoss wrangler."

Belle looked him over -- not too tall, maybe five-eight and one hundred sixty pounds. Under the dirt of the trail, he was neat. His tunic was buttoned, his neckerchief was tied appropriately and his boots, although dusty, seemed to have a shine. His hair, black and curly, had streaks of gray around the temple and over his ears. His eyes and his smile caught her attention.

A mouth full of white teeth almost covered his face as he smiled, and the whites of his eyes seemed to sparkle against the dark background of his skin. Wrinkles around the edges of his eyes accentuated the smile.

"Ned is not here, Smokey," Belle said, "but we are always looking for good cowhands. Why don't you take your horse down to the stable, tend to him and then take your poke over to the bunkhouse. I think one of the Garcia boys is down there doing the evening chores. He'll show you where you can wash up and Biscuit will be serving chuck in a little while. I'm expecting Ned and the other hands pretty soon, they have been moving cattle from the plains down into the creek bottom."

"Thank you kindly, ma'am," he said, politely, as he led his horse across the compound and towards the stables. Shep followed closely at his side, wagging his tail and introducing himself as a friend. Smokey reached his hand down and patted him on the head as he walked.

Removing the saddle from his horse, he set it on an empty saddle rack in the tack room. After rubbing him down, getting the salt and sweat-stained dust from his hide, he led his horse into one of the empty stalls and gave him a bait of oats which he found in the feed room.

A young Mexican boy appeared around the corner of the barn with a pitchfork in his hand. "Howdy," Smokey said, smiling.

"*Buenos Dias*," the boy replied.

They shook hands and introduced themselves to each other. The boys name was Pedro, and Smokey told him that Belle had instructed him to find an empty bunk in the bunk house.

"*Si, senor*," Pedro said, "I will show you."

Soon Smokey had his gear stowed and was washing up at the spring. He removed his shirt and trousers and shook most of the dust from them, then replaced them. With a brush from the tack room, he brushed his shirt and trousers, hat and boots and by the time Ned and the other cowboys rode in, his appearance had changed to that of a spic and span cavalry soldier.

"Well, howdy, Smokey," Ned said as the ex-soldier met him at the barn door. Smokey stood at attention and saluted and said, "Howdy, Mr. Ned," as he took the bridle reins of Ned's buckskin.

Ned had met Smokey when he was acting as scout for Colonel Mackenzie during the Indian wars, and had on occasion fought side by side with him while under attack.

"This ain't the army, Smokey," Ned said, smiling. "Stand at ease. Have you got a message for me from the major?"

"No, suh, Mr. Ned. I got me a discharge from the army and I'm looking for me a job," the black soldier said, as he stepped up and started removing the saddle from Ned's buckskin.

Ned stepped back and watched him -- it was apparent that he had already chosen Ceebara as his home, as he removed the saddle and carried it into the tack room, then started rubbing down the buckskin with a rag and brush.

"Tell you what, Smokey -- you join the boys for chuck and find a bunk in the bunkhouse, we'll talk about it in the morning."

"Thank you, Mr. Ned," Smokey replied, smiling, "but they ain't much to talk about, I 'spect as how this is where I wants to work!"

* * * * * * *

After breakfast the next morning, Ned, Cole and Chief walked down to the corrals and found Smokey in the pens with a rope in his hands. As the blue roan ran by him, he swung the rope and it settled neatly around the roan's neck. The stallion reared and screamed and began pulling Smokey around the pen. Smokey dug his boot heels into the soft sand, leaving two deep tracks as the horse pulled him around the pen.

Finally, the roan stopped, turned his head to the soldier and began to back, slowly. Smokey moved to the snubbing post in the center of the corral, made a couple of wraps a-round the post, and as the horse would make a step towards the post to release the tension around its neck, he would pull out the slack.

Soon the stallion's head was snubbed tightly to the post and Smokey was rubbing his neck and shoulders and talking to him gently.

"Better watch him, Smokey -- he's an outlaw!" Ned yelled as he sat astride the top rail of the fence. "Ain't no one been able to ride him or tame him since I bought him from a trader over at Tascosa. He bit a chunk out of the last man that tried to ride him. I 'spect I'm going to have to be rid of him."

"Yes, suh, Mr. Ned. I'll watch him, but I 'spect its time someone called his bluff. Just give me a few minutes and I'll have him tamed down, somewhat," the soldier said as he started rubbing the horse's back with a saddle blanket.

The roan didn't like the blanket at first, and fought, but soon realized that the more he fought, the more the rope a-round his neck hurt. He finally calmed and began to enjoy the rubbing that Smokey was giving him.

The saddle was a different situation. The stallion was determined that he wasn't going to allow that contraption to be buckled to his back. Smokey would ease the saddle up and before he could get it fastened, the horse's hind legs were in the air and the saddle was thrown over his head. But Smokey was persistent, and after thirty minutes and the saddle being thrown a dozen times, the stallion remained still while the cavalryman pulled the cinch tight.

Smokey left the horse snubbed to the post and walked over to the fence where Ned, Cole and Chief sat watching. He pulled a bag of Bull Durham and papers from his pocket and began rolling himself a cigarette.

"Looks like you've had a little experience taming horses before, Smokey," Ned said.

"Yes, suh, about thutty years worth," Smokey replied as he licked the rolled makings and stuck it between his lips. "I taken care of Massa McDougall's hosses before the war, and when he went off to war, I went with him. Him and me growed up together on his daddy's plantation and I figured I had took care of him for so long, wasn't no use in me letting him go off by his self and get his self kilt. He got his self kilt, anyway, in one of them battles by Washington City and I got myself captured by the Yankees."

He pulled a match from his pocket, struck it on the seat of his britches, and lit the cigarette before continuing. "When them Yankees saw I was colored, they thought I had been forced to fight with the Rebels, so I jes let them go on thinking it. The colonel put me in charge of looking after his hosses and I took good care of them until the war was over. That's when I decided to join up with the cavalry and come out west with the colonel to fight Injuns."

Cole and Chief listened with awe as Smokey told his story. They had seen the black soldiers at the fort -- Buffalo Soldiers the Indians called them because of their black, curly hair -- but had never been around them much.

"How come you decided to mess with that outlaw stallion, Smokey," Cole asked, "We got lots of horses that's already been broke."

"Well, suh, I heard Mr. Slim talking about no one had ever been able to tame him down and how he was such a bad outlaw. There ain't no outlaw hosses, Mr. Cole, they's just some hosses that's got their bluff up on us two-legged folks and tries to make us believe they's outlaws. I supposed that maybe if I could prove I could ride this old pony and tame him down, you might make a place for me on the ranch."

Turning he walked back towards the sweating stallion which had stopped fighting the rope and saddle and was watching him with hate-filled eyes. Smokey talked softly to him as he approached, patted his neck and shoulders and scratched him between the ears. The roan attempted to take a chunk of Smokey's arm with his teeth, but the rope was tied too short.

Tying his bandana over the horses eyes, blindfolding him, he slipped a tough rope halter over his ears and around his nose. Gently easing his left foot into the stirrup, he swung his right over the saddle, all the while talking softly to the stallion. Feeling the weight of the cowboy on his back, the stallion began to tremble. When Smokey had his right foot set firmly in the stirrup, he leaned forward, pulled the slipknot loose on the rope and jerked the bandana from around the horse's eyes.

Nothing happened -- the stallion blinked, turned his head slightly so he could see what was causing all the weight on his back, then took a couple of steps backward. He stopped, with all four legs spread as if balancing himself, then looked back and rolled his eyes at the black cowboy seated on his back, snorted and left the ground! He came down hard on his front feet while kicking his hind legs toward the sky. With his nose between his front legs, he bucked, twisted, spun, pawed and ran -- all the time snorting and squealing as if he were being attacked by a mountain lion.

Smokey leaned back with his weight firmly planted in the stirrups of the saddle, but his body limber as a wet rope. He seemed to anticipate every move the stallion was going to make, and kept his body in position to compensate for the moves. When the horse stumbled and went down to his knees, Smokey was nearly unseated.

Cole, Chief and Ned yelled their support, "Stay with him, Smokey -- ride him, Smokey -- ride him, cowboy!!"

Neither the horse nor the cowboy would give up -- for fifteen minutes the battle continued.

Finally, the blue roan stallion, sweat pouring from his body, stopped his bucking and began running around the corral, as fast as his feet would carry him. When he saw that was not going to rid him of the man on his back, he began to trot, then to walk and finally stopped. With all four feet spread and planted firmly on the ground, he dropped his head in defeat, breathing as if he would never get enough air to fill his lungs. A small puddle of water formed in the sand around his feet as the sweat poured from his body.

Smokey patted his neck and his rump as he continued to set the saddle. Finally, he stepped down and led the horse to the fence where Ned, Cole and Chief sat watching.

"That was the finest ride I've ever seen anyone make, Smokey," Ned said. "I guess you've won yourself a job at Ceebara. I pay fifty a month and pound, if that suits you?"

"Yes, suh, Mr. Ned, that suits me fine -- don't make no difference what you pays, I jes wants to be able to work with hosses and cows."

And so another hand was added to rolls of the Ceebara Ranch.

* * * * * * *

Smokey soon found his niche on the Ceebara ranch crew. Ned assigned him to the task of breaking the two-year old colts to the saddle, and he took on the job with a vengeance. Cole and Chief loved to sit on the corral fence and watch as he broke one after the other of the fine cow ponies.

Watching Smokey, Cole was amazed how he seemed to anticipate every move the horse would make. "How do you know which way the horse is going to turn, Smokey," he asked.

"Well, suh, Mr. Cole," the horse wrangler replied, "I watches his ears. If his left ear falls and his right ear stands up, then he's going to turn left. If his right ear falls and his left ear stands up, he's going to turn right. Then I jes leans the way he's fixing to turn."

"How do you keep your balance when his front feet come down so hard and he kicks his hind feet straight up to the sky?" Chief asked.

Smokey lay his hand on Chief's shoulder and replied, "You jes got to remember, Mr. Chief, that if his hind feets is up, they's got to come down -- and if his front feets is down, they's got to go up. You jes plants your feet hard in the stirrups and lean back so's you don't get overbalanced to the front. Most folks that gets throwed off a bucking horse, gets throwed to the front, not to the back."

Smokey was a good teacher and soon both Cole and Chief were covering their share of the colts. Kate watched from the kitchen window with pride, worried that the boys might get hurt but realizing that they were no longer babies and these were things they needed to learn as they grew into manhood.

4

The Panhandle Stockmen's Association had just about fallen apart. After the Colonel had been killed in Dodge City, Ned had decided he could no longer spend the time required as captain of the group and had resigned. No one else was willing to take the job on a volunteer basis. The ranchers were looking for a professional lawman to hire for the job, but thus far had been unable to find the right person.

Cattle continued to disappear, and rumors were being spread that Billy the Kid's gang was behind most of the thefts. True, he had taken his share of the missing cattle, but only a small portion of those that were missing.

He was having too many problems of his own, to have much time to spend rustling cattle. Sheriff Pat Garrett had arrested him and jailed him in Lincoln for the murder of Sheriff Brady, and while he was locked up, waiting for trial, he had recovered a pistol which had been hidden in the privy, next to the building where he was being held prisoner. He had shot and killed his two jailers and escaped.

Garrett continued to trail him all over the New Mexico Territory and a thousand dollar reward had been posted for his capture, dead or alive.

The Kid headed for Tascosa.

* * * * * * * *

District Attorney Temple Houston received word from Tascosa that a committee had been formed to organize Old-ham County with Tascosa as County Seat. The message stated that they needed his advice and help with the legal aspects of organization. He caught the next stage out of Mobeetie and arrived in Tascosa the same time that a small band of dust covered cowboys rode in from the west, trailing fifty head of excellent horses. The group was led by a small, bucktoothed and longhaired kid, no more than nineteen years old. His Colt was hung low on his right hip and tied down.

The Kid instructed the gang to take the horses to Mickey McCormick's livery stable as he stepped down from his horse in front of the Equity Bar. Jack Ryan, owner of the bar, smiled and spoke.

"Howdy, Kid, ain't seen you around for awhile. Where you been keeping yourself?" he greeted.

Smiling as he beat the dust from his shirt with his hat, the Kid stepped forward and shook the outstretched hand of the bartender, "Howdy, Jack -- we been buying horses over at

Las Vegas and thought maybe you fellers might be getting a little short on good horseflesh, what with all the cowboys and cows flooding the area."

"You've sure got that right, Kid," Ryan said. "Every rancher I know of has been asking about horses. Shouldn't have any trouble selling them if they're good cow ponies."

Ryan didn't say, but he highly suspected that the Kid was stretching the truth a mite when he said he'd been *buying* horses in Las Vegas -- *stealing* would be a better word.

"You know I don't handle anything but the best, Jack," the young cowboy responded, his teeth protruding from the broad smile, then added, "Reckon a man could get a drink of something stronger than water in this oasis. I'm drier than a catfish in the middle of the desert."

"Like you said, Kid, I don't handle anything but the best. Come on in, if you've got the gold, I've got the whiskey."

They both laughed as they stepped inside the cool interior of the adobe building.

As they disappeared inside the saloon, the stage arrived and was parked across the street . Temple stepped down from the stage and assisted the other passengers out, all female, as they disembarked. One of the girls was Elizabeth McGraw, who was affectionately called Frenchy by all her male, back room acquaintances.

Mickey McCormick, gambler and livery stable owner, had met Frenchy while on a gambling trip to Hide Town, fallen in love with her, and had asked her to join him in Tascosa. She stepped from the stage, brushed the dust from her dress and looked around, searching for Mickey. She spied him coming from the livery stable, turned and thanked her new friend, Temple Houston, as she rushed to meet the man she would eventually marry.

Temple, tipping his hat to the ladies, turned and headed for the saloon.

Walking across the dusty street, he made quite a dashing figure, dressed in soft buckskins. The jacket was cut short and buttoned tightly around his waist, with fringes dangling from the bottom and each sleeve. The trousers, open to the knee, were fringed and laced with colorful ribbons which matched the bright red band on his wide-brimmed hand woven Mexican sombrero. The hat was adorned with a silver eagle spread against the high crown. Brown, high topped boots, with a shine showing through the dust, covered his small feet. *Old Betsy*, his white handled Colt revolver was strapped outside around his waist.

Everyone, up and down the street, stared in awe as he walked briskly down the street and disappeared inside the Equity Bar.

Like Old Sam had said, *"If you want to be remembered, you got to look different from the crowd!"*

Ryan looked up as Temple stepped up to the bar. He couldn't help but smile as he looked the lawyer over from head to foot as he said, "Howdy, stranger, what'll it be?" Far be it for Jack to criticize the dress of a stranger, especially one who wore his Colt as if it was a part of him.

"Beer," Temple responded, "I ate enough dust to choke a mule on the stage and I reckon that beer is about the only thing that's going to wash it down. I also would like to have a little information."

"You came to the right place, I've got both, lots of beer and just a little information," Ryan said as he drew a glass of beer and set it on the bar in front of Temple.

The Kid, standing next to Temple, stepped back and looked him over, then laughed and said, "Damned if you ain't the fanciest looking dude I ever did see."

Temple returned the laugh, and replied as he reached out his hand, "Well, now, I rightly appreciate that compliment. Houston -- Temple Houston, district attorney from Mobeetie."

"Billy Bonney," the Kid replied as he took Temple's hand, "from Lincoln, New Mexico. Horses and cattle are my business."

"Seems I've heard of you, Billy -- Billy the Kid -- you've left quiet a reputation behind you."

The Kid smiled and replied, "Well, now, I appreciate that compliment, Mr. Houston."

Jack Ryan, hand shaking nervously, wiped the sweat from his brow with a bar towel, as he watched the most notorious outlaw in the west and the newly appointed district attorney of the Texas Panhandle, spar words which could have double meanings, either compliments or insults.

"Now why don't you fellers have another drink on the house," he said. "I don't want any trouble that might leave some blood on my clean floor."

Temple, looking the Kid square in the eye, said, "What makes you think there's going to be trouble. It seems to me that two like-minded men should be able to have a friendly discussion about how we dress without it causing any trouble.

What do you think, Kid?"

The Kid, returning the stare, replied, "I came to town to trade horses, not to indulge in any kind of activity that might leave blood on your floor, Jack. Besides, if I knew where I could get me some duds like Mr. Houston is wearing,, damned if I wouldn't be dressed just like him."

Temple laughed and slapped the Kid on the back, "I guess you'd have to go all the way to Mexico to find another set, Kid, but I do appreciate your good taste."

Ryan relaxed and asked, "Just what kind of information was you needing, Mr. Houston?"

"Mr. Houston was my father's name, Jack. Most of my friends just call me Temple. I'd appreciate it if you'd do the same -- you too, Kid."

"Alright, Temple, how can I help you?"

Pulling the letter from his coat pocket, he handed it to Ryan, "I received this letter from Mr. Henry Kimball, stating that you folks are ready to organize Oldham County, and needed some legal advice. I came to offer my help."

"Good, Temple. Why don't you have a seat at one of the tables and I'll see if I can rustle up the committee."

"Well, Jack, I'm so hungry I could eat the north end of a south bound skunk. I saw a sign down the street that said Scottie's Restaurant. I'll just see if he can rustle me up some grub while I wait." Turning to the Kid, he said, "Why don't you join me, Kid, looks like your bellybutton is scraping on your backbone -- besides, I think you and me may have some talking to do."

"You just made yourself a deal, Temple," the Kid answered, "Maybe I can sell you a horse while we eat."

They both laughed as they walked out the door. Ryan shook his head in disbelief, as outlaw and lawyer, disappeared into the street.

* * * * * * *

Ned continued to believe that one of the established ranchers was behind the disappearance of many of the cattle, although he had been unable to prove it. He continued to search for evidence along the Canadian River, where most of the ranch headquarters were located.

A lot of deep canyons spilled the water from heavy rains on the plains down into the Canadian River bottom. It was in those canyons where cattle could be driven and hidden until a herd was formed, driven out to the north and trailed into Dodge City. He voiced his suspicions to Belle and Kate one evening after supper while they were sitting on the veranda enjoying the quiet of the evening. Cole and Chief listened attentively. They were fourteen years old, nearly six feet tall, and thought they were already men. This sounded like something they might help solve.

"I know we are missing a lot of cattle, maybe a thousand or more. The other ranchers say they have come up short during the roundups. The western edge of the LE range is the border between Texas and New Mexico. Lee thinks the LE cattle are being driven west across the border, and tells me he thinks the Kid is behind it.

I hope that isn't true, but it looks as if he may be right.

"Major Littlefield, Deacon Bates, and Tom Bugbee have all come up short, and so far we haven't been able to find hide nor hair of the missing cattle. It would be pretty easy for one of the big ranchers to doctor the brands and just throw the cattle in with their herds. By roundup time, hair would be grown over the brands and we couldn't tell the brands had been changed."

"But if they all say they are missing cattle, it couldn't be one of them," Belle said.

"One of them may be lying to cover up his guilt -- how would we know what his count is? Besides, he may be holding the cattle in one or more of those deep canyons on his spread until he gets ready to make his drive into Dodge City, then just throws the doctored brands in with his own cattle and no one would ever know the difference," Ned explained.

After they had gone to bed that night, Cole and Chief discussed what they had heard about the missing cattle.

"I betcha we could locate them cows if they are holding them in some of those deep canyons north of the river," Cole said.

Chief agreed, "They'd have to leave a pretty good trail if there are that many missing. It would be much easier to trail them than it is to trail a bobcat, and we've trailed a lot of bobcats in those canyons."

"Yeah," Cole replied, "but what would we do if we found them? They would probably have guards out and we'd be in a lot of trouble if they caught us."

"Maybe we could just locate them and come back and tell your pa," Chief said.

"Yeah, that'd be the smart thing to do," Cole replied, sleepily. "We'll talk about it tomorrow."

Next morning, they went about doing their chores and began planning how they could look for the rustlers without Ned and Kate suspecting anything. "They sure wouldn't let us go if they thought that was what we were up to," Cole said.

* * * * * * * *

After meeting with the Oldham County Citizen's Committee and advising them on the legal process of setting up their county government, Temple returned to Jack Ryan's saloon, just as three riders on winded horses rode up to the hitching rail. They dismounted, tied their horses, brushed some of the dust from their bodies and walked stiffly into the saloon.

Billy and Temple had purchased a bottle and were sitting at one of the tables, pouring their drinks.

"Howdy, Jack, the taller of the three said, as he bellied up to the bar.

"Well, howdy, Bat. Haven't seen you around these parts in quiet awhile. Heard they was keeping you busy up in Dodge City as marshall."

"That's for danged sure, Jack. I've been as busy as a bitch dog with sixteen pups. We've been trailing four hombres who held up the Dodge City - Trinidad stage. Shot the driver and got away with about five thousand dollars in gold. Looks like their trail led right to Tascosa." Then turning to the two men who had come in with him, he said, "Boys, meet my old friend from buffalo hunting days, Jack Ryan -- Jack, I'd like for you to shake hands with my two brothers, Ed and Jim who are helping me to tame down Dodge City a mite."

Jack shook hands with the three Masterson brothers and poured them a drink, "On the house, boys," he said, "for old-times' sake." Smiling, he added, "Hope you didn't come to Tascosa to tame it down a mite. That could sure have an effect on my business."

Bat laughed and allowed as how no one was paying him to try to tame Tascosa.

Temple, hearing the introductions, stood and walked over to the bar. Sticking out his hand, he said, "Bat, good to see you again. Don't know if you remember me or not but I met you at Colonel Cole's funeral. Ned's told me some wild tales about your exploits as Colonel Mackenzie's scout during the Indian wars."

"Sure I remember you, Temple --how could I forget the son of Sam Houston," Bat said, then introduced Ed and Jim.

The four of them walked back and joined the Kid at the table -- Temple making the introductions.

The Kid stood and offered his hand in friendship, and Bat took it, smiling and looking at Temple, said, "We've met before, when the Kid worked for Ned on the Ceebara. Ned always said he was one of the best cowboys the ranch ever had."

Ed and Jim didn't know whether to shake hands with the Kid or draw their guns, until Bat said, "Now boys, just relax, Kansas ain't never set eyes on the Kid, and I reckon what takes place in New Mexico Territory is none of our business. Besides, I hear tell there's two sides to that story about who's responsible for the row over there in Union County."

"Thanks, Bat," the Kid said, relaxing. "I'd be pleased to buy you a drink."

The ice was broken and they all were soon laughing and telling stories of past events. The stories soon got around to who was the best shot in the West, and Jack said he figured it was the Kid, just from tales he had heard about all the men the Kid had killed in gunfights.

Ed Masterson disagreed, saying that he hadn't seen anyone who could draw as fast or shoot as straight as his brother Bat.

Mickey McCormick and Frenchy had joined the crowd of revelers and Frenchy spoke up, "I've got a fifty dollar gold piece that says Temple can draw faster and outshoot either one of them."

Frenchy had seen some of the demonstrations of Temple's ability with the six gun on the streets of Mobeetie.

Jack had seen some of the Kid's fancy shooting and figured he'd be safe in calling Frenchy's bet.

"Well, I'll take twenty-five dollars of it on Bat," Ed said, and you can have the other twenty-five on the Kid."

They all walked out of the saloon and into the middle of the street. "O.K., how we going to prove who's the best shot and fastest draw," Jack asked.

Temple, reaching into his vest pocket, pulled out a plug of Star chewing tobacco and handed it to Jack. The tobacco, two inches square had a silver star embedded in one side. "This ought to do," he said, "throw that in the air and we'll see who can shoot the star out of the middle."

"Better get something larger than that," Jack said, looking the tobacco over. That star ain't much bigger than a buffalo nickel."

"It's alright with me if it's alright with Bat and the Kid," Temple said.

"Who's first," Jack asked.

"It's Temple's tobacco, let him go first, the Kid said.

Jack took twenty paces down the street and said, "O.K. Temple, here it goes," and threw the chewing tobacco into the air.

The sun reflected from the tin star and as it reached it's apex, Temple, quick as a flash drew Old Betsy and fired. The tin star disappeared, leaving a neat hole in the center of the plug.

"Well, I be damned," Bat said. "I wouldn't have believed it if I hadn't seen it. That's too good for me!"

The Kid smiled and said, *"Quien lo baja mejor!"* (Who could do better) as he slapped Temple on the back and congratulated him -- refusing to even try.

Frenchy collected her fifty dollars and invited all the men back into the saloon for drinks on her. "Easiest fifty bucks I've ever made," she laughed.

* * * * * * * *

"Ned," Temple said as they sat in the darkened corner of the Lady Gay in Mobeetie, Temple's temporary office, "I'm making a trip to Austin on business next week and I was wondering if you would accompany me?"

"Well, I don't know, Temple. We're pretty busy at the ranch," Ned replied.

"I'm going to insist, Ned -- there are things going on down there that I think you and the ranchers should be aware of -- things that may change the whole aspect of the twenty-six counties here in the Panhandle."

"I guess you're going to have to explain what you're talking about, Temple. Change it in what way?"

"Well, to put it all in a nutshell, the recent survey of the counties has opened up a hornet's nest. As I understand it, the Legislature has instructed the State Land Office to platt all of the land up here that hasn't been outright purchased from the state into six hundred and forty acre blocks, described as *sections*. That's one square mile to each section. A checkerboard system of platting will be incorporated and alternating sections will be designated as school and university lands, the other sections will be designated railroad lands. That's lands that you ranchers are grazing your herds on.

"The school lands will be reserved for settlement by homesteaders and the railroad lands will be given to the big railroads in exchange for building railroads all over the state. They say they will give a railroad sixteen sections of land for every mile of railroad they build. That's going to gobble up a helluva lot of land in our twenty-six counties."

"Sixteen sections for every mile of railroad! That's crazy, Temple! I don't believe anyone could be that stupid!" Ned screamed.

Cowboys and buffalo hunters who were drinking and gambling in the Lady Gay all turned to see what had Ned so excited.

"What's the railroads going to do with all that land," Ned asked.

Temple pulled a cigar from his pocket, struck a match and lit it before answering. "Like I say, Ned, I don't know that much about it, that's the reason I think we should go to Austin and look the horse in the mouth. That's the only way we can be positive what the politicians are planning."

"I shouldn't have anything to worry about, Temple, Cee-bara is a land-grant from the Republic of Texas, before Texas even became a state. Your daddy helped the colonel to get it and I don't see how they can take it away from us and give it to the railroads."

Temple frowned. "Politicians can do any damned thing they please if they can get a majority vote. Don't say they can't, and don't believe they won't. As far as they are concerned, this area up here is theirs to do with as they please, and I believe that free grazing and land grants are a thing of the past."

"When do we go?" Ned asked as he pushed his chair back and stood to leave.

"Monday, if that's alright with you. That'll give you four days to get ready and meet me here. There's a stage to Henrietta leaves at nine o'clock Monday morning. We can catch a train there for Fort Worth and ....."

Ned didn't wait for Temple to finish. Walking to the door of the saloon, he looked back and said, "See you Monday morning!"

* * * * * * * *

"Ma, me and Chief are going to ride the Canadian River pasture to search for bogged cattle. Quicksand is going to be worse since that last rise in the river, we may be gone overnight," Cole said as they were having breakfast.

Cole, fourteen, going on fifteen, had begun to make decisions without being told. If he saw a need for something to be done, he did it. Ned had been gone for eight days, the Canadian River had been on the rise because of recent rains upstream, and Cole knew that if his Pa was home, he would have someone check the river.

"Alright, Son, but ya'll be sure and take your slickers and bedrolls and some grub if you're going to be gone overnight. No telling what kind of weather you'll run into," Kate said.

Cole wasn't lying -- he just wasn't telling the whole story. He and Chief figured on checking out a couple of the canyons where rustled cattle might be held while they were checking for bogged cattle.

Smokey wasn't prying, but he couldn't help but hear them talking about their plans while they were saddling their horses. "I don't think that's too good an idea, Mr. Cole, just the two of ya'll out there looking for rustlers. If they was to catch you spying on them, they's liable to put a hole in you and leave you for buzzard bait."

"We'll be careful, Smokey. If we find anything, we'll just slip back to the ranch and tell Pa when he gets back from Austin. Don't you go telling Ma and getting her upset. We'll be back by dark tomorrow," Cole said.

They tied on their bedrolls and a sack of jerky, ground coffee and cold biscuits, mounted up and headed north. By mid-morning they had reached the river and followed its banks upstream. They found a couple of mama cows bogged and their calves bawling next to the river.

Cole slipped his lariat from the saddle horn, made a loop and threw it over the nearest cows horns, while Chief shed his pants and waded into the knee deep water. Grabbing the cows tail, he began to twist and holler while Cole put the spurs to Comanche, his chestnut gelding.

With the help of the horse and Chief, the cows legs soon pulled free of the quicksand and Cole dragged her to river's bank. Chief waded out of the water, mounted Badger, his paint, without putting on his pants, released his lariat, made a loop and threw it under the cow's belly. She stepped into the loop, he jerked the slack from the rope and had her hind feet caught snugly. Badger immediately backed up, pulling the cows rear legs into the air. Cole backed Comanche until the cows front legs were pulled from under her and she fell. Cole dismounted and walked to the cows head, spoke to Comanche and he moved forward, putting just enough slack in the rope for Cole to remove his lariat from the cows horns. He remounted and Chief moved Badger forward. The cow kicked her rear legs a couple of times and his lariat fell free. The cow jumped to her feet, looked around for someone to attack, spotted her calf, ran to it, then turned tail and trotted up the slope.

Repeating the process, they soon had the other cow free. Chief pulled on his trousers, remounted and they continued their ride upstream. No more cattle were found, and as the sun slipped slowly towards the western horizon, they stopped beneath the limbs of a huge old cottonwood tree and made camp.

Sitting around the campfire, munching on cold biscuits and jerky and drinking coffee, they talked about their plans to scout out the first canyon which was located about thirty minutes ride upstream.

"If we don't find any tracks after the first mile, we'll come back and go on to the second canyon," Cole said.

Chief nodded in agreement, his mouth full of the biscuits and jerky. "I think second canyon is where we will find the rustlers," he said, after swallowing the mouthful of food. "It is wider and deeper and has plenty of good grass and water to hold a large herd. If I wanted to steal cows, that's where I would take them. Remember we trailed that big buck deer up that canyon last year."

"You're probably right," Cole answered. "Maybe we'll just go on to that canyon first. If we don't find anything, we'll check out the other one on the way back to headquarters."

As the fire died to glowing embers, they rolled out their blankets, removed their boots and stretched out. Without saying a word, they each pulled their revolvers from their gun belts and lay them close by. They were soon asleep, dreaming of rustlers, running irons and gun fights.

* * * * * * * *

"Governor, this is Ned Armstrong, owner of the Ceebara

ranch just north of Mobeetie," Temple said as he shook the Governor's hand. Ned stepped forward and took the out-stretched hand of Governor Ireland.

"Pleased to meet you, Sir," Ned said.

"The pleasures all mine, Ned," the Governor said. "I've heard tales about your and Colonel Cole's exploits for several years. Been wanting to take a trip up there and see that wild part of the state but just can't seem to find time. We'll have dinner together while you're in town and you can tell me all about the pleasures of building a ranch while trying to protect your scalp from the redskins. Sorry to hear about the colonel's death."

Turning back to his desk, he picked up a gold inlaid cigar box, opened it and offered a cigar to each of them. They bit off the end of the cigars and spit the tips into the spittoon next to the desk, puffed as the Governor struck a match and held it to the tips of their stogies. Flipping the extinguished match into the spittoon, the Governor sat down and asked, "Now then, Temple, I'm sure you didn't travel six hundred miles just to have a friendly smoke with me. What's on your mind?"

Temple, never one to mince words, got right to the point. "Governor, I got word that the legislature's been doing some stupid things concerning our twenty-six counties in the Panhandle. And if what I've been hearing is true, I expect it's going to cause a heap of trouble for you and the rest of the politicians."

"Well, tell me what you've been hearing and I'll tell you whether it's the truth or just a bunch of rumors," the Governor said as he blew a plume of smoke towards the ceiling.

"Well, Sir," Temple said, "First of all, I've heard that the state plans on dividing the Panhandle into alternate sections of land, keeping half of the land for schools and giving half away to the railroads. If that happens, the ranchers are going to be harder to tame than Quanah Parker and his Comanches. Most of that land is already divided into ranches and covered up with longhorn cattle. What does the state expect the ranchers to do -- sell their cattle and move out? I thought the idea was that we wanted the country organized and settled."

"Certainly we want it organized and settled, Temple. And we're not aiming to push the ranchers out. We need the railroads, and the only way we have of getting them to build is to pay them with land. We're giving the railroads five years to sell their land, and the ranchers are free to buy all of it they want. The school land can be leased from the state for grazing -- and who's in the best position to lease the grass? The ranchers are! Now, I don't see any reason for the ranchers to get upset over that kind of a deal."

Temple stood, and paced back and forth in front of the Governor's desk, chewing on his cigar. Stopping, he looked the Governor in the eye and said, "The ranchers figure they already own that land. They came in there with their cattle, some of them while it was still under the control of the Indians, when no one else thought it was worth a damn, and carved out the best cattle grazing country in the world. They've fought Indians, buffalo hunters, rustlers, blizzards and droughts -- and now that they've kinder got it tamed, the politicians figure on taking it away from them. I can tell you, Governor, they ain't going to set still for it!"

The set of Temple's jaw and the glint in his eye convinced the Governor that he meant what he said. Turning to Ned, he asked, "You're a rancher, what have you got to say about this, Armstrong?"

"I think Temple has told it pretty straight, Governor. Seems like a pretty ridiculous plan to give sixteen sections of land to the rich railroad folks just for building a mile of railroad. And even if the ranchers could afford to buy the land from the railroads, there's no way they could ever put together a paying business with the state owning half the land inside their boundaries. Personally, I wouldn't want no part of a ranch that I was forced to partnership with the state politicians."

"You've got it all wrong, Armstrong. First of all, that land is worth less than thirty cents an acre. A hundred dollars a section will buy you all of the railroad script you want. What we're proposing to do is allow every person to file on four sections of the state land, prove up on it and it will belong to you without costing you a dime. By buying the four alternating sections from the railroad, that would give you eight sections in one block. That's over five thousand acres for an investment of only four hundred dollars!"

"Five thousand acres! My God, Governor, five thousand acres wouldn't even run my horse remuda. My ranch covers a million acres! I'm running over thirty thousand head of longhorns and a thousand head of horses! And sometimes, after a dry year, the million acres ain't enough to feed them all. Looks to me like you need to make that trip up to Panhandle and see just exactly what we're talking about."

Temple interrupted. "Governor, if the politicians are so all-fired anxious for the railroads to build in Texas, trade them land in the area where they build. Seems to me you're asking them to build in East and Central Texas and trading them land in West Texas. We haven't seen any railroads in the Panhandle, nor anyone planning on doing it any time soon!"

The Governor stood, his temper beginning to flare, pointed his finger at Temple, and said, "You know damned well, Temple, that we don't have any state lands in East and Central Texas -- it has all been filed upon or purchased outright. The only land we have to barter is in that God forsaken country up North and out West. And if this state is ever going to get back on its economic feet after the carpet baggers finished with it, we've got to have railroads!"

"Well, Governor, looks like you've laid it on the line, the politicians are going to sacrifice the twenty-six Panhandle counties on the alter of economic greed," Temple replied. "We don't have any representation in the State Legislature and very few votes in our district, so you are going to run roughshod over the greatest cattle country in the whole damned world!"

Turning, he pointed his cigar at the Governor and continued, "And railroad lands are just a part of our gripes. It seems the politicians in Austin have decided they need a new fancy State House where they can meet and pass laws affecting us folks who have *taxation without representation*. Since the treasury is busted, they've decided that they will trade three million acres of some of our best ranch land to anyone who will build a new capitol building -- and that three

73

million acres is located slap-dab in the middle of some of our established ranches. The LS, LE, LX, and LIT are running cattle on that grass -- and I haven't heard anything about buying them out or reimbursing them when the deal goes through."

"Now, Temple, you know damned well that the legislature reserved that land for the purpose of trading it for a new state capitol building last year. Anyone who has been running cattle on it has been trespassing and has no legitimate gripe concerning our plans to follow the wishes of the legislature," the Governor replied. "They should be thankful that they were able to use the grass this long without being out a dime."

This was something new to Ned, he had never heard about the legislature's plan to trade a block of three million acres for a new capitol building. "Governor," he said, "those ranchers have been running cattle on that land since 1876, long before you say the legislature reserved it for horse-trading purposes. Seems to me, the legislature has overstepped its authority. I've always heard that possession is nine points of the law, and we've got possession!"

"You apparently are not familiar with the law, Mr. Armstrong. That is state land and the legislature can do any damn thing it pleases with the land as long as they can get a majority vote in a duly established meeting of the legislature."

"What do you propose that we tell those ranchers when we return home," Ned asked.

"My advice is that you tell them they had best start making plans to move their ranches elsewhere -- the contract has already been signed with an Illinois syndicate to take over the acreage," the Governor answered.

"Well, Sir," Ned replied, "Since the state has so much authority over our country, what are your plans concerning my ranch?"

"I don't understand," the Governor replied, "how does your ranch differ from any others?"

"The Republic of Texas made a land grant to me, setting meets and bounds on a million acres along the Canadian and Red Rivers, in 1844 before entering the Union as a state. Is the state going to honor that grant?"

"I guess you will have to take that up with the State Land Board," the Governor replied. "Since we are now the State of Texas and not the Republic of Texas, I would assume that your ranch will be treated no different than any of the others in the area. The railroads have probably already taken title to those sections designated in your platt, and you will be obligated to deal with them."

"And the school lands -- what about the school lands? If the state owns half the lands, when are they going to tell me I have to get off of those lands?" Ned asked, angrily!

"That has yet to be determined," the Governor answered. "A committee has been looking into the possibility of arranging some kind of lease deal, maybe in the range of four cents an acre annually. But like I said, you can file on four sections which will be yours, free and clear."

Ned had heard enough! He walked to the hat rack, picked up his hat, pulled it onto his head and said, "Sounds like we've already been roped and hog-tied, Temple, I'm going back to the Panhandle where the air is cleaner and people can be trusted!" With that, he walked out of the Governor's office.

Temple retrieved his hat, turned to the Governor and said, "Governor, we've been friends a long time. You and the general were friends and I realize that it was your influence that got me the district attorney's appointment in Wheeler County. But I've got to tell you, I think you're wrong on this one. You saw Ned's reaction and he's pretty level-headed compared to some of the other ranchers in my district. You may have to send the Rangers in if you try to push them off of that land!"

Without waiting for a reply he slammed the door and followed Ned down the hall.

* * * * * * * *

Cole and Chief rode warily into the canyon, keeping their horses on soft ground to muffle the sound of their hooves. While Chief kept his eyes glued to the ground for sign that would indicate cattle had been driven into the area, Cole kept his eyes on the canyon walls and the trail ahead.

They walked their horses slowly, listening.

"There, Cole," Chief said, pointing to a trail coming in from the side. "Many cattle have been driven."

He dismounted and examined the ground closely. Looking up at Cole who was still sitting on Comanche, he said, "Looks like six shod horses were driving the cattle. The trail is maybe three days old."

Cole nodded, "Looks like we've hit pay-dirt, Chief. We'll ride ahead slowly, and keep a sharp eye out. We danged sure don't want them to see us before we see them. They probably have guards posted."

Chief remounted and they rode slowly up the canyon. After riding about a mile from the river, the canyon widened and the grass was green and deep, offering a good place to hold stolen cattle. The canyon walls were steep, making a natural fence to keep the cattle from straying.

Chief held up his hand and placed his fingers to his lips. Motioning, he indicated he had heard something. They both sat immobile in the saddle and strained their ears to detect the sound again. The ears of both horses shot forward, hearing sounds that the boys couldn't hear. Then it came, a mama cow bawling for her calf. Then another, and another. The sound was coming from just around a bend in the canyon.

Dismounting, they led their horses into the shadows of a hackberry thicket and tied them. Slipping their Winchesters from their saddle boots, they walked slowly and silently up the edge of the canyon, keeping in the shadows as much as possible.

"Hell's Bells, Pete," they heard someone say, "I'm getting tired of sitting out here on our asses while the rest of the boys are entertaining the girls in Tascosa. I'll be glad when the boss sends someone out to relieve us."

"Them's my sentiments, exactly, Curley," another voice replied. "Come on over to the fire and pour yourself a cup of coffee. These goldanged old mossy horns ain't going nowhere."

The two boys heard the tinkling of a coffee pot as Curley took the pot off the fire and poured himself a steaming cup.

Dropping to their knees, Cole and Chief crawled through the grass for another hundred yards until they could see a-round the bend in the canyon. There before them lay the camp of the rustlers and in the background they could see hundreds of cattle grazing along the small stream's banks. Swung from the branches of a cottonwood tree was the fresh dressed carcass of a butchered steer. They lay immobile, watching, as Curley and Pete drank their coffee and con-tinued to discuss what they were going to do with the girls and the whiskey when they were relieved from their guard duty.

Cole continued to watch and listen, hoping that the name of the boss of the rustlers might be mentioned. He was so en-grossed in what was going on in front of their position that he failed to keep watch on their rear.

Suddenly the barrel of a rifle was shoved into his back and a voice said, "O.K., you two -- let go them rifles real slow like and stand up."

Cole and Chief looked up and two dirty, rough looking cowboys stood over them with rifles pointed at their backs. Cole's heart stopped. How could he have been so careless to not watch his rear? Now he and Chief were in more trouble than the two cows they had pulled from the quicksand.

They did as they were told, released their rifles and stood. One of the rustlers stepped forward and relieved them of their revolvers, then marched them into the camp.

"Look what we caught, Curley," the one with the crooked nose said, laughing, "a couple of coyotes what was trying to steal some of our chickens!"

Pete and Curley jumped up, subconsciously pulling their pistols from their belts. There was no need, Cole and Chief were already disarmed and looked scared and beaten.

"What you two think you're doing, spying on our camp?" Pete asked.

"We wasn't spying on your camp, mister, we've been trailing a buck deer all the way from the Canadian River and his trail led right up this canyon," Cole quickly replied.

"Who are you and where are you from?" crooked nose asked.

Once more, Cole quickly lied, "Just a couple of cowhands from over in Indian Territory. We heard that the ranchers in the Panhandle were looking for hands and we need the work."

"They's just a couple of kids, still wet behind the ears, Pete," Curley said. "And that one," pointing to Chief, "Is sure as hell a red skin. They're probably telling the truth and don't mean no harm."

"Looks to me like they're mounted pretty good just to be a couple of drifters," Pete replied, pointing to the boys' horses which were being led into camp by a third newcomer. "I say we string them up and be done with it. You know what the boss said, he don't want no one messing up this deal."

The one leading the boys' horses, not much older than Cole and Chief, spoke up, "Now wait a minute, Pete, I didn't sign on to do no hanging. I say we just tie 'em up and wait for the boss -- he said he'd be here in a couple or three days and we'd start heading the herd over to New Mexico Territory."

"I don't know what kind of deal you fellas have going, but

me and Chief ain't particular. If you need more help, we'd sure like to sign on," Cole said, looking at each of the men who surrounded him.

Pete bent down, picked up a log and threw it on the fire, kicking sparks into the air, "O.K., tie 'em up -- we'll wait," then looking Cole in the eye, he continued, "but if you try to run, I'll shoot you down like I would a stray dog!"

Turning, he spoke to crooked nose, "Burt, you ride back to Tascosa and find the boss. We'll let him decide what to do with these two."

"Why don't I just ride over to the ranch, he's more apt to be there," Burt said.

"No," Pete replied, "he said don't ever come looking for him at the ranch."

* * * * * * * *

"Miss Kate," Smokey said, "them boys should have been back before now. I 'spect as how I had better go see if they've got themselves into trouble."

"No need in worrying, Smokey," Kate replied, "they probably found more bogged cattle than they expected. And I know, Cole, if he found a bobcat or deer to trail, he may be late coming in."

"No ma'am, Miss Kate," Smokey said, dropping his head and refusing to look her in the eye, "Them boys weren't going to look for bogged cattle, they were goin' to look for rustlers. I heard them making plans and tried to talk them out of it but Mister Cole wouldn't listen. He made me promise not to say anything to you about what they was up to."

Kate gasped, "Why didn't you tell me, Smokey! No telling what kind of scrape they've got their selves into!"

"I wanted to, Miss Kate, but Mister Cole made me promise!" Smokey replied.

"Do you know where they were going?" Kate asked.

"Yes 'um, I know 'xactly where they was going. When I was serving in the cavalry we chased some Cheyennes up that canyon during the Indian wars," Smokey answered.

Ned was still in Austin and Slim and the other hands were rounding up in the Red River pasture, a good day's ride to the south. Kate didn't hesitate, "Saddle horses for me and Miss Belle," she said as she turned and trotted to the ranch house, "we'll leave as soon as I change clothes."

Smokey wasted no time, he caught the ladies' two horses and one for himself, saddled them and led them to the house. Kate and Belle, rushed through the door, dressed in their soft buckskins and carrying rifles. Both had gun belts buckled a-round their waist and were carrying a sack filled with grub. They tied bedrolls behind the saddle, took the reins from Smokey, shoved their rifles into the saddle boots, and quick-ly swung into the saddle.

Smokey kicked his horse, a tall, muscular sorrel, into a lope out the compound's gate, and turned him west.

* * * * * * * *

Before leaving Austin, Ned and Temple paid a visit to the office of the State Land Board. The Commissioner ushered them in, introduced himself, and asked what he could do for them.

"We've just been meeting with the Governor," Temple said, "and we want to verify some things that he told us."

After explaining their concerns, the commissioner replied, "Well, Mr. Houston, the Governor told it like it is. I'm just the Land Commissioner, but I'm obligated to uphold the law of the State, and the Legislature has already acted. Unless you can get the law reversed, then I would say that it's just a matter of time until the ranchers are either going to have to purchase the railroad land and lease the state land -- or move off."

They left the Land Office even more angry than before, retrieved their bags from the hotel and caught the first train back to Fort Worth. On the return trip, they discussed the situation, trying to determine the best course of action for the ranchers.

"You're the district attorney, Temple -- what would you do if you were in our shoes," Ned asked.

"Legally," Temple responded, "the ranchers don't have a leg to stand on. You heard what the legislature has done -- it's the law, whether we agree or not. So I guess if I were in your shoes, I'd start laying plans to first, fight it -- negotiate the best deal possible with the state -- and that failing, I'd try to find someone with a lot of money and political clout, to sell out to."

"Sell out! Who'd want to buy our holdings if the State says we don't have any holdings?"

"Well, no one has announced publicly that you don't have

any holdings -- and I understand there's a lot of foreign investors that are looking to get into the cattle business in the
Texas Panhandle. Now, with this big Chicago Syndicate agreeing to build the State Capitol building in return for three million acres in our district, I expect there's going to be a lot of
those foreign investors ready to buy anything they can get
their hands on," Temple said, smiling slyly as he pulled a cigar from his pocket and lit it.

Ned didn't respond and continued to sit, deep in thought.
Then it dawned on him what Temple had insinuated. He
slapped his leg, laughed and said, "Well, we aren't beat yet.
We'll show these danged politicians that two can play their
game!"

* * * * * * * *

Smokey led the way to the canyon, dismounted and examined the tracks. "They're a couple of days old, Miss Kate,
but these are the boys tracks, I'd know those hoof marks anywhere. But there's three more horses that came after them. I
'spect we'll find them up this canyon."

Kate nodded without answering, pursed her lips and
kicked her roan into a trot up the trail left by the five horses.
Belle followed close behind.

Mounting and catching up with the ladies, Smokey cautioned, "Miss Kate, I knows you want to catch up with the
boys as soon as possible, but we best slow down some. Why
don't you let me ride on ahead, maybe a couple hundred yards
and scout out the trail. One horse goin' to make a lot less

noise than three -- if I see anything, I'll wait for you to catch up."

"I think he's right, Kate," Belle said to her daughter, "We don't want to rush into something and maybe make matters worse for the boys. We need to be using our heads, not our hearts."

Wiping a tear from her cheek, Kate reined the roan to a stop and nodded for Smokey to proceed.

They had gone nearly two miles when Kate saw Smokey stop, turn his horse and ride quietly back to their position.

"There's a camp just around the bend, Miss Kate -- I seen the smoke from their campfire. You ladies stay here with the horses while I scout ahead and see 'bout the situation. Soon's I look it over, I'll be back," he said.

"Alright, Smokey -- we'll take the horses into that stand of willows and wait until you return. If we hear gun shots, we're coming a running!"

Smokey dismounted, pulled his saddle gun from the boot and walked quietly up the trail. Leaving the trail, he climbed the talus slope and slipped around several boulders until he was directly above the rustlers' camp.

He could see four men sitting around the camp fire drinking coffee and talking, a fifth was sitting his horse on the other side of a herd of cattle which was resting peacefully along the stream's bank. Cole and Chief, with hands tied, were sitting dejectedly on the tongue of a chuck wagon.

Smokey watched as one of the men, picking himself up from the ground, walked to the fire and poured two cups of coffee and handed them to the boys. They held the cups with both hands and sipped slowly from the hot tin cups.

Satisfied that he had the terrain painted firmly in his mind, he turned and slipped silently back to the willow thicket.

"The boys is there, Miss Kate, and they looks like they are none the worse for wear. They gots their hands tied, but looks like their feet are free. There's five men, four at the camp and one on a horse a short distance up the canyon. The horses are all saddled as if they are expecting to go someplace," he said.

Kate and Belle levered shells into the chambers of their rifles, checked their Colts, and Kate said, " Let's go get the boys!"

"No, ma'am, Miss Kate, I don't think that's a good idea," Smokey said. "I looked the situation over real good, and I'm afraid if we rush the place, the first thing they're going to do is shoot the boys. I want you and Miss Belle to take positions along the slope behind some of those boulders where you got a good view of the camp. Miss Belle, you take yonder side and Miss Kate, you go up this side. I'll watch and when you gets in position where you can site down on them with your rifles, wave your hands and wait for me to make my move. Don't do no shooting unless you see me pull my gun or do something unusual. I'm going to try to get them boys out of there before them owlhoots got a chance to hurt them."

"Smokey, you're not going into that camp alone," Belle said.

"Yes, ma'am -- I is! Don't you go fretting none, I got a plan. You wait and don't do no shooting unless I start it first.

Miss Kate, you get your sites on the two on the left side of the fire and Miss Belle, you get your sites on the two on the right side of the fire, and wait for my signal."

Kate and Belle finally reluctantly agreed, and slipped slowly to positions which overlooked the camp. When they were in place, they waved and Smokey mounted his sorrel and walked him slowly around the bend. They could hear him singing, as if he didn't have a worry in the world. "Going to Louisiana with my banjo on my knee, going to Louisiana my true love for to see. Rained all day the day I left, the weather it was dry, the sun's so hot I froze to death, Louisiana don't you cry!"

He rode straight into the camp as the four men jumped up from the ground and pulled their pistols.

With one hand holding his horses reins and the other on the saddle horn, Smokey pulled up next to the fire. "Howdy," he said with his white teeth showing through a friendly smile. "I saw the smoke from your campfire and smelled that coffee and that beef roast cooking over the fire and my nose just led me right in!"

Pete, with his Colt pointed straight at Smokey's chest said, "Mister, you best have a good story to tell why you come onto us like this or you're a dead man."

Looking at Cole and Chief, he showed no recognition, and said, "Name's Smokey. I been serving in the cavalry over at Fort Elliot. Got into an argument with a white corporal who said I was cheating at cards so I shot him. They throwed me in the guardhouse and said they was going to hang me! Well, sir, my neck wasn't made for no hangman's rope so the first chance I got, I beaned my guard over the head with a scantlin', stole a horse and lit out. I fought Indians in this canyon and figured it would be a good place to hide out for a spell. Didn't reckon as how I'd run into you fellers."

Pete looked doubtful, but said, "Well, step down off that horse and pour yourself some coffee while we decide what to do with you."

Smokey swung his leg over, and stepped down. With the horse between him and the rustlers, he looked at the boys and winked. Smiling, he walked to the fire, blew the ashes out of a cup and poured it full of boiling coffee. "Looks like these boys must have done something you fellers didn't like," he said, motioning with his head towards Cole and Chief.

"That's right," Curley said, "we caught them spying on us -- and we don't like spies!"

"Can't say as I blame you none," Smokey said, " 'specially, if them ain't your cows that you're holding here in the canyon."

"Nigger," Curley said, with a snarl, "You saying we're rustlers?"

"No, suh," Smokey answered, still smiling, "but if you is, maybe you need some help. The army ain't going to think too kindly 'bout me killing that corporal. Rustling ain't no worse than murder, and maybe I could help out around here for some grub and a little protection."

Curley relaxed and smiled, "What you think you could do to help us out?" he asked.

"Well, suh, I can do lots of things -- hoss wrangling,

cooking, mule skinnin', and fightin'. I don't 'spect I'd be much good herding cows, but I'd be willing to learn."

Pete looked at the other rustlers and said, "Why don't we give him a chance to prove himself. I'm tired of eating Burt's cooking. And he could spell us off keeping the cattle from straying until the boss shows up."

The other men holstered their guns and nodded their heads in agreement. Pete said, "O.K., Smokey, I guess we can give you a try until the boss shows up. Look the chuck wagon over and see if you can find anything to cook that'd beat the beef and beans we've been eating for the past week."

"Yes, suh!" Smokey replied. "If you got some canned peaches, flour and sugar, I can make a cobbler pie that'll make your mouth water!"

Kate and Belle, watching from their hidden position in the rocks, with their rifles sighted in on the rustlers, couldn't believe what they were seeing. They didn't know what Smokey had told the outlaws but it looked like he had convinced them that he didn't mean any harm.

Smokey led his horse to the chuck wagon and tied him to one of the wheels. "Reckon I couldn't cut me a piece of that beef and drink a cup of coffee before I starts to work? Seems I ain't had nothing to eat now for two days."

"Sure, Smokey, ain't no hurry," Pete said.

Smokey pulled the Bowie knife from his belt, turned his back to the gang and started cutting a chunk from the roast which was hung from a spit over the fire. Looking Cole in the eye, he mouthed "Be ready!" without uttering a sound. Cole nodded.

Quickly, Smokey vaulted the fire, and with a quick slash, cut the ropes holding Cole's hands and pushed the two boys down. At the same time, two shots rang out from the hillside and Curley and Burt were knocked backwards as the bullets found their mark.

Smokey's revolver appeared in his hand as he rolled over and shot Pete through the neck before the outlaw could get his Colt from his holster. Another shot rang out from the hillside and the fourth man, who was running for his horse, went down with blood pouring from his shoulder.

Keeping Cole and Chief prostrate on the ground, Smokey rose to his knees and looked around, keeping his gun pointed towards the four men lying bleeding next to the fire. Three of them were dead, the other was moaning and trying to stop the blood from the wound in his shoulder.

Kate and Belle appeared from their hidden positions and rushed down the talus slope. Belle -- seeing the fifth man, who had been herding the cattle turn his horse and kick him into a wild run up the canyon -- stopped, threw her rifle to her shoulder and fired.

The outlaw reeled in the saddle but continued to ride hard up the canyon.

Cole, using Smokey's knife, cut the rope which bound Chief's hands as Kate rushed up. He put his arms around her and squeezed as she began to cry. "Ain't no need in crying, Ma, we're alright," he said.

Belle looked Chief over and decided he wasn't hurt, "I ought to take a sapling to both of your backsides," she said, angrily. "Running off like that, without telling us what you was up to!"

"Yes, ma'am," Cole responded, cringing from her outburst. He and Chief, both nearly six feet tall, knew that if this small frontier woman was a mind to, she *could* take a sapling to their backsides.

Instead, she drew both of them into her arms and said, "Don't you ever put this kind of scare into us again."

"Yes, ma'am," they both replied, hanging their heads in embarrassment.

Kate looked around at the three dead bodies lying next to the fire and the young wounded cowboy who was moaning a short distance away. "Smokey," she said, "They don't deserve it, but I guess we best dig a hole and bury these owlhoots. Ma, why don't you see if that one that's still alive needs any help. I'm going to take Cole and Chief and see if that one that got away is still around."

Comanche and Badger stood saddled, tied in a rope corral with the other horses. Cole and Chief mounted up and followed Kate up the canyon. They traveled only about a half mile when his trail left the canyon floor and followed a dim trail to the top of the canyon walls. Chief dismounted and looked the ground over.

"Here's blood, Miss Kate," he said. "Looks like he's carrying a little lead."

"Well, let's go back. He's not going to be looking to come back and give us trouble if he's wounded. We've got work to do."

After burying the bodies, Kate gave orders for the boys to head the cattle back down the small canyon to the Canadian

River. "We'll push them across the river and let them scatter out. I doubt that whoever is responsible for this rustling is going to try to work this area again for awhile. We need to get this wounded boy back to the ranch house and doctor him up. Maybe he can give us some information on who's heading up this operation."

Smokey hitched the mules to the chuck wagon, tied the dead rustler's mounts to the rear and led the herd back down the canyon. They pushed the herd across the river and allowed them to begin drifting south, parked the chuck wagon next to the river and made camp. Belle made the wounded cowboy as comfortable as possible while Kate and Smokey prepared a quick meal.

Daylight found them on the trail to Ceebara headquarters, a days journey for the mules and chuck wagon.

"Don't know if this wounded cowboy is going to make it or not," Belle said, "he's lost a lot of blood from that shot in the shoulder."

* * * * * * * *

"You know better than to go off like that without telling where you're going and what you're going to do, Cole," Ned said angrily when he heard the story.

He and Temple had returned from Austin and he was waiting at the ranch house when Belle, Kate, Cole, Chief and Smokey rode in.

"Yes, Sir," Cole said, with head bowed, but then added, "I know it was wrong Pa, but we found out something that you should know."

"What's that?" Ned asked.

Cole raised his head, looked Ned in the eye and answered, "Them cows that the rustlers had corralled in the canyon. I looked them over real close while we were driving them out -- weren't no running iron been used on them, all the brands were old burns -- and there were C Bar A , Quarter Circle T, LS, and LE brands on them, but weren't no LX cattle in the bunch."

"Huh -- that's interesting -- no LX cattle at all? There's LX cattle running all over that country next to Cheyenne Canyon," Ned said. "Strange the rustlers didn't pick up any of that brand. Are you certain?"

"Yes, Sir. I looked through them real good. No LX brands," Cole answered.

Looking puzzled, Cole continued, "And another thing, Pa. When that rustler named Pete told the one named Burt to ride into Tascosa and tell the boss about us being held, Burt says, *Why don't I just ride to the ranch, he's more apt to be there?* And Pete says, *No, the boss said don't ever come looking for him at the ranch.*"

Ned smiled. "You did well, son. You almost got yourself killed, but that's information I've been looking for, for a long while."

"What's it mean, Pa," Cole asked.

"It means that the boss of that bunch of rustlers is either one of our ranchers or works for one of the ranchers. Now we just need to find out which one. Maybe this wounded cowboy you brought in can shed a little light on that question."

The young cowboy, unconscious, was lifted from the chuck wagon and carried into the ranch house and Belle and Kate began to wash the wound with drinking whiskey, clean it up and bandage it.

"He's not going to be able to answer any questions for awhile, Ned," Belle said as she completed the dressing. "He's lost a lot of blood and is still unconscious. Probably be morning before he comes around."

Ned never learned what the wounded cowboy may have known about the boss of the rustlers -- the kid died before morning.

* * * * * * * *

The sweating and winded horse trotted into the town of Tascosa and stopped in front of the Equity Bar. The cowboy, covered with blood, weaved in the saddle and then fell unconscious to the sandy street.

Slippery Sue, one of Jack Ryan's saloon girls, looked out the window and screamed, "There's a dead cowboy in the street!"

The saloon emptied and the crowd stood around the unconscious cowboy. "Charlie," Ryan ordered, "Get the Doc, he's still alive. Some of you men carry him into the saloon and lay him on one of the tables."

Outlaw Bill, foreman of the LX looked down on the prostrate form of the wounded cowboy and his face turned white. He recognized him as being one of the new men he had left guarding the hidden herd of cattle in Cheyenne Canyon. Unobserved, he slipped away without being noticed, untied his horse from the hitching rail and rode quietly out of town.

* * * * * * * *

The meeting was held in the newly erected courthouse in Mobeetie. Ranch owners and managers from all over the Panhandle had come in answer to a call from District Attorney Temple Houston and C Bar A owner, Ned Armstrong.

None of them knew the purpose of the meeting, only that the word had gone out that it was an emergency. Charles Goodnight of the JA, Henry Campbell of the Matador, Hank Cresswell of the Bar CC, Tom Bugbee of the Quarter Circle T, Deacon Bates of the LX, Major George Littlefield of the LIT, Lee of the LS and the Reynolds brothers of the LE, all were present .

"Men," Temple said as he called the meeting to order. "I want you to know this meeting is unofficial. I am here, not as your district attorney, but as a friend. Ned and I just returned from Austin, and we've got bad news. Seems as how the politicians down state have decided that this country is theirs to do with as they please. Ya'll know that there has been a survey going on for the past year, and that survey is being made for three reasons. First of all, to designate the boundaries of the twenty-six counties known as the Texas Panhandle. Secondly, the entire area is being platted into one mile square sections of six-hundred-forty acres each. Every other section is designated State School Land, and the adjoining sections are designated as Railroad Land."

"What you mean, Railroad Land," Bugbee asked. "Are we

going to get a railroad into the area?"

"Afraid not, Tom," Temple replied. "Seems like the legislature has determined they will give your grass away to the railroads, sixteen sections for every mile of railroad that is built anywhere in the State."

There was a roar of disapproval at that statement. "They can't do that, can they Temple?' Major Littlefield asked. "That's over ten thousand acres of grass for just one mile of railroad -- and the railroads not even being built in our area!"

"They've already done it, George. Half of the grass you're grazing now belongs to the railroads and half of it belongs to the State. It's just a matter of time until you're going to be asked to either purchase the railroad lands or get off. Seems like they've given the railroads five years to sell the lands. The State School lands are a different proposition. They're talking about allowing you to continue grazing those lands on a lease basis, maybe four cents an acre per year."

"Damned if I'm going to pay them a red cent," Lee said, angrily. "We came into this country when there was nothing but injuns and buffalo and carved out these ranches with our blood and sweat. Now they expect us to pay them for the privilege of running our herds? They come around trying to collect and they'll carry dead bodies back to Austin."

"What's the third reason for the survey, Temple?" one of the Reynolds brothers asked. "You said there was three."

"Well, seems like the politicians have traded away three million acres of our land to a syndicate out of Chicago in return for them building a new state capitol building. And that three million acres is going to lay smack-dab in the middle of the LS, LE and probably the LIT. It's just a matter of time before we're going to have rangers come in and tell you to get your cattle off of syndicate land, once they get the survey completed."

Pounding the table, Lee shouted, "I bought my land fair and square from the Mexican sheep men. Took thirty thousand dollars in gold coin and paid each of them a fair price to take their sheep back to New Mexico and leave the land for my cattle. Not only that, but I've spent five years building the LS headquarters and trailing thousands of head of cattle up from South Texas. Who's going to pay me for all of that?"

"No need shouting at me," Temple replied, angrily, "I'm on your side, I'm just telling you what the letter of the law says."

Lee, a crusty old cattleman who had come into the area as a teamster during the buffalo hunting days, and had amassed a fortune buying hides and hauling them to market in Dodge City, was not about to give in without a fight.

He and his partners, the Reynolds brothers, had established the LE ranch along the border between Texas and New Mexico Territory. When they couldn't agree on how to run the ranch, Lee sold out to the Reynolds, moved across the Canadian River to the south and established headquarters for the new LS ranch on the Alamocitas Creek.

"I'll see this new company in hell before I'll give up my grass," he said.

The other ranchers nodded in agreement.

"Maybe we should just secede from Texas and start our own state," Hank Cresswell said. "We'd still be larger than most of the other states in the Union."

"You know we wouldn't stand a chance in hell of doing that, Hank," Ned said. "We've got maybe a dozen ranches, and less than a thousand cowboys going against the whole state of Texas. That'd be like a tick crawling up a bull's ass with rape on his mind!"

"You're the lawyer, what do you think, Temple," Goodnight asked.

"Well, first of all, colonel," Temple replied, "we need to recognize that the legislature has already passed the laws, and until we can get the laws changed, we are going to have to obey them. Now I don't expect the politicians are going to send troops up here anytime soon and tell you that you're trespassing on state and railroad property. I do expect them to start trying to collect the four cents an acre lease. And the railroads, even though they have been issued script on their land, are not going to be too anxious to kick you off their sections until they first try to get you to purchase them. We're talking about millions of acres of land that they can't even identify until they get a survey completed and some pretty good platt maps drawn up of the area.

"I have been getting a lot of inquiries from foreign investors that are interested in buying cattle ranches in the Panhandle. Most of you men have established good ranch headquarters and are in agreement as to where your ranch boundaries are located. Maybe you should think about trying to sell out to some of those foreigners."

"Whose going to want to buy land that doesn't even belong to us?" Deacon asked.

"Well, they don't know it doesn't belong to you. And they seem pretty anxious to dump a lot of money into the area. If they are willing to pay your price for the ranch and the cattle, let them worry about what they are going to do about the railroads and the state," Temple said, smiling.

"What about those of us that don't want to sell. What do we do?" Tom Bugbee asked.

"I'd just sit tight and let the railroads and politicians make the next move. Temple answered. "Try to quietly buy the railroad script as cheap as you can get it. The State Land Commissioner says that you can buy all you want for one hundred dollars a section, maybe cheaper. That's about sixteen cents an acre. You can also file on four sections of school land. Your cowboys could also file on four sections each, then you could buy their land from them. If you just happened to file on the land which has the best water, and buy the railroad land with the best water, there's not going to be very many people that will come in and try to homestead on property that doesn't have any water."

Heads began to nod in agreement.

"How do we contact those foreign investors?" Major Littlefield asked. "If that new syndicate is going to gobble up some of my ranch, I'd just as soon sell and let someone else fight that battle."

"I'll give you a list of the ones who have contacted me," Temple replied, "and you can get in touch with their representatives."

Deacon Bates said nothing but was thinking that there was two things he needed to do as quickly as possible -- find a buyer for the LX and start selling the stolen cattle which he had been holding on grass in the Rabbit Ears area of New Mexico.

After the fiasco in Cheyenne Canyon, he had instructed Outlaw Bill to hold the stolen cattle north of the established ranches until fall, then head them into Dodge City and ship them back east.

5

After the incident with the rustlers in Cheyenne Canyon, most of the cattle thefts seemed to stop. The Kid and his gang had left Tascosa and were back in New Mexico Territory. Ned noticed a few signs of one or two head being driven towards the dugouts of some of the sod busters, but figured they would be butchered for food for the hungry families. He wasn't going to complain about that, he had seen some of the children who looked as if they were malnourished and was glad that Ceebara cattle might put a little meat on their bones. Life on the Plains was tough on families who were trying to put down roots in this harsh land. He noticed one family who had penned a couple of C Bar A cross-bred cows with young calves and were trying to break them to milk. He smiled at that, thinking that what milk they took from the wild cows would be well earned. He said nothing, noticing six kids standing next to the sod house who looked as if a little milk would do them good.

Citizens of Oldham County circulated a petition for organization and soon joined Wheeler County as the second organized county in the Texas Panhandle, with Tascosa designated as the County Seat. The unorganized counties of Potter, Randall, Swisher, Deaf Smith, Dallam, Castro, Hartley, Moore and Sherman -- an area equal in size to the state of Delaware -- were attached to Oldham County for legal purposes. Cape Willingham, former ranch foreman of McAnulty's Turkey Track and superintendent of the mail route from Dodge City to Tascosa, was elected first sheriff of the county. Temple Houston's district now had two courts to conduct, Mobeetie and Tascosa, one hundred miles apart, and he was kept busy traveling by stage and horseback between the two towns.

The Texas Panhandle was making a change, a change that was inevitable but one which did not set well with most of the ranchers. Most of the land along the Canadian and Red Rivers had been claimed by the big cattlemen. Survey of the twenty six counties was in progress, there were rumors that a huge portion of the area along the western boundary was being traded to a bunch of Yankees out of Chicago, in exchange for the construction of a new capitol building in Austin. How many of the ranches would be swallowed up in the trade was unknown.

Hundreds of cowboys had flooded the area, seeking work on the ranches, and with them had come the gamblers, prostitutes, outlaws and cattle rustlers.

News of free land being offered to homesteaders was circulated nationwide and an influx of sod busters was beginning to take place.

But something else had come into the area which threatened to completely change the lifestyle of the people who had settled this huge, free grazing, last frontier of the State of Texas.

Devil's rope! A name coined by the Indians for barbed wire!

In 1873, J.S. Glidden, an Illinois farmer and inventor had developed a process for winding two wires together with a sharp barb inserted every six to eight inches. He began to market it in the farming country of Illinois on a limited basis, but not until the birth of the cattle industry in Texas did his invention really get off the ground.

He hired a young salesman, Henry Sanborn, who traveled to Sherman, Texas, on the Red River, in 1875 and started exhibiting his product. He soon ordered four carloads of the wire to be delivered, one each to Sherman, Dallas, Austin and San Antonio.

Sanborn sold the Sherman and Dallas loads piecemeal, to small businesses. Business was so good, he sent for an old friend, Jud Warner, to help in sales. Warner was able to move the entire Austin load to one buyer, John Webb, an Austin merchant.

Sanborn and Warner then went to San Antonio to dispose of the last load. They persuaded the town fathers to allow them to build a barbed wire enclosure in the downtown plaza. Bringing in twenty five of the wildest longhorn bulls they could find, they turned them loose in their "corral."

The bulls made a run to escape and hit the wire -- the

barbs sank deep into their hides and they returned to the center of the corral, looked the situation over and made another lung to escape. Once again, the *Devil's rope* turned them back and they returned to the center of the enclosure.

Local cattlemen, who had been invited to witness the demonstration, were sold on the newfangled fencing material and purchased the entire car load supply.

With this success behind them, Glidden and Sanborn decided to tackle the huge ranching country in the Texas Panhandle, and in 1881 purchased 143 sections of range land about twenty miles southeast of Tascosa, from the railroads and the state, and proceeded to fence it with the new *Devil's Rope*. Soon, 120 miles of new barbed wire fence surrounded the Frying Pan Ranch.

Sanborn, always looking for ways to advertise the wire, invited ranchers of the area to the Frying Pan for a celebration, barbecue, dance and inspection of the newly constructed fence. Charles Goodnight, recognizing the benefits of the wire, returned to the JA and began constructing what he called a "drift fence" on the north side of his ranch holdings. The fence, running east to west, was erected, not to hold his cattle in but to keep strays from the northern ranches from drifting onto his ranch and eating his grass.

Owners of the Shoe Bar, Leigh Dyer, Goodnight's brother-in-law, and L.G. Coleman, constructed a similar fence to the east of Goodnight's and when joined together, the two fences stretched for one hundred miles across the prairie.

Goodnight also strung a wire across the southeast end of Palo Duro Canyon to contain his cattle within the confines of the canyon.

Later, another cooperative drift fence was stretched across the entire Texas Panhandle, from the Oklahoma border on the east to the New Mexico border on the west, across Hartley, Moore, Hutchinson and Hemphill counties, to stop the drift of cattle from as far away as Kansas.

Fencing of the Texas Panhandle had begun, and with it, came additional problems for the cattle ranchers!

Sod busters and small nester ranchers began laying claim to lands inside the big ranches, fencing their claims and applying for homesteader rights.

* * * * * * * *

Temple Houston was in Tascosa, along with Judge Frank Willis, to hold court when news arrived that the wooden capitol building in Austin had burned to the ground. The news traveled fast because 'Court Day' in Tascosa had become a day of celebration when all of the Panhandle citizens within fifty miles came to town to witness the antics of the early legal 'experts'.

Temple Houston could be counted upon to give the spectators a thrill as he prosecuted the criminals on the docket. His knowledge of the law, the Bible, Shakespeare, and Greek mythology were combined to offer a display of showmanship to the entranced courtroom audience. His antics were emphasized by his dress, whether in a long, black coat, white shirt, string tie, black trousers and boots -- or his fancy Mexican buckskin outfit. Unless ordered by the judge, he usually had

Old Betsy strapped to his waist.

Rustling and assault cases predominated the court docket, and murder trials were rare. Murder in Tascosa was considered murder only if the victim had been given no chance to draw. Temple learned to play on the heartstrings of the jury, walking in short, nervous steps before the box, auburn hair flowing, gray eyes darting back and forth and snapping as his head dropped in thought. Jurors enjoyed his antics but would usually yield to their sympathies and allow the prostitutes and cowboys to go free.

On one occasion, it was reported, Temple was visiting in a county court session when a madam who operated a house of ill repute was brought before the court. Some of the *privileged* citizens wanted her business closed down and her run out of town. The judge asked if she had a lawyer. She said no. Then the judge said he would have to appoint counsel for her. Temple arose and said, "Please, your honor, and I'll defend the lady, if she will allow me," -- and she did.

The prosecution gave its evidence and asked for conviction. Temple rose to his feet, paced around the court room as he briefly discussed the evidence, then bent forward nearly touching the twelve men in the jury, and in a clear, low voice began:

"Gentlemen: You heard with what cold cruelty the prosecution referred to the sins of this woman, as if her condition were of her own preference. The evidence has painted you a picture of her life and surroundings. Do you think that they were of her own choosing? Do you think that she willingly embraced a life so revolting and horrible? Ah, no! gentlemen, one of *our* sex was the author of her ruin, more to blame than she.

"Then let us judge her gently. What could be more pathetic, than the spectacle she presents? An immortal soul in ruin! Where the star of purity once glittered on her girlish brow, burning shame has set its seal forever! And only a moment ago they reproached her for the depths to which she had sunk, the company she kept, the life she led. Now, what else is left of her? Where can she go and her sin not pursue her? Gentlemen, the very promises of God are denied her, for He said: "Come unto me all ye that labor and are heavy laden and I will give you rest." She has indeed labored, and is heavily laden, but if, at this instant she were to kneel down before us and confess her Redeemer and beseech His tender mercies, where is the church that would receive her? And even if they accepted her, when she passed the portals to worship and to claim her rest, scorn and mockery would greet her; those she met would gather around them their spirits the more closely to avoid the pollution of her touch. And would you tell me a single employment where she can realize "Give us this day our daily bread?

"*Our* sex wrecked her once pure life. Her own sex shrinks from her as they would the pestilence. Society has reared its relentless walls against her, and only in the friendly shelter of the grave can her betrayed and broken heart ever find the Redeemer's promised rest.

They told you of her assumed names, as fleeting as the shadows on the walls, of her sins, her habits, but they never told you of her sorrows, and who shall tell what her heart, sinful though it may be, now feels? When the remembered voices of mother and sisters, whom she must see no more on this earth, fall again like music on her erring soul, and she prays God that she could only return, and must not -- no -- not in this life, for the seducer has destroyed the soul.

"You know the story of the prodigal son, but he was a *son*. He was one of us, like her destroyers; but for the prodigal daughter, there is no return. Were she, with her wasted form and bleeding feet, to drag herself back to home -- she, the fallen and the lost, what would be her welcome? Oh, consider this when you come to decide her guilt, for she is before us, and we must judge her. They sneer and scoff at her. One should respect her grief, and I tell you that there reigns over her penitent and chastened spirit a desolation now that none -- no, none -- but the Searcher of all hearts can ever know."

Temple paused, brushed his unruly hair from his eyes, and stared squarely at each juror before continuing. The courtroom was so quiet that a Mocking bird could be heard singing a plaintive song from the limb of a cottonwood tree outside.

Temple, in a soft voice, continued:

"None of us are utterly evil, and I remember that when the Saffron Scourge swept over the city of Memphis in 1878, a courtesan there opened wide the doors of her gilded palace of sin to admit the sufferers; and when the scythe of the Reaper swung fast and pitiless, she was angelic in her ministering. Death called her in the midst of her mercies, and she went to join those she tried to save. She, like those the Lord forgave, was a sinner, and yet I believe that in the day of reckoning her judgment will be lighter than those who would prosecute and seek to drive off the earth such poor unfortunates as her whom you are to judge.

They wish to fine this woman and make her leave. They wish to wring from the wages of her shame the price of this meditated injustice; to take from her the little money she might have -- and God knows, gentlemen, it came hard enough. The old Jewish law told you that the price of a dog, nor the hire of such as she, should come not within the house of the Lord, and I say unto you that our justice, fitly symbolized by woman's form, does not ask that you add ought to the woes of this unhappy one, one only asks at your hands the pitiful privilege of being left alone.

The Master, while on earth, while He spake in wrath and rebuke to the kings and rulers, never reproached one of these. One He forgave, another He acquitted. You remember both -- and now looking upon this friendless outcast, if any of us can say unto her, *I am holier than thou*, in the respect which she is charged with sinning, who is he? The Jews who brought the woman before the Savior have been held up to execration of the world for two thousand years. I always respected them. A man who will yield to the reproaches of his conscience as they did has the element of good in him, but the modern hypocrite has no such compunctions. If the prosecutors of this woman whom you are trying had brought her before the Savior, they would have accepted his challenge and each one gathered a rock and stoned her in the twinkling of an eye.

No, gentlemen, do as your Master did twice under the very circumstances that surround you. Tell her to go in peace." (From *Temple Houston, Lawyer With a Gun - Glenn Shirley*)

The jury acquitted the woman as soon as they reached the jury room.

According to witnesses in the court, there was not a dry eye in the room, including the judge, when Temple finished.

Even though Temple's plea had been entirely extemporaneous, it gained him everlasting fame, and was regarded by the legal profession as a masterpiece. The court stenographer was besieged for copies, and thousands were printed and circulated. A framed copy was placed on a pedestal in the Library of Congress with a card above which reads: *"One of the finest examples of American oratory ever uttered."*

Old Sam's boy had come of age!

* * * * * * * *

The days court session had been completed and Ned, Cole and Chief, having also arrived for a meeting with the local cattlemen to plan the cooperative fall roundups, joined Temple and the crowds as they headed for the only other place of entertainment in the community, one of the many saloons that lined the street. The cattlemen were meeting in the Equity Bar when the peace of the town was shattered by strange sounds coming from the east.

W.S. Mabry, the new county surveyor, like many of the inhabitants of Tascosa, was wondering about the sounds and the dust which was rising from the stage road in the direction of Fort Elliot. He shaded his eyes with his hand, trying to make out the cause of the dust.

An old buffalo hunter, resting in the shade of the overhang on the porch of the hotel, spat a brown stream of tobacco juice into the dirt street and shouted, "What the hell's going on, a goldanged invasion?"

Cole and Chief were the first to run from the saloon to the street to see what the hunter was talking about. They could hear the noise before they could actually see what was entering the town.

The first thing that appeared through the dust was the heads of four mules, two abreast, ears flopping and pulling a dust covered Army ambulance.

Temple, Willis, Ned and the ranchers stepped from the saloon and watched as the procession passed by.

Following the ambulance another set of four mules appeared pulling a large wagon, loaded with supplies. Men in Army uniforms drove the teams, as the mules moved slowly down the main street of Tascosa. The sides of the street filled with people as they exited the buildings to see what was causing all the commotion. A dog fight in the middle of the street would cause most of the occupants of the small frontier town to exit the buildings to watch the action -- this unexpected visit by the U.S. Army drew even greater interest.

The mules, ears now switching to and fro, indicating

their displeasure at the barking dogs and shouting by-standers, tugged the two heavy vehicles through the deep sand of the street. Sweat covered their bodies as they moved slow-ly through town without stopping.

The ambulance was covered with a tarp draped over wag-on bows and rolled up on each side like curtains on a porch which allowed air to circulate and cool the lone occupant in-side. This was Tascosa's introduction to Amos Babcock, a member of the Capitol Syndicate, who had traveled all the way from Chicago by rail, then to Fort Elliot by stage, to in-spect the land which would eventually be named the XIT cat-tle ranch. Orders had been sent to Fort Elliot, all the way from Washington City, to provide Mr. Babcock any thing which he requested -- thus the reason for the Army vehicles and personnel.

Witnesses said he sat, covered with dust, unmoving, in the middle of the ambulance before a desk-like table, wear-ing a business suit and soft fedora hat. Short and heavyset, he looked neither right nor left, but kept his eyes glued to the book which he was reading! It seemed that he was either un-aware of the town, or it was not worthy of his notice.

He was not reading, however, and was taking note of eve-ry thing and everybody with furtive glances as the wagons moved slowly down the street. County Clerk, C.B. Vivian, a onearmed, good-natured former cowboy would later describe the gentleman as a bored, suspicious, puffed-up toad.

The wagons passed through town and stopped next to Mickey McCormick's Livery Stable. Babcock stepped down from the ambulance and stretched his legs, and after giving orders to the Army drivers to tend to the mules, began walking back down the street towards the center of town. Ignoring the people who were staring at him as if he were an alien from a distant planet, he stopped under a sign which described the establishment as that of County Surveyor, W.S. Mabry.

Mabry, who had returned to his office after the wagons had passed, was busy with his maps at a small table when the stranger entered. He looked up from his work and greeted him, "Howdy, come in and have a seat. I'm W.S. Mabry, County Surveyor."

"Good afternoon," the man said, taking a letter from his pocket and handing it to Mabry as a way of introduction.

Mabry looked at him, then at the letter which was from the Texas State Surveyor's Office, and identified the bearer as Colonel Amos C. Babcock from Illinois, a member of the Capitol Freehold Land and Investment Company, Ltd., which had contracted to build the Texas Capitol building in Austin. The letter instructed Mabry to extend every courtesy to Colonel Babcock.

After shaking Mabry's hand, Babcock took a seat, and began to explain the purpose of his visit.

"Perhaps you have heard, the State Capitol building in Austin has burned to the ground, and my company," he said, "has contracted with the State of Texas to build a new granite capitol building to replace it. The legislature has agreed to trade my company three million acres of land in a single tract in the Panhandle in payment for the building."

Stepping to a table which had a map unrolled on its top,

Babcock looked closesy, tracing his finger along the edge which described the border between Texas and New Mexico Territory. "This property, I am told, stretches from the northwest corner of the Texas Panhandle, south for two hundred miles along the New Mexico-Texas border, and probably includes this collection of mud hovels. I have come to examine our property."

Mud hovels! Mabry couldn't believe what he had heard, "Do you mean to tell me," he asked incredulously, "that you traded for three million acres of land, sight unseen?"

"That is true," Babcock answered, "but we have investigated the possibilities of a profitable venture, and have determined that other cattle ranches are returning a large profit on investments in this area. We intend to do as well."

"I guess you know," Mabry said, shaking his head in disbelief, "that the land which you describe incorporates several established ranches. Those ranchers are not likely to take too kindly to you taking over their land."

"That's no problem of mine," Babcock replied, "The state has guaranteed possession of the land. And since no one actually holds title to the land, anyone who is now running cattle on the property will be considered trespassers. I would say that they had best start making plans to move their operations."

This statement definitely was not one which would make friends in Tascosa and the surrounding area.

After the wagons had passed, Ned accompanied County Clerk Vivian to the surveyor's office. Mabry introduced them to Babcock, who repeated his tale and told the three of them that he was looking for good men to be local representatives of his company. He explained that he would like for Mabry and Vivian, since they apparently were well acquainted with the area, to organize his inspection expedition and informed them that they would be well paid for their time.

"I will need one more wagon, more supplies, and several cowboys to go along as helpers," he explained.

Always ready to make an additional buck, the two Oldham County officials agreed to help organize and accompany him on the trip.

Ned asked, "When do you expect to take title to this land, Mr. Babcock?"

"Actually," Babcock replied, "we can begin immediately, but I prefer to examine the property first. The Texas legislature has agreed that we may take possession in increments, as progress proceeds on erection of the capitol building. Of course, hiring a manager and cowboys, building a headquarters and purchasing enough cattle to stock the range is going to take time. I believe we can be up and operating within two years."

"So you are saying that the ranchers who are presently settled on the property will have to vacate within the next two years," Ned said.

"I am saying," Babcock replied, "that they should begin vacating our property immediately. We do not intend to allow other people's cattle to eat our grass."

The next few days, news of Babcock's purpose for visiting the "mud hovels" of Tascosa took precedent over the court docket.

Outlaw Bill, drinking with some of his cowboys in Cone's saloon, complained, "I told you boys that surveying crew that came in last year was up to no good. The State's done sold us out. Next thing you know, they'll be sending in the rangers to put a stop to free grazing, and close down Hoggie Cone's and the Equity and run our gals out of town."

"Not without a fight," Deacon Bates said, as he downed his drink and asked Jack for another.

* * * * * * * *

Homesteaders -- sod busters to the cowboys -- began to flood the area after the State Land Office announced that anyone could file on four sections of state land in the Texas Panhandle, with the option to purchase another four of the adjoining sections which had been given to the railroads.

Dugouts and sod houses sprang up haphazardly across the prairie, anywhere there was water available. Longhorn cattle would walk for miles to the small streams and playa lakes seeking water, and paid no mind to the newly erected homesteads, trampling gardens, knocking down lean-tos and destroying newly planted crops. On several occasions, the large bovines had walked onto the roofs of the half-dugouts and fallen through the sod roofs.

The sod-busters discovered that the newfangled wire would keep the cattle off their property and began stringing the wire around gardens and small fields.

Tascosa and Mobeetie mercantile began a booming business in the sale of the new fencing material, freighting it in

115

from Dodge City, Fort Worth and Springer, New Mexico.

One of the sod-busters, a large German immigrant by the name of Henry Friedman, wasted no time in erecting a barbed wire fence around forty acres along the bottom of the Rita Blanca canyon, a few miles west of Tascosa, where he intended to plant a crop of wheat.

LE Cowboys, whooping it up after an evening in the saloons and painted ladies cribs in Tascosa, running their horses back to the ranch headquarters, hit the fence at full speed, tripping their horses and throwing their riders to the ground. Bedlam reined in the dark, as horses and men, tangled in the wire, fought to free themselves. Some of the horses, still thrashing on the ground were cut so badly that the cowboys were forced to shoot them. When order was finally restored around the bloody scene, three horses lay dead, others were cut and bleeding, and several cowboys, with shirts and chaps torn to shreds, were trying to stop the blood from their scratched and cut arms and legs.

Cody and several of the cowboys who were able to pull up before getting entangled in the wire, uncoiled their ropes, looped them over the fence posts and began tearing out the fence. Henry, hearing the screaming and cursing, stepped from the dugout, dressed only in his long johns with a Winchester held in his hands. Cody, riding by at full gallop, pulled his Colt and fired. The big German was knocked back into the doorway of his dirt hovel as the slug entered his chest. He was dead when he hit the ground. His wife became a widow, and his children fatherless.

The barbed wire wars had begun!

* * * * * * * *

"Guess I'll be heading back to Fort Sumner," the Kid said to Ryan as he paid for the drink.

"Why not stay around for awhile, Kid? I've heard that Garrett's sworn to kill you if you show back up in New Mexico," Ryan advised.

The Kid laughed. "Pat's been trying to get me ever since he was elected sheriff. I 'spect he ain't no smarter now than he was when he first turned on me. Besides, I got a hankering to see my pretty senorita, Duvelina. I'll be back, Jack, just as soon as I put together another hoss herd."

But he didn't return. Pat Garrett gunned him down in the home of the Kid's friend, Pete Maxwell in Fort Sumner, the night of July 13, 1881.

* * * * * * * *

Temple was correct in his belief that the ranchers who wished to sell would have plenty of opportunities as soon as news of the huge trade between the State of Texas and the Capitol Syndicate reached the shores of England and Scotland.

One of the first groups of foreign investors to invade the Texas Panhandle was the British syndicate known as the Prairie Land and Cattle Company. The firm had been capitalized for the sum of 650,000 pounds sterling and began to gobble up ranch land in Colorado, New Mexico and Texas.

Major Littlefield decided he was not going to wait for the railroads or state to put pressure on him to purchase the land. He actually owned only a small acreage where he had established his headquarters and free grazed hundreds of thousands of railroad and state lands. The railroads offered to sell him railroad script for as little as thirty-five cents an acre, but he refused. Instead, when the British Syndicate approached him to purchase the LIT, he jumped at the chance to sell. For the sum of $248,000 he sold his LIT brand, 14,000 head of cattle, 250 saddle horses and the small acreage where he had established his headquarters near Tascosa.

The Prairie Land and Cattle Company now controlled an unbroken range that reached from Tascosa, up through New Mexico to the Arkansas River in Colorado, a strip more than 250 miles long. Unknowingly, they had taken over control of property which had been deeded to the new Capitol Syndicate.

Littlefield gathered his poke and headed south.

* * * * * * * *

Ned and Tom Bugbee were drinking buttermilk in Miss Mollie's kitchen -- Ned, Cole and Chief had been riding their north pasture next to the Canadian when they spied the Bugbees checking cattle across the river.

"Ride on over, Ned, and join us for a glass of Miss Mollie's buttermilk," Tom shouted.

Miss Mollie's buttermilk was known throughout the Panhandle by cowboys and travelers who happened to pass next to the Bugbee's ranch house. It may have been the welcoming hospitality of Tom's pretty wife as much as the taste of the cool buttermilk that had spread the word across the grasslands.

Cole looked at Ned and said, "Let's go Pa. A glass of cold buttermilk would sure taste good."

Ned smiled and allowed as how he figured Cole was right. The three of them splashed across the shallow Canadian and joined Tom and Miss Mollie on the other side.

"Well, Tom -- I hear you've got a new neighbor," Ned said as they sat at the huge dining table.

"Yep," Tom replied, "that bunch of Englishmen act like they're serious about getting into the cattle business. I hear tell they've got control of everything from Tascosa north to the Arkansas."

"What about you, Tom? You plan on selling out or trying to hold your spread together?" Ned asked.

"Been giving it a lot of thought, Ned. I don't rightly see how I can afford to pay the railroads for all of their land that make up the Quarter Circle T -- and still have to contend with the state on the other half. And I can tell you, rustlers have been taking a pretty good cut out of my herd. Me and the boys kinder made a rough count last week and it appears that a couple thousand head are unaccounted for."

"I know what you mean, Tom. We haven't tried to make a count but looks like we may have lost that many or more. I certainly would hate to loose you as a neighbor but I can understand the temptation. They tell me that the major got nearly a quarter million for his outfit."

"That's the truth, Ned. The major told me himself -- feller from another British outfit dropped in last week and made me an offer. Wanted to know how many cattle I was running and when I told him about twelve or thirteen thousand head, he offered me $350,000 for my spread without batting an eye! Gave me a week to make up my mind -- said they were also dickering with McAnulty for the Turkey Track which joins me on the north and east."

"Be hard to turn a deal like that down, Tom," Ned said.

"I know, Ned. Be like pulling eye teeth, though -- me and Mollie put a lot of hard work into getting this spread built up and I'd hate to part with it."

Tom looked at his hands, callused and brown, and fell into deep thought. Ned didn't say anything and Miss Mollie walked over and put her hands on her husband's shoulder, then spoke. "Ned, we talked it over last night and decided it was too good a deal to turn down. I 'spect we'll be selling out."

* * * * * * * *

Ned hated to think about loosing the Bugbees and Little-fields for neighbors but it looked as if most of the other ranchers had decided to wait for the railroads and state to make the next move. He and Goodnight began staking out the best watering holes on their ranches and filing homestead rights.

* * * * * * * *

Nesters and cowboys continued to battle over the barbed wire fences going up. Cowboys, who had been using certain trails across the prairie, objected when they found that a fence had been erected, blocking their way to headquarters or town. They began carrying wire cutters in their saddle bags, cutting wire and pulling up fence posts.

The nesters, who had filed homestead papers on the property, took the law into their own hands and began firing on cowboys who were caught in the act. The cowboys usually fired back.

It wasn't just the nesters whose fences were targeted. The two drift fences erected across the Panhandle, the two hundred and fifty mile fence which enclosed Glidden's Frying Pan, and fences which had been erected on the JA to keep Goodnight's registered shorthorn's separate from the longhorn's, fell under the wire cutter's pliers.

"I tell you, Temple," Colonel Goodnight said, "this wire cutting is going to erupt in an all-out shooting war if something is not done to stop it. Trail herds coming from South Texas and heading for Colorado or Montana, leave our fences in a helluva mess. I realize that some of my own cowboys have cut wire on nester's property and probably have cut JA wire just to make a shorter route to visit their lady friends in Tascosa and Mobeetie. It makes no difference who's responsible, I intend to put a stop to it."

"I agree, Colonel," Temple replied. "The nesters have been lodging complaints for the past six months against cowboys who have been tearing down their fences. The State Legislature has been notified of the problem and it is my understanding that they are developing laws which will put a halt to the problems."

"What kind of laws?" Goodnight asked, anger flaring in

his eyes.

"Well, for one thing, they are trying to put a little order in the way the fences are constructed. The latest word I have, is that the law will state that any fence erected must have an access gate constructed no more than two miles from the nearest gate. Their thinking is that if a cowboy or traveler knows that there is a gate within one mile of his location, he will seek that gate rather than cut the fence."

"That sounds reasonable enough," Goodnight said, nodding in agreement. "What else have they got in mind? Knowing those down-state politicians, they've surely got something up their sleeves besides sticky fingers and the long arm of the law."

Temple thought about how to approach the crusty old cattleman with the next bombshell that had come out of Austin. He decided the best approach would be to lay it all out in the open.

"Looks like they're going to put a stop to the fencing of all state lands, Colonel. News has got to them that you ranchers have been erecting fences enclosing state school lands within the boundaries of your own ranches," Temple explained.

He was right, Charles Goodnight was not in agreement with that action. He pounded the table and cursed, "How the hell do they expect us to fence off the property that we've purchased from the railroads, with the state owning every other section within our pastures? Some of my pastures cover fifty thousand acres!"

"All I know is what I've heard, Colonel. I suspect that

they figure it's a good way to force you ranchers to pay lease money on the school lands. I suppose that there would be something in the legislation which will say that if you've got a long term lease on the school lands, you will be allowed to put fences wherever you please."

The two men were meeting in the new town of Clarendon, which had sprung up on a site where Carroll Creek entered the Salt Fork of the Red River. It also was on the wagon road from the JA to Mobeetie. The Reverend Lewis Carhart, a minister of the Methodist Church, had founded the town as a colony for his church followers, and the town had grown to the point that settlers in the area were requesting the State to designate it as the county seat of Donley County. Goodnight and Houston had been called in to assist in getting the county organized.

Location of a Christian colony on Carroll Creek, fifty miles from the den of iniquity known as Mobeetie, was hard to understand. It was providential, however, that it was on the trail from Goodnight's ranch to the county seat of Wheeler County. Goodnight, although a rough talking old reprobate, allowed no drinking or gambling on the JA, and could see that a county seat in a Christian community which neither allowed saloons, brothels or gambling halls would be a fine addition to the area, especially since it was the nearest town to his ranch headquarters. His ranch hands, however, soon found that it offered none of the pleasures they were seeking on their days off, and nick-named it *Saint's Roost* --- a name that became better known in the area than Carhart's original name of Clarendon.

Goodnight's partner, John Adair, was a Bible toting Christian and was exceptionally proud of the new *sinless* county seat. He could never understand how Goodnight could use such foul language while at the same time supporting all of the efforts of the new Christian community in its efforts to bring Christianity to this wild country. Goodnight never professed to be a Christian but Miss Molly, his devout wife, used her influence to guide the colonel's support of the Christian community.

One day, after the colonel had uttered a string of expletive's when a wild longhorn cow crashed through a corral gate, Adair asked, "Colonel, haven't you ever read the Bible?"

"Hell yes," Goodnight answered angrily. "It's a damned good book and I intend to read it again some day!"

* * * * * * * *

Millions of acres of prime grass lands on the Llano Estacado had no access to water, other than playa lakes, which were dry more often than wet. Rainfall in the area averaged less than twenty inches a year, and few streams had permanent flowing water. Most of the land along the flowing streams had been filed upon by the ranchers, leaving little land capable of supporting the efforts of homesteading families.

That was destined to change.

"Colonel," Charlie Goodnight asked, "I'd like for you to bring that new well drilling machine over to my place and see if I've got any water under my grass."

He was visiting with Colonel B.B. Groom, who operated the Diamond F ranch in Carson county. Groom had been experimenting with a horse drawn well drilling rig and had successfully found water and had erected a windmill which was pumping a clear stream of water into a wooden stock tank.

Groom agreed and within a year, Goodnight had a half dozen windmills stabbing the Panhandle skies, corralling the wind and pumping much needed water for his expanding JA ranch.

Had he realized the long term effects of the windmills, he probably would have never allowed the first to be drilled. Windmills which would pump water for cattle would also pump water for homesteaders. Hundreds of them began to move onto the plains, homestead four sections of land within the boundaries of the JA and the other ranches, erect sod dugouts, drill water wells and erect fences. This activity forced him to do what he swore he would never do, proposition the state to lease the school lands before they could be filed upon by the homesteaders.

However, the Land Board had decided that four cents an acre was too cheap and had raised the ante to eight cents an acre.

"Ned," Goodnight said, as they sat visiting in Mark Huselby's cafe on the main street of Mobeetie, "I'm going to Austin and offer to lease all of the state lands in my ranch for four cents an acre -- want to go along?"

"I sure do, Colonel," Ned replied, "if you think its the thing to do, I'll make the same offer."

"I spoke to Munson with the T-Anchor and he's in agreement," Goodnight said. "We plan on leaving day after tomorrow."

The three of them arrived in Austin, along with Attorney Buck Walton, and because all lease tenders were to be made in cash, went to Brackenridge's bank on Congress Avenue, and borrowed over $100,000, taking it in gold coin. They loaded a wheelbarrow with the money, hired a black porter to push the wheelbarrow, strapped on their six-shooters and marched up Congress Avenue to the Land Commissioner's office. A large crowd accompanied them.

Marching into the land office, they offered the money in payment for their leases at four cents an acre. Treasurer Lubbock refused to accept it, saying the lease price had been doubled.

"It's my understanding," Ned said, "that the lease price was set by the Legislature at four cents an acre."

"Four cents is too cheap," the commissioner said, "we've decided that eight cents is more in line."

"Who is *we*," Goodnight demanded.

"The Land Board," Lubbock answered.

"And who is the Land Board?" Ned asked.

"The Governor, the Attorney General, the Comptroller, the Treasurer, and the Commissioner of the General Land Office," Lubbock answered.

"Seems to me you have overstepped your authority," Attorney Walton said, "My clients are here to make payment for lease on all of the land within their ranches, at the rate of four cents an acre in accordance with the law. Are you going to accept it?"

Treasurer Lubbock, looking at the six-shooters strapped to the side of the ranchers, sweating profusely, refused the payment.

Attorney Walton thrust a receipt under his nose that stated payment had been offered and refused, the Treasurer signed it.

Goodnight and the other ranchers marched back down Congress Avenue, escorting the black porter pushing the wheelbarrow load of money, turned into the lobby of the bank, and repaid the loan. The bank charged them interest on the use of the money in the amount of $175.

This incident proved to be a smart move on the part of the cattlemen. The Austin politicians eventually filed suit against the ranchers for non-payment of lease levies, threatening stiff fines and jail time. The signed receipt not only forced the suit t o be dropped, but also influenced the state to reduce the lease levy to four cents an acre.

6

September arrived with the threat of fall in the air. Flocks of geese and ducks could be seen high in the sky, flying south.

"Winter's going to be early, Cole," Ned said as he listened to the honking of the high-flying geese. Cole looked up and marveled at the neat V formation of the honkers.

They were in the Red River pasture, with several cowboys from other ranches of the area, bringing the cattle down from the plains.

Setting their horses on a high promontory above the almost dry river bed, Cole could see several groups of riders, each driving a small herd of cattle through cuts in the caprock, weaving around huge boulders which had weathered away from the parent rock and rolled down the talus slope. Dust was kicked up by the hooves of the cattle and horses as they slowly descended from the high plains to the valley below.

"Pa," Cole said, "look at the size of those crossbreds. They must weigh a couple of hundred pounds more than the straight longhorns. Those Scottish Shorthorn bulls we bought four years ago have really changed the quality of our herd."

"You're right, Son," Ned replied. "Got shorter horns and shorter legs, too. We'll find out how well they will trail when we take them to Dodge City this year. Probably going to slow down the drive. I 'spect those short legs won't be able to stay up with Big Red's lead."

Cole laughed, "Well, ole Red's getting old, maybe he'll slow down a mite."

Seeing Chief coming down the slope with Slim and Waddie behind a sizable herd, Cole kicked Comanche in the ribs with his spurs to join him. Ned watched with pride as the two boys good-naturedly jostled each other as Cole joined the group. The boys had become as close as brothers, even though one was blonde haired and light skinned while the other was black haired and brown skinned. They had grown into the two best cowboys on the ranch, whether breaking broncs, roping calves or building fences.

One thing worried him though, he had watched as they practiced quick draws with their revolvers and saw how accurate they were when they shot at running jack rabbits. They were good. He had cautioned them to never draw the guns in anger, and to never threaten anyone with them unless it was to protect themselves. He had seen too many young hotheads buried in Mobeetie's Boot Hill, who thought they couldn't be beat.

For the past two years, Ned had been constructing working pens next to the Red River, large enough to hold five thousand head of cattle. The pens were a simple design, with ten pens in a row, each large enough to hold five hundred head. The pens opened into a long alleyway which led to a large working pen, where the herds were cut according to brands. Twenty smaller holding pens were on the other side of the alleyway.

After the cut, C Bar A cattle were pushed back into one of the holding pens, and cattle belonging to other ranches were driven into the pasture to be headed back to their home range by visiting cowboys.

Ned always appointed three cowboys from other ranches to act as arbitrators when there was a question about a brand.

For two days cowboys had been arriving with herds from as far away as forty miles, and the last of the roundup was now arriving. Dust filled the air around the huge corral and cowboys could be heard shouting and whistling at the herd. Now and again a contrary cow would break from the herd and head in a run back towards the way she had come, thinking her calf had been left behind, but would be turned back into the herd by a couple of the riders.

One wary old mama, with five foot horns, bolted the herd next to Cole and Chief and headed for the hills. She refused to turn and offered her horns to the nearest horse. The two boys unfurled their ropes, Cole threw his loop and caught her by the horns. When she made a run at his horse, Chief threw his loop under her belly and caught her two hind feet. As the two ropes tightened, the angry cow was thrown to the ground.

"Let's let her lay here for a spell, Chief," Cole said. "Maybe she'll realize who's boss!"

Chief laughed, "We may be boss while she's down," he said, "but I 'spect she'll still have them horns when she gets up."

After the cow stopped struggling, Chief moved his horse forward, allowing the lariat around her feet to go slack. She kicked a couple of times and the rope came loose. As she jumped to her feet, Cole kicked Comanche into a trot and headed for the corral. Chief's paint, Badger, moved to her rear and nipped at her tail to let her know she had better follow Cole. They dragged her into the pens and once again, Chief threw his rope under her belly and caught her heels. She fell to the ground and Chief kept his rope tight as Cole moved his horse forward, dismounted and removed his loop from her horns. Remounting, he said, "O.K., Chief, let her up."

Chuck wagons from each of the ranches were circled under the huge cottonwood trees and smoke from cook fires curled up towards the cloudless sky. The smell of mesquite roasted beef filled the air as the last of the herds were guided into the half-mile long wing fences which funneled into the corral alley. Dirty and tired cowboys removed saddles, watered their horses in the small stream, and stretched out on saddle blankets in the shade of the trees, waiting for the cooks to complete their cooking.

Up and down the line of chuck wagons cooks could be heard shouting, "Alright, you mangy bunch of cowhands, come and git it afore I throw it out to the coyotes."

Beans and meat, biscuits, coffee and cobbler disappeared in short order as the hungry cowboys consumed two and three helpings each. Afterwards they sat around the campfires, telling tales of past experiences with wild broncs, angry cows and painted ladies.

Cole and Chief took it all in, moving from campfire to campfire, especially the tales about the painted ladies. Cole punched Chief in the side and whispered, "It's time we made a visit to Hidetown to see if them painted ladies is all these men say they are." Chief nodded his agreement.

The next day, the cattle were sorted as to brands, cows and calves were mated, and unbranded calves were ear-marked and branded. Several branding fires were built in the large working corral, and teams of ropers were kept busy, heeling the calves and dragging them to the fires where other cowboys held them down while one ear-marked them, another castrated the bulls, and another pushed a hot iron to their sides and burned the brand deep.

"That's a LX calf," a dusty cowboy yelled to a roper.

"What's the matter -- you blind? His mama's carrying the LS brand," an LS rider shouted.

The LX rider refused to agree, and answered, "You dumb, greenhorn, you trying to steal one of our calves?"

Wrong reply! The LS rider, pushed his horse next to the LX cowboy's horse and swung a right, catching the LX rider on the shoulder. The LX rider responded, grabbed the angry LS cowboy by the shirt and they both fell from their horses and began a brawl in the middle of the corral.

Cole, seeing the confrontation, motioned to Chief, and they quickly unfurled their ropes, rode to the struggling cowboys and threw their loops, each snagging a cowboy by the legs. Backing their horses, they tightened their ropes and threw the fighting cowboys to the ground and dragged them apart.

Branding crews stopped their work and shouted support for one or the other of the fighting riders.

Ned rode up, dismounted and approached the two angry cowboys. "We've got a committee to settle these disputes -- you don't need to try to settle it with fists. First thing you know, someone's going to pull leather and we'll be burying a dead cowboy. Now, why don't you boys shake hands and get back to work."

The boys brushed the dirt from their hats, pulled them back onto their heads, and warily approached each other. The LS cowboy offered his hand and the LX cowboy took it. Satisfied they had made their pointd, they smiled, remounted and returned to work.

After the last calf was identified and branded, the strays were put to the trail and driven back to their home range by the visiting cowboys. Ned and his crew cut out the three year old steers and headed them to ranch headquarters on Red Deer Creek, in preparation for the long drive to market at Dodge City.

Roundups such as this were continued all across the prairie lands of the Texas Panhandle, from the JA in Palo Duro Canyon to the Turkey Track in the northern Panhandle, until all of the cattle had been gathered, worked and returned to their home range. Each ranch made preparations for their own trail drive to market.

* * * * * * * *

Deacon intended to be the first to market, getting his steers loaded and shipped before the other herds arrived. Not because of the price, but because he didn't wish to have the brands on his herd put to close scrutiny by his neighbors.

The LX herd was put on the trail the first week in September, heading due north from ranch headquarters on the Canadian River, crossed the Dodge City - Tascosa trail and continued north to the Cimmaron. Outlaw Bill was waiting on the Cimmaron with the stolen herd which had been summered well north of the Panhandle ranches.

Hair had grown over the brands and it was hard to identify any of them, especially the LE, LS and the LIT, since they were well mixed with LX brands.

"Howdy, Boss," Outlaw Bill said as Deacon came in with the new herd.

"Howdy, Bill," Deacon replied. "How many head made the summer up here."

"Counted near-about two thousand head -- how many in your herd?"

"We brought a thousand head, that should be enough to make 'em all look like LX's. I already wired for box cars and they should be waiting when we get into Dodge. We need to head 'em into the pens and load out soon's we get there. No use in taking a chance on association inspectors taking a closer look."

"Where you plan on taking them?" Bill asked.

"St. Louis -- less chance there of inspectors taking a close look at the brands. Probably would bring more at Kansas City or Chicago, but I think St. Louis would be safer."

* * * * * * * *

A rider from Fort Elliot loped into the Ceebara Ranch compound and dismounted in front of the ranch house veranda. Ned stepped out and greeted the dusty cavalry corporal.

"Looks to me like you could use a good cold drink of water, corporal," he said.

The black soldier nodded as he tied his horse to the hitching rail, "Yas suh," he said, "I'd appreciate a cold drink. That stuff in my canteen done got hot and dirty."

Walking to the porch, he pulled the telegraph message from his pocket and handed it to Ned. "Major said I should get this message to you as soon as possible so I near about rode my hoss into the ground."

He knocked some of the dust from his uniform as Ned read the message from the Panhandle Stock Association's brand inspector in Dodge City.

"LX herd arrived in Dodge City today -- stop -- scheduled to be shipped to St. Louis day-after-tomorrow --stop -- many head with doctored brands -- some LS, LE, LIT, C Bar A, Quarter Circle T in the herd -- stop -- Deacon Bates and Bill Moore with herd -- stop -- Request advice -- stop."

Ned led the way into the cool interior of the ranch house and told the soldier to be seated at the huge dining table. Belle appeared with a pitcher of cool water and a steaming cup of coffee. Setting them on the table she said, "You're just in time for dinner, corporal. We'll have it on the table in just a few minutes."

"I'm much obliged, Ma'am," he said, as he drank the water in one gulp.

Ned sat down next to him, with pen and paper. He wrote, "Try to delay train as long as possible -- stop -- do not let

Bates know that you are aware of the brands -- stop -- take train with cattle to St. Louis if necessary -- stop -- I will meet you at Dodge House or River Hotel as soon as possible -- stop."

Handing the paper to the corporal, he said, "Tell Major Biddle to send this immediately to Ben Hilton in Dodge City, and find Temple Houston and tell him I will meet him at the Lady Gay Saloon in Mobeetie tonight."

Belle and Kate appeared carrying steaming plates of steak, potatoes and beans and set them next to Ned and the corporal. "Kate, better pack me a bag while I'm eating. Looks like we may have caught Deacon Bates red-handed with a herd of stolen cattle. I'll be leaving to catch the stage for Dodge City just as soon as I can get ready."

Turning once again to the corporal, who was shoveling beans and steak into his mouth as if he hadn't eaten in a week, Ned instructed, "Corporal, when you finish your meal, you'd best go to the barn and find Smokey. Tell him to put your saddle on one of our fastest horses and leave your mount here. You get back to the fort as quickly as possible and get that message off."

"Yas suh," the corporal replied, as he placed the last of the meal into his mouth. Standing, he turned to Kate, "I'm thanking you, Miss Kate, for the meal. I best be going now." He turned, and walked quickly from the room.

An hour after the corporal had ridden from the compound, Ned, Cole and Chief mounted their horses, bedrolls lashed to their saddles, and kicked their horses into a gentle lope out the compound gate. As they rode, Ned told Cole that he was going to Dodge City with the sheriff to arrest Deacon Bates and Outlaw Bill, and he was depending on him and

Chief to take the herd to market.

"It's getting late, and if we don't hurry, the snows are going to be flying before we get them to the railroad. You pick ten of our cowhands to help you -- you've made the drive enough times that you know the trail -- and I know I can depend on you."

Cole beamed, "Thanks, Pa, I'll take care of it."

"Look up Vince Abercrombie when you get there and make him pay top dollar. Vince is a good friend but he's no different than all the cattle buyers, he's going to try to steal them if he can," Ned advised.

"Don't worry, Pa, I'll get some more bids before I let him have them," Cole replied.

It was well after dark when they arrived in Mobeetie, the horses covered with sweat and dust. Tying their horses to the hitching rail in front of the Lady Gay, Ned and the boys pushed open the swinging doors and entered. The saloon was filled with cowboys, hunters, gamblers, painted ladies and travelers. A honkey-tonk piano was being banged by a balding man who was dressed in stripped trousers and a plaid shirt. A bewhiskered buffalo hunter was accompanying him on a beat up banjo.

Pushing through the crowd, Ned spied Temple sitting at his corner table, playing cards with Cap Arrington, the newly elected sheriff of Wheeler County. Arrington had been one of the first Texas Rangers to arrive in Mobeetie and had made a name for himself by running some of the more noted troublemakers out of town. A sawed-off shotgun lay on their table.

"Howdy, Ned," Temple said, then nodded to the boys, "Got your message to meet you here but didn't find out what the big rush was all about."

"Howdy, Temple. Howdy, Cap," Ned answered as he sat down.

"What'll you have to drink," Temple asked, "looks like you're about as dry as a mallard duck in the middle of the desert."

"You're right about that," Ned responded. "Me and the boys didn't even stop to relieve the pressure from our bladders! Beer will do me fine -- sarsparilla for the boys."

"Aw, Pa, when you going to realize that me and Chief are grown up enough to drink beer?", Cole asked.

"Better stop your complaining, Son. You're lucky that I even allow you to come into a sin hole like the Lady Gay," Ned replied.

Temple laughed and motioned for one of the girls to bring the drinks.

Cole and Chief eyeballed the young girl who was exposing a lot of flesh, top and bottom. Cole blushed when she placed her arm around his shoulder and winked, then whispered something in his ear.

"Maybe you need to notice a little closer, Ned. Maybe them boys are old enough for a lot of things that comes with growing up," Temple said.

Smiling, Ned said, "Ain't no need in rushing things, Temple."

"What's so all-fired important that you rode them horses into the ground to get here," Temple asked.

Ned responded, "Well, looks like we finally got the number one chief rustler, Temple, if we can get him corralled and hog-tied."

"Great!", Temple responded, "Who is it?"

"You know I was telling you I suspected one of the big ranchers but didn't want to make any accusations until we got some hard evidence. Well, Ben Hilton, our brand inspector in Dodge City wired me that a herd had come in with all kinds of brands doctored to look like LX's -- and Deacon Bates and Outlaw Bill are with the herd."

Temple's mouth fell open. "The hell you say -- the Deacon and Outlaw Bill?"

"That's what Ben says. I wired him back and told him not to make any moves until I get there. Looks like Deacon has made plans to ship them to St. Louis."

Turning to the boys, Ned nodded, "Cole and Chief put me onto the trail when they found that herd of rustled cattle in Cheyenne Canyon. They was smart enough to look the brands over real close and said there wasn't any LX cattle in the whole bunch. That pretty well cinched my suspicions, but I didn't know whether it was just Outlaw Bill's doings, or if Deacon was involved."

Temple turned to Sheriff Arrington, "Better get your bags packed, Cap, and go along with Ned. We can't let that rich sonofabitch get away with this! I want you to find him, arrest him and bring him back. We'll hang the bastard, stealing from his own neighbors and friends. I'll get the arrest warrants written up and have them ready."

Sheriff Arrington stood up and said, "Guess I'd best get started packing, the stage for Dodge City will be leaving at sun up. See you in the morning, Ned."

"Alright, Cap," Ned replied.

"You planning on taking the boys with you, Ned?" Temple

139

asked.

"No, we've got a herd ready to drive to market and I'm putting the boys in charge. They've made three drives, already -- know the trail and know cattle. They should be able to take care of it as good as me."

That night, in their room at Mark Huselby's hotel, Ned gave orders to Cole. "Son, you need to understand, taking on the job of trail boss is going to be entirely different from trail hand. Because of your age, some of the older cowboys are not going to want to take orders from you. You've got to start off proving to them that you know what you're doing, that you're willing to work right alongside of them, and if they refuse to obey your orders, you may have to convince them with your fists."

Cole, six feet tall and weighing one hundred sixty pounds even though he was only sixteen years old, smiled at his Pa. "I'll pick men who know me and who I can work with, Pa. If I need some back up, Chief and Smokey won't let me down."

"Alright, Son, but remember all the things you have learned on the other drives. Don't push the cattle into any swollen streams, don't try to rush them, let 'em graze at their own speed, watch our for roving bands of Indians and outlaws, and find the best watering holes for your night-time stops. Thirsty cows will cause you trouble."

"I understand, Pa," Cole said. "What about money? You know when we reach Dodge City the first thing the hands are going to want to do is celebrate, so I'm going to need to pay them some of their wages before I get the cattle sold."

Ned reached into his pocket and pulled out a talley book and pencil, and began writing. "We've got money in the

140

Dodge City Bank and Trust. Give this note to Mr. McCabe, it will introduce you and authorize him to advance you whatever funds you request. You'd best not give the men all their wages at once, they'd probably spend it all in one night on whiskey and gals, and wouldn't be worth a dang to you for a week."

Cole laughed, looked at Chief and said, "You wouldn't do nothing like that, would you Chief?"

Without cracking a smile, Quanah's son said, "No sir, Mr. Cole -- you know white man's fire water and Indians don't mix -- and I ain't got any hankering for them white gals that just want to get in your pants and steal all your money."

Ned looked at Chief, shook his head and smiled, "I thought Comanches never lied, Chief."

After they all three had a good laugh, Ned said, "I want you to rent a wagon and team from Dickerson tomorrow, buy enough supplies for the drive. You'll probably need a hundred pounds of beans, two dozen slabs of sow belly, two hundred pounds of flour, fifty pounds of sugar, fifty pounds of Arbuckle coffee, salt and pepper, two cases of canned peaches and canned tomatoes, and maybe some dried apples and cinnamon for Biscuit's apple pies. Your cowboys will be willing to take orders from you a lot better if you keep their stomachs full."

"Reckon I ought to take Slim along, Pa. He's been top hand ever since you first came up from Waco?"

"No," Ned said, "The other men would be looking to him as boss, and I want you to take full responsibility on this drive."

Cole didn't say it, but it made him feel good that his Pa

had so much confidence in him.

* * * * * * * *

Thirty-six hours after leaving Mobeetie, and after four stops to change teams, the stage arrived in Dodge City. Ned went immediately to the Santa Fe depot and was told that the train had left the day before. He purchased tickets on the next train for himself and Cap, and was told that the train would be leaving in eight hours.

They walked to the Dodge House, paid for a room and bath, and after bathing, both fell exhausted onto the bed. Six hours later, they awakened, dressed and walked downstairs to the restaurant, ate a big breakfast, then carried their bags to the train depot.

As the train moved slowly to the east, Cap said, "I hope the Deacon doesn't get wind that he's been found out -- with his money and influence he might be able to buy his way out of this."

"Ben's a good man," Ned said, "I don't think he's going to do anything until we get there."

* * * * * * * *

The stolen herd was unloaded at the stockyards in St. Louis and the two rustlers checked into the River Hotel, while they waited for the buyers to look over the herd.

"Probably going to take them a day or two to figure what they're worth. We'll just sit tight and let them make the first offer," Deacon said.

"Yeah, I think that's smart, Boss. Didn't look like there was too many cattle in the pens. If we can get three or four buyers bidding on them, they ought to bring a good price."

They bathed and changed clothes and walked down to the restaurant. A well-dressed businessman stepped over to their table. "Bates?" he asked.

"That's right," Deacon answered, "Who's asking?"

"Satterwhite -- Walton Satterwhite -- cattle buyer for St. Louis Packing. I hear that new herd that was just unloaded from the train belongs to you."

"You mean that herd that's carrying more flesh than any that's ever been shipped out of Dodge City?" Deacon asked, smiling.

"Well, now, that remains to be seen," Satterwhite said. "But I must admit, it's a fine looking herd, and my company might be interested in taking them off your hands."

"What are you thinking they'd be worth to your company?" Deacon asked.

"I'd probably need to take a little closer look before I made a commitment. How many head you got?"

"Twenty-nine hundred and eighty-five," Deacon answered.

Outlaw Bill was thinking -- "one thousand LX's and nineteen hundred and eighty-five mixed brands" -- but he didn't say it.

"Tell you what," Satterwhite said, "I'll look the herd over real close, talk to my boss and have you a bid ready early tomorrow morning. How's that?"

"Sounds good to me," Deacon replied, "but you'd better sharpen your pencil pretty good because we've got a couple more buyers that are looking."

"Who would that be?" Satterwhite asked, concerned.

"Now, you know that wouldn't be ethical. Whoever offers the most is the one I intend to sell to -- hope it's you."

Satterwhite smiled, turned and walked from the restaurant.

Ben Hilton watched from a darkened table across the room. "Ned and Cap had best be getting here soon, or there ain't going to be any evidence left," he thought to himself.

* * * * * * * *

The next morning, Satterwhite returned and joined Deacon and Bill for breakfast. As they ate, he said, "Looks like I can't pay more'n six cents a pound, Mr. Bates -- and that would be with a two percent cut of the old and cripples."

"I 'spect you'll have to find you another herd, Mr. Satterwhite. I've already had a better offer than that," Deacon said. He was lying, but Satterwhite didn't know that he was.

"Care to tell me what they offered," he asked.

"Couldn't do that," Deacon responded as he shoved a fork full of ham and eggs into his mouth. "But I would tell you that you're not far off, maybe a couple of cents a pound and no cuts."

Satterwhite shook his head, "The boss would hang and quarter me if I paid that much. Best I can do is seven cents, and be damned with the cut."

Deacon laid his fork down, pushed his hand across the table and said, "You just bought you twenty-nine hundred and eighty-five head of Texas cattle, Mr. Satterwhite, "Let's shake on it."

Satterwhite took his hand and they shook, consummating the deal. "Stop by my office when you finish your breakfast and I'll have the papers made out. We'll run 'em across the scales this afternoon."

* * * * * * * *

The cattle weighed out an even thousand pounds each, bringing a total of $209,895.00. Deacon had the money divided three ways, $70,000.00 to Bates and Beal Cattle Company for the thousand head of LX's, and $69,947.50 each for himself and Outlaw Bill for the nineteen hundred eighty five head of stolen cattle.

After depositing their money in the Bank of St. Louis, they were ready to celebrate but their celebration was stopped cold when they saw Ned Armstrong and Cap Arrington entering the lobby of the hotel.

"Sonofabitch!" Deacon said, as they stepped back into the shadows of the alley next to the hotel. "They must have followed us here. If they know about those rustled cattle, we've got a problem."

Bill spoke, "Well, I'm not waiting around to find out what they know. I'm taking my money in gold and catching the next train to Las Vegas, New Mexico where I've been building me a herd of my own with mavericks and rustled cows from the ranches around Tascosa. If you've got any sense, you'll high-tail it out of here, too. That Texas Ranger would as soon shoot you as look at you!"

145

"I think you're right," Deacon said, "I've still got a home and property in Boston, so I think I'll head east and cool my heels in the Atlantic Ocean until this all blows over."

They slipped into the hotel, retrieved their bags, stopped by the bank, then caught the first train out, Outlaw Bill to Pueblo, Colorado and Deacon Bates to Boston.

Ben Hilton met Ned and Cap in the hotel and they all headed for the stock pens where the stolen cattle were being held. "Yep," Cap said, "looks like maybe a third of them are branded LX, the rest have had a running iron blot out the original brand. I'll have the packing company read the brands from the inside after the hides are removed so we can see that the proper owners are compensated. Right now, we need to apprehend these owlhoots before they head for tall timber."

The hotel manager accompanied them to Bates' and Moore's room, unlocked the door and Ned and Cap rushed in with pistols drawn. But they were too late, the room was empty.

"Well, we've got two choices, the railroad or the river boats -- they've got to take one or the other," Ned said. "I'll check the river, you take the train station, Cap. We'll meet back here when we locate their trail."

They parted and took horse carriages to each of their destinations.

"Sorry, sir," the river boat ticket salesman told Ned, "I haven't sold any tickets at all today. The next steamboat is not due to depart until day after tomorrow."

Ned climbed back into the carriage and instructed the driver to carry him back to the hotel. Cap was waiting with their bags at the door.

"They took the train, Ned. Deacon's headed for his home in Boston and Outlaw Bill took a train to Pueblo, Colorado. I bought us tickets on the next train to Boston, it won't be hard to find Deacon there in his old stomping grounds. We'll try to pick up Bill's trail after we hog tie the Deacon and bring him back to Texas."

"It may be hard to get him back to Texas, Cap. I understand that his family is pretty well hooked politically in Massachusetts. You'll have to get extradition papers to get him out of the state. I doubt that a county sheriff and a cowboy is going to be carrying much influence with a bunch of Yankee politicians."

"Yep, I know," Cap replied, "but I've still got my Texas Ranger badge and my ranger papers in my valise. Maybe we can bluff our way out."

* * * * * * * *

Two days later, Ned and Cap stepped from the train in Boston. Dressed in their western clothes, they drew a lot of stares from other travelers at the station.

"I feel like a whore in church," Cap said, as he noticed a crowd whispering and pointing fingers in their direction.

"I know what you mean," Ned replied, "but we'd probably be staring at them if they showed up in Mobeetie dressed in those city slicker duds."

Cap laughed.

A black man, dressed in a blue uniform, stopped them and said, "Could I carry your bags and get you a cab, sirs?"

"That would be fine," Ned replied, "we don't know anything about this town. Maybe you could recommend a good hotel."

"Yes, Sir," the man said as he picked up their bags, "follow me."

He pushed his way through the crowd, into the train station, and out into the street. Whistling, he stopped a passing carriage and told the driver to carry them to the Cosmopolitan Hotel. "That's the best in the city, and right next door is the Revere Emporium where you gentlemens can purchase some Boston style suits and shirts, if you're a mind to."

Ned laughed, "We look that bad, do we?"

"No Sir, not bad, just different," the black porter smiled, showing a mouthfull of white teeth.

"Well, hopefully, we won't be staying that long," Ned said as he handed the porter a large tip.

"Thank you, Sir," he said as he flipped the gold coin in the air. "You may look funny but you sure knows how to tip!"

* * * * * * * *

Ned and Cap checked into the hotel, and discussed their next move over lunch. "I've been thinking, Cap," Ned said. "Maybe we should first try to take Deacon back legally. What's the name of the document that forces a prisoner to accompany you across state lines?"

"You mean extradition papers?"

"Yeah, that's it. Where do we get one of those?"

Cap thought a minute, "I suppose the Governor would have the final authority."

"Well, let's pay the Governor a visit. You never can tell, he may dislike Deacon as much as we do."

Cap smiled, "It ain't going to hurt nothing to try. Let's go see the Governor."

The Governor heard the commotion in his reception room. A white faced aide opened the door and said, "These two gentlemen insisted on seeing you, Sir. I told them you was busy but ---"

Ned and Cap pushed him aside and Cap said, "Governor, I apologize for acting like a jackass, but it's very important that we have a few minutes of your time, and your staff refused to even announce our presence."

Governor Brown, anger flashing in his eyes, said, "It better be important or I'll have you arrested. Who are you and what is so important that you have to break into my office like this?"

" My name is Arrington, Sir, and this is Ned Armstrong. I am a Captain in the Texas Rangers and have a warrant for the arrest of one of your citizens for cattle rustling in the Texas Panhandle," Cap said as he handed the papers to the Governor.

"Well," the Governor said after reading the warrant, "so the Deacon's finally got caught in one of his crooked deals." He laughed as he continued, "Captain Arrington, you might be interested in knowing that Deacon Bates is an old political enemy of mine. He was always able to wriggle out of his crooked shenanigans here in Massachusetts, and it does my heart good to learn that he is wanted in Texas for a crime. Rustling cattle -- that's a hanging offense in Texas, isn't it?"

"Yes, Sir, it is," Ned said, "but he'll be given a fair trial. If he's found guilty, he can be fined, sentenced to jail, or hung. That's up to the judge and the jury."

The Governor laughed, "I'd say hanging would be a just reward for the Deacon. What do you gentlemen want me to do."

"We need you to sign extradition papers, Governor," Cap said, " so we can take him across state lines legally."

"I'll be glad to sign whatever documents are necessary. Why don't you wait in the reception room and I'll have the documents drawn up immediately," he said.

Ned could hear him chuckling as they walked out the door.

* * * * * * * *

The carriage, carrying Ned and Cap, stopped in front of the white brick mansion on Boston's north side. "This is it, gentlemen," the driver said, "the Bates Mansion."

"Thank you, driver," Cap said, "please wait, we shouldn't be but a few minutes."

Cap wasn't one to mince words, and his vocabulary contained many highly polished phrases. He hitched his gun belt a little tighter and nodded to Ned, "Let's go get the crooked sonofabitch."

Ned followed him to the door.

A black servant opened the door and Cap pushed him aside and walked in. Deacon was sitting in the library, a drink in his hand and a book in his lap. He looked up and cursed, "How the hell did you know where to find me?" he asked.

"Ain't hard to follow a skunk," Cap answered, "the smell gives them away every time. I 'spect you'd best get a bag packed, I'm taking you back to Texas."

"You can't take me back, you don't have any authority in Massachusetts," Deacon whined.

Cap pulled his Colt, pointed it at the cattle thief, and said, "This is all the authority I need."

"I demand to see my lawyer, you can't force me to leave the state without legally drawn up extradition documents."

"I recognize that, Deacon, but I've got a warrant for your arrest signed by the district attorney in Mobeetie, and extradition papers signed by the Governor of the State of Massachusetts. I 'spect that's all we're going to need to transport you back to the scene of your crime. We've got three tickets on a train that leaves in just two hours, now git up, and let's git your bag packed, we're going to Texas."

7

Cole picked ten of the best cowboys, besides Chief, Smokey and Biscuit Banes, and called them all together the night before they were to leave on the drive the next morning. "Men," he said, "Now I know ya'll kinda look on me as a kid, but Pa has put me in charge of getting this herd to Dodge City, and I intend to get it done. If any one of you feels like he can't take orders from me, just say the word and you can remain here. I'll understand. Otherwise, I'll expect you to do your jobs just like you would if Pa was in charge."

There were a few nods, and "we know you can do it, Cole. You're the boss."

"Alright, most of the time during the day I'll be riding ahead, scouting out the trail, looking for water and a place to bed down each night. Some of you will be riding swing, others flank and others drag. There's one thing I want you all to remember, ain't no telling what kind of trouble we might run into -- I hope none -- but Chief will be riding point and if I see any kind of trouble brewing, I'll ride out where he can see me, get off of my horse and walk around the horse in a circle. If that happens, Chief is going to send a message back down the herd to each one of you and I want you to leave your position and hightail it to the front of the herd."

"What about the cattle, Cole, if we leave our position they're going to scatter?" Waddie asked.

"Makes no matter, forget the cattle and come running. I don't intend to send for you unless it's a real emergency." Cole replied.

Smokey was placed in charge of the horse remuda and the old Ceebara cook, Biscuit Banes was going along as cook. The chuck wagon and hooligan wagon were loaded, both pulled by a team of four young mules -- Sandy, a blonde headed kid of fifteen, was to drive the hooligan wagon and assist Biscuit with the cooking and Smokey with the horses. The herd hit the trail at daylight, led once again by Big Red, the old Brazos River steer that had led the first herd of longhorns up from Central Texas.

Cole took command with confidence, riding up and down the line, sending the wagons on ahead to make dinner camp. Chief was positioned as point man, swing and flank men were spotted at proper intervals and two of the youngest cowboys, the Garcia brothers, were designated as drag riders. Smokey, with sixty head of trail-broke horses, followed the chuck wagon

Kate and Belle, mounted on their two roan mares, watched from the hillside. With both Ned and Cole gone, they would have to take over the responsibilities of the ranch. Kate wiped a tear from her eye, realizing that Cole had grown into a man. Cole and Chief waved as they kicked their horses into a lope and took positions at the head of the herd of three thousand cross-breds. If everything went well, they would be arriving at the stock pens in Dodge City in less than two weeks.

Cole had decided that it would be best to push the cattle to the open, rolling hills on the south side of Red Deer Creek, before turning east. He didn't want the cattle to have the brush and trees along the creek bank for protection until he got them trail broke. He remembered his first trail drive, when he allowed a rogue steer to break from the herd and hide in a plum thicket. He still had scars from the scratches he received while trying to haze the steer back into the herd.

The swing and flank riders were kept busy the first day, teaching a few of the unruly old longhorns that they were expected to stay with the herd. The cross breds were easier to handle, and by night, the herd was moving in a well organized line. Cole rode his horse Comanche about a mile ahead of the point, scouting the best route for the herd. When he wanted the herd to turn right or left, he would stop his horse on a rise where he could be seen by Chief, wave his hat and ride a short distance in the direction he wished the herd to turn. Chief would then motion to the swing riders and one side would crowd the leaders while the other side gave ground. The herd would slowly swing in the direction indicated by Cole.

The first night was spent on the south side of the Cana-

dian River at the fork of Red Deer Creek. The cattle were allowed to graze the lush grasses along the river's edge while
Biscuit and Sandy set up camp underneath the spreading
branches of a large cottonwood tree, built their fires and began supper. Smokey kept his horses upstream a couple
hundred yards. Everyone was in high spirits, the cowboys realizing in only a few days they would be enjoying the entertainment that Dodge City, one hundred and twenty miles to
the north, had to offer.

The herd was restless during the long hours of the first
night, unused to the strange sounds coming from the huge
trees surrounding their bedding ground. Cole doubled the
night watch, to make certain they didn't bolt during the night
and head back to the ranch.

The men discussed plans for crossing the river while
they ate their breakfast of beans, bacon, biscuits and coffee.
Rains up river had put nearly two feet of water in the stream
bed for a span of three hundred yards. Waddie and Chief were
designated as quicksand spotters and rode their horses back
and forth in the water, shouting for the lead animals to be tak-
en up or downstream when they discovered areas of danger.

The crossing was made without incident, although the
chuck wagon team became excited when they stepped into a
bed of quicksand -- Biscuit screamed at them and busted their
tails with the leather reins and was able to get through the
danger area. After crossing, Big Red raised his head in the air
as if to smell the proper direction, then headed north across
the rolling sand dunes, a trail which he had traveled ten
times before. The herd of crossbreds, content to accept the

massive old longhorn as boss, followed in his tracks.

Cole allowed the cattle to seek their own grazing speed, then rode ahead, searching for water for the noonday stop. A small, spring fed creek, offered a good camp ground, and Cole waited until Biscuit arrived with the chuck wagon, pointing out where the cook should place his wagon.

That was his first mistake -- the cattle drive cook considered those decisions to be made by him alone. Cole might be ramrod of the cattle drive, but he was the boss of the chuck wagon. Anyone who had ever been on a cattle drive knew that they didn't give the cook any orders or back talk -- twenty feet on either side of the chuck wagon was his domain, and he ruled that domain with an iron hand.

After looking the situation over, he slapped his mules on the rear with the reins and rode past Cole, who was still sitting on Comanche. Cole watched in disbelief as Biscuit guided the mules another hundred yards and picked a spot on the windward side of the creek.

Riding up, Cole asked, "What was wrong with the spot I picked."

"First thing was wrong was that you picked it! That's my job! Second thing that was wrong was when the cattle gets here, the wind is going to be putting their dirt and sand in the middle of my grub -- over here, the wind is going to be blowing towards the herd and away from me. Third thing that was wrong, was I want my water to be clean, and I'm upstream from where the cattle are going to be drinking. Now, anymore questions, Cole? "

Biscuit had known Cole all his life, and knew he was

capable of making decisions for the rest of the crew, but he'd do the decision making for the vittles cooking, that was and always had been the rule at the cow camps and on the trail drives.

Cole smiled, remembering what Ned had told him before giving him responsibility over the herd, "One thing you need to remember, son, only a fool argues with a skunk, a mule, or a camp cook!"

"I 'spect you're right, Biscuit -- I know'd better but just wasn't thinking. From now on, I'll keep my nose out of your business."

The old cook nodded, satisfied that he had made his point.

* * * * * * * *

After the noon meal, the cattle were allowed to rest and drink for about an hour before being pushed on northward. Big Red had gone through the routine so many times in the past that he was up and taking the first steps onward before the point man was good in the saddle. "Well, come on you or-nery old mossy horn," Chief said, "if you're in that big a hur-ry, I'll try to stay out of your way."

The cattle had filled their bellies with grass during the leisurely morning drive, and were ready to pick up the pace. Big Red had trouble staying ahead. Most of the unruly long-horns had learned there was no way to break away from the herd without being headed and slapped with a rope by one of the flank riders. They remained in place and the herd, like a huge exclamation point, moved slowly northward. By night-fall they were fifteen miles closer to their destination.

The cook had his fires made, biscuits, steak and beans cooking and coffee boiling by the time the herd reached the campground on the next spring-fed creek. Riders who had the first night watch were the first to ride in, dismount, fill their plates with the hot food, eat and then mount the new horses which Smokey had saddled for them. Riding back to the herd, they began to slowly circle the cattle, singing softly to let them know that everything was alright. The other riders rode in, dismounted and unsaddled their mounts before filling their plates with the hot biscuits, beans and steak. The cook had a surprise for them, peach cobbler cooked in a large dutch oven. He gave Cole an extra helping of the cobbler as a sign of peacemaking. Looking at the young trail boss, he winked without saying a word. Their little confrontation was a secret to be known only by the two of them.

Smokey roped the night riders horses and saddled them for the men, who then tied them to the hooligan wagon before curling up in their bedrolls. Some of the men sat around the campfire, smoking cigarettes and drinking coffee. One of the Garcia brothers had brought along his guitar and was softly playing and singing a Mexican love song.

When the north star made its appearance, Biscuit picked up the tongue of the chuck wagon and pointed it towards the star. "Why'd you do that, Biscuit," Ben, a young wrangler from Jack County asked.

"One of my jobs," Biscuit replied. "That way, we will always know which way to go in the morning if the sky is cloudy or if fog has come in during the night."

That got the cowboys to talking about the stars. Looking up, the stars sparkled like a million diamonds in the dark sky. "Yonder's the Big Dipper," Biscuit said, pointing to the constellation overhead. "You can learn to tell time by looking at its position in the sky. Right now, it's telling us it is nine o'clock."

Nine o'clock and they would be rolling out of their sacks by four a.m.! Time to stop the palaver and get some shut-eye.

Soon, the only sounds around the camp were the loud snoring of the men, an occasional bawl of one of the steers, and the lonesome wail of a coyote from the distant hills. Now and then, the soft singing of the night riders could be heard, as they made their ride around the herd.

"Whoopie tie yi yo, get along little dogies,
It's your misfortune and none of my own.
Whoopie ti yi yo, get along little dogies,
For you know that Dodge City will be your new home."

Every two hours, the night riders would ride into camp, shake the next guards awake, who would put on their hats, pull on their boots, mount their night horses and take their place around the herd.

Down low on the horizon, faint flashes of lightning could be seen, too far away for the sound of thunder to be heard.

The next day on the trail began at four a.m. with the last change of guards before breakfast, riding into camp. They awakened the cook and then headed for their bedrolls to catch another half hour of precious sleep before they would have to get up, eat, and once again mount up for the day's ride.

Biscuit kicked Sandy awake, started his fire, put on the coffee pot and started rattling pots and pans as he began to prepare breakfast. The sour dough, which he had started the night before, had risen and was ready to be shaped into biscuits, fitted into the dutch oven and placed on the hot coals. The sounds coming from the chuck wagon told Smokey that it was time for him to ride out and look for the remuda.

"Come on, Sandy," he ordered, "let's go pen the horses."

Next up were Cole and Chief, who would be the first to eat so they could ride out and be in position when the herd began drifting from the night's bed ground.

The cook soon had the coffee boiling, his biscuits cooked, bacon and beans hot over the fire. He yelled for the men to come and get it before he threw it out to the coyotes. They arose, put on their hats, then struggled into their boots. By the time the men had finished their breakfast, Smokey and Sandy had the horses in the rope corral, ready to be roped and saddled.

Sandy caught his mules first, and hitched them to the hooligan wagon, then harnessed the chuck wagon mules and tied them to the wagon, ready for Biscuit when he completed breakfast.

One by one, the men threw their dirty dishes in the 'wreck pan" lying under the chuck box lid, tied up their bed rolls, and walked to the remuda corral.

Each rider had been assigned six horses and each horse had a name. "Catch ole Buck for me, Smokey," Waddie said.

Smokey uncurled his rope, walked into the herd until he spotted ole Buck, threw the loop which settled gently over the horses head. He led the horse out of the corral and Waddie slipped his bridle on and released the rope.

The next cowboy shouted out the name of the horse he wanted to ride that morning, and Smokey had him quickly roped, and ready for the next request. The cowboys saddled the horses and rode out to the herd. The last night guards headed for the wagon, ate a hasty breakfast before they rejoined the herd as it slowly began to move out on the trail.

Big Red, who had bedded down away from the main herd as if he were too good to associate with the other cattle, looked back, bellered and followed Chief onto the trail. The rest of the herd followed, obediently.

The day passed without a major incident, but Cole rode nervously, continually glancing to the west where the storm clouds of the night before could be seen in the distance. Riding back to Chief's position on point, he said, "I don't like the looks of those clouds, Chief. Probably ain't going to reach us until sometime tomorrow, but you remember what happened two years ago when the cyclone hit us on the Cimarron. We need to be prepared just in case it hits tonight."

"I 'spect you're right, Cole," Chief replied, "I watched that lightning on the horizon last night -- pretty strong storm."

Comanche dropped his head and nibbled on the dry grass as Cole, with his hands crossed on the saddle horn, continued to look to the west, "Even if the storm misses us, it could put the Cimmaron on the rise and we should reach the river by tomorrow evening."

Chief nodded in agreement, then asked, "Did you notice the dust between the storm and here?"

"No -- where?" Cole asked.

Chief pointed to the southwest, "Back there," he replied.

"Yeah, I see it. Could be a buffalo herd moving, or maybe another trail herd. Most of the ranchers should be heading for Dodge City with their herds. Colonel Goodnight told me he was planning on making a drive this month, and his trail is west of ours."

"Probably Goodnight," Chief replied.

"Keep the herd moving north. I think I'll make a ride to the west and see if it might be the colonel," Cole said as he kicked Comanche into a lope.

* * * * * * * *

The dust cloud continued to parallel their drive, and in less than an hour, Cole was close enough to see that it was a large cattle herd moving slowly to the northeast. Two miles ahead of the herd, he recognized the big blue roan that Goodnight was usually mounted upon. He loped over.

"Howdy, Colonel," Cole greeted.

"Well, howdy Cole. I was wondering who was kicking up all of that dust to the east. Looks like we're going to get to the Cimarron about the same time," the old cattleman replied.

"Yes, sir," Cole answered, as he rode close and shook Goodnight's hand. "Looks like we won't be more'n a mile or two apart when we camp tomorrow night."

"I 'spect you'd best swing your herd a mite to the east and I'll adjust ours a little to the west so we don't get too close together," Goodnight said. "We sure don't want them to get mixed."

"How many you got, Colonel?" Cole asked. "We're trailing near about three thousand head."

"About the same size herd as mine," Goodnight replied. "Our count was thirty-five hundred when we left the canyon," then asked, "Where's Ned?"

"I figured you probably knew," Cole answered, "He and Sheriff Arrington caught a stage to Dodge City last week. He got a wire from Ben Hilton that said Deacon Bates was in Dodge with a herd that was carrying a lot of brands other than the LX."

"Well, I be damned," Goodnight exclaimed. "Deacon Bates a cattle rustler!"

"Yes, Sir," Cole said, "Ben said it looked like Mr. Bates was shipping the herd to St. Louis. Pa put me in charge of the herd and we left the ranch three days ago."

They discussed the weather, the distance to Dodge City, and other minor problems they each had experienced on the short drive, then Cole turned Comanche back towards his own herd and kicked him into a ground eating trot.

They circled the herd and made camp on a small playa lake before night, and once again began the ritual of preparing the evening meal. The lightning in the west was now close enough that they could hear the thunder. The herd was restless and nervous.

* * * * * * * *

However, the storm ran its course without reaching their campground and soon rained itself out.

"Storm will re-form tomorrow evening," Biscuit told Cole, "and will hit the herd tomorrow night."

"That's what I was thinking," Cole said. "Maybe we'll reach the Cimarron before it gets to us and we can cross before night."

"I wouldn't count on it, Cole," the old cook said, "I'll bet a sack of beans that the river is already on the rise. It's been raining the last three nights upstream, and the rise travels faster than the storm."

Cole gathered the men around the campfire and gave some instructions. "Men, we may be in for a blow tomorrow night. I was hoping we could cross the Cimarron before it got on the rise, but we're probably already too late. If it is too high, we'll have to make camp on the south side tomorrow night and wait it out. There won't be any sleeping, tomorrow night, we'll all have to be on night watch to try to keep the herd from stampeding."

Corky, a twenty-two year old cowboy who had signed on just two weeks before the drive had begun, said angrily, "You can't expect us to work day and night. No, sir. I'm going to sleep tomorrow night!"

"I didn't ask you, I told you, Corky. We'll all be in the saddle tomorrow night," Cole ordered as he stepped close to the disgruntled cowboy.

"I'm tired of taking orders from a kid," the newcomer

said, "I 'spect I'll just have to show you that you can't boss me around."

Before Cole realized the extent of the cowboy's anger, a big fist slammed into his chin and he was sent sprawling. Chief, who had been watching from the back side of the fire, stepped forward but was stopped by Cole's order, as he rubbed his chin.

"Leave him be, Chief. It's me he's got a quarrel with," Cole said as he picked himself up from the ground.

He circled the big cowboy, warily, with his fists doubled and arms bent in front of his chest. Corky threw another looping right, but Cole was prepared for it, ducked and brought his own right up in a smashing blow to his opponents nose.

Corky's head snapped back and blood flowed from the broken nose. Cole stepped back, dodging a left which barely missed his right ear, then seeing an opening, quickly brought his right fist forward in a straight jab, catching Corky's cheek and at the same instant put all his force behind a left upper-cut, landing solidly on Corky's chin. The big cowboy's feet left the ground and he fell flat on his back, unmoving.

Cole walked to the water barrel on the side of the chuck wagon, dipped a bucket in, walked back to the prostrate cowboy and splashed the water in his face. Corky's eyes opened, he wiped the water from his face and slowly got to his knees.

"Like I said, Corky. We all ride night herd tomorrow. If you don't agree, you can ride out tonight," Cole said, picking his hat up from the sand.

Corky smiled sheepishly, "If you say so, boss. I guess I'll stay on."

Cole nodded and stuck out his hand. Corky took it and they shook.

* * * * * * * *

As Cole suspected, the Cimarron was flowing six feet deep when they reached it an hour before sundown the next day. He could see the Goodnight herd, circling for their bedding ground two miles upstream. Hanging low on the horizon was the dark, ominous clouds of the thunderstorm -- the wind had already shifted from the direction of the cloud and lightning and thunder were crashing in the distance.

Biscuit had a fire going with beans and steak cooking by the time the herd had been bedded. "Everyone back on your horses as soon as you finish eating," Cole said, "Might as well put on your slickers before mounting up, looks like we're in for a toad floater. Remember, if they start to run, get out of their way and try to keep them circling to the left -- that'll keep them from mixing with the JA herd."

Darkness had fallen and the herd was still standing and milling, as nervous as the cowboys. When a huge bolt of lightning hit one of the steers at the rim of the bunch, they all bolted as one -- and headed upstream! Although they tried, the cowboys couldn't get the herd turned to the left, and as luck would have it, the JA herd was stampeding downstream. Cole, through flashes of lightning, could see the JA herd coming in their direction, their horns shining with balls of electricity bouncing from one horn to the other -- St. Elmo's fire, he had heard it called. It was an eerie feeling, watching the two herds on a collision course, with the St. Elmo's fire sparkling and bouncing across the herds. Riding hard, he passed one after the other of the cowboys and shouted for them to forget the cattle and ride towards the river, otherwise they would be caught in the middle of the two herds.

Rosco, a tall, gangling kid of sixteen, was in the lead and Cole was shouting for him to turn back, but the thunder of the hooves, the wind and the rain drowned out his shouts. The last he saw of Rosco was when a flash of lightning lit up the sky, and the two herds met, with the young cowboy in the middle!

Like two freight trains meeting, the cattle crashed into each other and hundreds of steers went down with the others struggling over their bodies. The two herds, now mixed into one huge herd, turned away from the river and continued to run south. JA cowboys and Ceebara cowboys were now riding together, trying to circle the herd. The rain continued to fall for two hours, and the cattle refused to stop until the rain stopped. The cloud moved on to the northeast and the sky cleared, with the moon and stars brightly sparkling in the heavens. Puddles of water on the prairie reflected the pristine beauty from above. The steers, tongues hanging from their mouths, finally stopped and the cowboys rode slowly around the herd until daylight, trying to calm them down and keep them from bolting again.

With the rising of the sun, a prairie of devastation greeted their eyes. Dead cattle were scattered from the point where the two herds had collided for five miles down the stampede tracks. Cole and Charles Goodnight, covered with mud, met as they circled the herd.

"Damnedest stampede I ever did see," the old man said. "Weren't no one's fault and there wasn't anything we could do but let them run theirselves down. Got anyone hurt, boy?"

"Yes, sir, Colonel," Cole replied, removing his hat and wiping the sweat from his brow, "at least one I know of. I saw one of my boys in the lead when the two herds met and I saw him go down. I'm riding back that way to see if I can locate him."

"I'll ride along," Goodnight said.

They rode back through the dead cattle, counting as they went. One hundred and fifty carcasses were counted before they came to the spot where Cole had last seen Rosco. They found him and his horse, lying in a pile of ten dead steers. Cole dismounted, removed his slicker and draped it over the dead cowboy.

"I'll send our hooligan wagon after him," he said, wiping a tear from his eye.

"I know you're feeling right bad, son, but don't blame yourself. These things happen on cattle drives. There's many a cowboy buried in unmarked graves across these plains from such accidents as this. I've buried over a dozen of my own men in the past. Even lost my partner over on the Pecos from a Comanche arrow."

"Me and the boys will bury Rosco and then we'll help you separate the cattle, Colonel," Ned said.

"No, young feller -- we're going to help you give this cowboy a decent burial and then we'll drive this bunch of or-nery steers into Dodge City together. There ain't no way we could ever get 'em separated out here on the prairie," Goodnight said.

A grave was dug and Rosco was lowered gently into its depths. Colonel Goodnight said a few words and Jesse Garcia strummed a lonely dirge on his guitar as the Ceebara cowboys shoveled dirt over the body. Biscuit carved *Rosco* on a rough board which he had pulled from the *cooney* under the chuck wagon -- no one knew his last name -- and began to drive it into the ground, the clang of the hammer echoed sadly up and down the Cimarron Valley.

* * * * * * * *

They waited two days before the water in the river receded enough for the crossing to be made safely. Now the drive consisted of a little over six thousand head, two chuck wagons, two hoodlum wagons, one hundred forty horses, two cooks, twenty-five cowboys, the colonel and Cole.

The second day after crossing the Cimmaron, Cole and Colonel Goodnight were riding about two miles ahead of the herd, following the old Ceebara Trail when they were surprised by the approach of several mounted riders coming at a lope.

"What you suppose that is, Colonel," Cole asked.

"Beats hell out of me, Son -- but looks like they're in a hurry. We best be on the lookout for trouble," Goodnight replied.

Cole slipped his Winchester out of the saddle boot and laid it across the saddle horn.

There were twenty of them, all heavily armed and they brought their horses to a halt in front of Cole and Goodnight.

"Howdy," the leader, a huge bull of a man, long black hair and beard, and with a plug cut out of his right ear, said, as he rested his hand on the butt of his pistol. The gotch ear was the result of a forty-five caliber bullet which missed its intended mark by about three inches to the right.

Goodnight, not to be bluffed, rested his hand on the butt of his pistol and answered, "Howdy."

Cole nodded without saying anything, slipping his finger inside the trigger guard.

"Looks like you fellers got a good many cattle coming behind you," the leader said.

"Looks like it," Goodnight said.

"Care to say how many," the leader asked.

"Can't say as I would," Goodnight answered.

"Well, Mister, we need to know how many, 'cause we're fee collectors. This is our land and we charge a dollar a head for passage," came the reply.

"Now that's very interesting," Goodnight said. "I been traveling this trail for several years and I was always told this was Indian Treaty Land. Never been asked for no *fee* before."

"Well, it used to be Indian land, now its my land, and I'm telling you that if'n you want to cross it, you got to pay a fee."

Goodnight could see that there was no use in arguing the point, they had at least forty guns to his and Cole's four. "Well, Mister, I guess we'll just have to pay -- we got to get these beeves to Dodge City. 'Course we don't carry that kind of money in our saddle bags, we'll have to ride back and get it out of the chuck wagon."

Cole smiled, he could see what the colonel had in mind - - with twenty-five cowboys, all armed, back at the herd, he would have more bargaining power. The problem was getting the hands all together at the front of the herd before this band of Jay Hawkers rode in.

While Goodnight discussed an agreement with the Jay Hawkers, Cole rode to the side, dismounted and pretended to be checking the hoof of his horse. He picked up the hoof and pretended to dig out a pebble, put it down then stepped away from Comanche and began to slowly circle him, all the time pretending to be looking for something wrong.

"What'cha doing out there, boy?" one of the Jay Hawkers hollered.

"Horse got a limp -- I was looking to see what might be wrong with him. I 'spect it was that rock I dug out of his hoof." Cole continued to circle Comanche, and the Jay Hawkers paid him no more mind.

Chief, watching from a mile off, decided Cole was actually sending him a message to get the hands to the front of the herd. He loped back to the first flank rider and shouted, "Get the hands all to the front, there's trouble brewing!"

Within a few minutes all of the riders, including the JA cowboys, were riding hard to the front of the herd. Big Red continued his slow gait to the north and the herd followed.

Convincing the Jay Hawkers that payment would be made, Goodnight and Cole led them back to the herd, where they were met by all of the trail riders, rifles in their hands and ready for any kind of trouble that might be approaching.

Cole and Goodnight turned their horses and faced the blackmailers, "This is as far as you skalawags are going," Goodnight said, "unless you want to go another six feet underground. These boys have orders to shoot to kill if any one of you so much as acts like you might want to pull leather."

Gotch ear nervously placed his hands on the saddle horn and said, "Ain't no use in you boys getting all riled. We were just trying to make an honest living."

"Honest living, be damned!" Goodnight said, then turning to Cole, he asked, "What you reckon we should do with these road agents, Cole?"

"Well, Colonel, I reckon we could line them all up and let the Chief scalp them, but that might be a little too harsh. Why don't we just let them go with the understanding that if we see hide or hair of any of them within ten miles of this herd, we shoot them on the spot."

Goodnight smiled, "Sounds fair enough to me." Turning to the outlaws, he said, "My name is Goodnight and this is my partner, Cole Armstrong, and if we ever see any one of you close to our cattle again, we intend to shoot first and ask questions later. Now get your asses out of the way of our herd, we're going to Dodge City!"

The outlaws turned as one, and kicked their horses into a run back towards the Arkansas River, thankful to get away from this Texas herd.

Reaching Dodge City without further trouble, the huge herd splashed across the Arkansas River and followed Big Red docilely into the stock pens, one hundred and ninety head less than when they had left the *Llano Estacado,* two weeks ago.

Cole carried the note that Ned had given him to the bank and withdrew enough money to pay his cowboys, who, after a bath at the Dodge House, immediately hit the saloons and brothels along Front Street. It didn't take them long to get into trouble.

Shanghai Pierce and fifteen trail hands had arrived from South Texas with three thousand head of longhorns, and the saloons were filled with thirsty cowboys anxious to wash the trail dust from their gullets -- and to compete for the attentions of the prettiest dance hall girls. The Ceebara cowboys, including Cole and Chief, were just as anxious.

Colonel Goodnight and Shanghai Pierce, being old friends, were eating a steak at the Dodge House, and the young cowboys from both herds were on their own.

"We got to learn what whiskey tastes like and what the girls have got that the older cowboys talk about all the time, Chief," Cole had said, smiling, "and I reckon now is as good a time as ever." They pushed their way into the Alhambra saloon. Corky was inside and had already started an argument.

Corky had his eye on Diamond Lil, queen of the Alhambra, and didn't intend for Colorado, one of the South Texas cowboys to win her affections. The two exchanged some liquored-up profanity and Corky flattened the trail rider from Victoria with a half empty beer bottle. The battle was on!

Five of the South Texans moved in to protect their downed friend, and Corky had his hands full. Cole and Chief, the only other Ceebara cowboys in the Alhambra, seeing their fellow drover in trouble, jumped into the fray with fists flying. Using their back-to-back method of battle, they quickly put two of the Pierce drovers on the floor.

Colorado, recovering from the knock on the head, rising to his knees, grabbed Corky's legs and pulled him to the floor. They were rolling around across the saloon floor, first one then the other on top, punching and gouging.

When two of the South Texas boys waded into Cole, he failed to block a round house right which caught him in the eye and he went down, dragging his adversary with him. Chief was left standing, confronted by the other three inebriated cow hands, and when it appeared he was in for a beating, one of the girls yelled from the door that Marshall Earp was on the way. Colorado and the other five Pierce cowboys headed for the door. Lillian Handie, a pretty soiled dove who had a room in the back of the Alhambra, grabbed Cole by the hand and led him quickly to the rear. Squirrel Tooth Alice did likewise with Chief, and Diamond Lil ushered Corky to the back.

Lilllian closed the door behind them and led Cole to the bed, pushed him down, removed his hat and began examining his eye. A small drop of blood was hanging from his nose. She pulled her hankie from the cleavage below the top of her gown and wiped away the blood.

The coal oil lamp sitting on a small table in the corner cast a dim light in the room. There was one cane bottom chair pulled up against the table with some crumpled lingerie hanging from its back.

"You alright, cowboy?" she asked.

"Yes, ma'am," Cole replied, rubbing his cheek and looking nervously around the room.

"My, you're a handsome lad," Lillian said, as she ran her fingers through his tousled hair.

Cole, sitting on the bed could not help but stare at the bare flesh of her upper torso as she stood in front of him, with her bosom only twelve inches away from his face. His heart raced as he savored the smell of her perfume. He had admired the pretty painted ladies in Hide Town and Tascosa, but only from a distance -- never had he been this close to one before.

"Seems to me I ought to know you," the pretty painted lady said.

"Yes, ma'am, I think so," Cole replied. He recognized her as being one of the young ladies on the wagon train two years before when the cyclone hit the Ceebara herd and the supply wagons on the Cimmaron. "I remember you was one of Miss Pearl's girls on the way to Mobeetie when that cyclone hit and tore up the wagon train."

A look of recognition crossed her face, "Durned if you ain't right! I remember you and that Indian boy helped us with our teams -- Cole, that's what your pa said was your name." She laughed, remembering, "He said you boys was too young to enjoy our entertainment."

Cole blushed, "Yes, ma'am, but I'm two years older now." "Well, Cole, my name's Lillian. You do know what we do in these back rooms, don't you?" she asked.

Cole stammered, "Ye-ye-yes, ma'am -- well, I-I think I do. I ain't never been in one but I hear the men talking about it."

Lillian stepped back, placed both her hands on her hips and laughed. "Well, what do you know -- I got me a innocent one."

Cole didn't know whether to run or laugh along with this pretty lady. But this was what he and Chief had been planning. He couldn't let Chief down.-- he didn't run.

"Ma would beat me within an inch of my life if she knew what I was planning on doing," he thought.

"Get them boots off, cowboy," she said, "I'm going to enjoy teaching you the facts of life!"

Cole obeyed, bent over and began pulling off his boots.

Lillian reached out and began unbuttoning his shirt, ran her soft hands over his smooth chest, then unlatched his belt. "Stand up," she ordered, as she pulled the shirt from his back. His pants fell around his ankles and he stood, embarrassed, dressed in nothing but his long johns.

Lillians deft fingers made short work of the long johns and laughed as Cole quickly jumped under the covers of the bed and watched as she began to slowly undress. It didn't take her long, because she didn't have much on to begin with.

She quickly crawled under the covers, pulled him close and placed a moist kiss on his trembling lips. Then she began to teach him the facts of life!

Cole was a fast learner!

* * * * * * * *

Returning home with their prisoner, Cap and Ned reported to D.A. Houston. "Well, Temple," Arrington reported, "You

176

sent me after the thieving sonofabitch, and I calaboosed him!"

Deacon Bates was incarcerated in the jail at Mobeetie while Temple made plans to prosecute him on the charge of cattle rustling and theft over five thousand dollars. However, time was running out for Temple to declare his candidacy for State Senator from the newly formed Thirty-first Senatorial District. He resigned his position as district attorney and Lawyer Luscious Dills was appointed to take his place. The trial was scheduled for November, but when Deacon agreed to pay each of the ranchers for the stolen cattle and to pay a stiff fine, Dill dropped the charges.

"I hate to see him released, Ned," Dill said, "but the other ranchers would rather have the money than to see him hanged, and you need to recognize that a good defense lawyer could probably get him off by swearing that he had nothing to do with changing the brands and actually believed that those were his cattle."

"Maybe he didn't change the brands," Ned angrily replied, "but he danged sure was paying the men who did."

Dill shook his head, "If he were to swear that Outlaw Bill was behind the whole thing, who's going to say he was lying. That's a big country out west, and we don't have any idea where Outlaw Bill is hiding. We've talked to all of the cowboys on the ranch and none of them will admit being involved. I'm convinced a jury would acquit him. His reputation is ruined in this country, so my advice is to take your money and be done with the whole affair."

Ned reluctantly agreed. "Alright, Luscious, you're the D.A., but I'll tell you one thing, if we find anymore Ceebara cattle with the LX brand, I'll hang the owlhoot myself!"

Although David Beales was apparently unaware of the Deacon's illicit activities, he could see that the LX reputation had been ruined. The American Pastoral Cattle Company of London had made an offer to buy the LX, so he sold out, lock, stock and barrel. The ranch encompassed 187,000 acres of deeded land plus 250 sections of school land -- extending from the northern edge of Palo Duro Canyon to Chalk Hollow in Moore County. The LX brand was burned on 40,000 head of cattle and 1000 horses.

Although the brands remained, the LX, LIT, Quarter Circle T, Turkey Track and Bar CC, which lay mostly north of the Canadian River, were now in the hands of foreign investors. Lands belonging to the LE and LS ranches along the Texas - New Mexico border were doomed to fall with the encroachment of the three million acre XIT British capitalized ranch, which was in the formative stage.

Outlaw Bill Moore, through the years as manager of the LX, had built a herd of his own with mavericked and rustled Panhandle cattle and had established his own ranch at Coldwater Springs in No Man's Land. It was there he finally holed up until Bates was released, then sold his Coldwater interests for $70,000 and established a new ranch in western New Mexico. He continued to build his herd with rustled Texas Panhandle cattle.

8

As ownership of the huge ranches in the Texas Panhandle continued to change hands, more and more foreign capital was injected into the area, and management of the cattle empires was transferred from local owners to bank headquarters in England and Scotland.

The cowboys, who had always "ridden for the brand", no longer felt a sense of loyalty to the foreign owners. The original owners -- Major Littlefield of the LIT, Tom Bugbee of the Quarter Circle T, Deacon Bates of the LX, Dick McAnulty of the Turkey Track, Hank Cresswell of the Bar CC and Leigh Dyer of the T-Anchor -- had been working owners, asking nothing of their cowboys that they were not willing to do themselves. They also allowed any of their cowboys who wished, to run a few of their own cattle under their own brand.

That had all changed with the new owners. They would visit the ranch only once or twice a year, and never dirtied their hands with real ranch work, taking the attitude that they were better than their hired help. Ranch managers were hired to do that, drawing wages like the other cowboys. No longer were the cowboys allowed to run their own brands with the ranch herds.

Most of the huge ranches employed as many as one hundred cowboys, and paid them only twenty-five dollars a month plus board and horses. Much of the time, their shelter was only the stars over their head as they spent their time on the prairie, many miles from headquarters or the nearest town.

Camp cooks received the same pay as the cowboys and wagon bosses were paid fifty dollars a month. Top ranch managers such as Outlaw Bill Moore of the LX, Cape Willingham of the Turkey Track, and J.E. McAllister (Mr. Mac) of the LS, received much higher salaries, but were still subservient to the absentee owners.

The independent cowboys resented the changes, and began to take actions to better their situation. Many continued to run their own brand and built their herds by branding ranch mavericks which had failed to feel the sting of the branding iron in last years round up. Others began talking of a cowboy organization which would give them bargaining power with the ranch owners. Still others quit their jobs and took up the lucrative occupation of cattle rustling, stealing cattle and driving them to ranges in New Mexico Territory.

* * * * * * * *

The saloons in Tascosa were buzzing with the news. Tom

Harris, wagon boss with the LS, Waddy Peacock of the LIT and Roy Griffin of the LX had camped with their crews at the LS supply depot above the mouth of the Frio Creek in southeastern Deaf Smith County, and after a big meal cooked up by their chuck wagon cooks, decided to do something about the situation. After much discussion, they elected Tom as their leader and drew up a list of demands to be presented to the ranch owners. The demands were written in the form of a petition, to be signed by all cowboys who agreed with the demands.

We, the undersigned cowboys of the Canadian River, do by these presents, agree to bind ourselves into the following obligations, viz:

First, that we will not work for less than $50 per mo. and we further more agree no one shall work for less than $50 per mo. after 31st of March.

Second, good cooks shall also receive $50 per mo.

Third, anyone running an outfit shall not work for less than $75 per mo.

Anyone violating the above obligations shall suffer the consequences.

Cowboys carried copies of the proclamation and a demand that the time-honored right for the cowboys to run a few of their own cattle on the open range, to all the ranch owners.

Ned, Cole and Chief were visiting the JA headquarters to look over some Hereford bulls that Goodnight had offered for sale, when Tom Harris rode in with a copy of the cowboys

181

demands. Colonel Goodnight, a long time friend of Harris, welcomed him and invited him into the ranch house for coffee.

After a few comments about the weather, condition of the grass, and small talk about cattle, the colonel asked, "What brings you our way, Tom? I supposed that you would be as busy as a banty hen feeding a nest full of chicks."

"Yes, sir, Colonel, we are pretty busy. My wagon crew has been working drift cattle over on the Frio around the LS supply depot. Waddy Peacock with the LIT and Roy Griffin with the LX had their wagons over, and we been trying to cut some of their strays out of our LS herd," Tom replied.

"That still don't tell me why you showed up over here in the Palo Duro. You know that any time we find strays in our bunch that we cut them out and head them back to their home ranch," Goodnight said.

"Yes, sir, Colonel, I know that. That's not what I came for," Tom said. Then, as if he were having a hard time getting said what he wanted to say, continued. "Me and the boys had a meeting over there on the Frio, and we got to figuring that the cowboys deserve more pay than what they're getting. We formed us an organization and are asking the ranchers to give us a better deal."

Ned spoke up, "First time I've heard anything about it, Tom. My boys seem to be satisfied with the pay they're getting."

Goodnight, never one to mince words, with anger flashing in his eyes, said, "Tom, I've been making decisions for most of my life how much a man who works for me is worth. I don't expect I need anyone telling me how much I should pay."

"Yes, sir, Colonel -- that's the reason I wanted to talk to you personally. I know you and Ned pay more than most of the ranchers in the country. It's those big, absentee owners that try to run their ranches from Kansas City, Chicago or England and Scotland that we are dissatisfied with. You still let your men run a few cattle of their own with your herds, but these new owners told us that we can't do that any more."

"What kind of demands are you boys making," Ned asked.

Handing Ned a copy of their demands, Tom said, "Well, first of all, we want the right to run a few of our own cattle, and be allowed to share in unbranded mavericks that are picked up in the cooperative roundups. Second, we're asking that regular cow hands and cooks be paid at least fifty a month, and wagon bosses be paid at least seventy-five a month."

"Hell, Tom -- I'm already paying my top hands that much, and my wagon bosses are being paid a hundred a month," Goodnight shouted. "Sure, I've got some nester boys working for me that I only pay twenty-five a month. They don't know a damned thing, so I figure they're over paid until they learn how to herd cows or build fences."

Ned spoke up, "That's the way it is on the Ceebara, Tom. And you know that I've helped several of my top hands to file on land and start their own spreads. I don't see why you'd be asking us to do more."

"We ain't, Ned. Like I said, those big foreigners have bought up the LIT, LX, Turkey Track, Quarter Circle T, Bar CC and some of the other Canadian River ranches, and treat us cowboys like we are their servants, and we feel we deserve to be treated better. Some of our cowboys have lost their lives to rustlers, stampedes and floods. We just feel like we're worth more than twenty-five dollars a month, and by organizing, we'll have the power to negotiate with them. I come to tell you what we're going to do, and hope you understand. We've been friends a long time and I don't want you to feel like I don't appreciate it."

"What about Lee, does he know about this?" Goodnight asked.

"No, sir, he don't. But you know him, Colonel, I don't see him more'n twice a year. He leaves running the ranch up to Mr. Mac while he stays holed up in his bank in Leavenworth, and he's kinder lost contact with us cowboys. He's been going along with the syndicates on this grazing of our own animals and the pay scale," Tom said.

"Last time I seen him, Tom, he said he was paying you a hundred dollars a month as wagon boss. Seems like you're asking for a cut in wages," Ned said.

Tom smiled, "He ain't paying me any more than I'm worth, Ned. But there's a lot of wagon bosses that ain't getting half that much, and I feel like I'm obligated in try to help them and our other cowboys. If I don't, first thing you know, some of them tight fisted Scotsmen are going to corral him in one of those fancy clubs in Kansas City and convince him that I"m being overpaid."

Goodnight, running his fingers through his gray hair, spoke, "Tom, you're my friend, but you mark this down in your talley book, if I catch you or any of the cowboys in this so called organization trying to cause trouble on my ranch,

I'll hang you to the nearest cottonwood. Now, I 'spect you'd best mount up and take your news elsewhere."

Tom rose, put on his hat and walked to the door, turned and said, "I'll pass the word, Colonel. Most of our problems lie along the Canadian River, I don't 'spect you'll be hearing any more about it."

"Tom," Ned said, as the wagon boss untied his horse and mounted, "I'll be telling my hands about the deal. Any of them who are dissatisfied will be free to pack their poke and leave with my blessings. But I'll be paying them what I think they are worth, and I can tell you right now, some of them are getting paid more than what you are asking."

"Fair enough, Ned," Tom said as he kicked his sorrel into a trot back up the trail and out of the canyon.

Walking back into the ranch house, Goodnight said, "Ned, I know what the cowboys are up against. John Adair is just like all those other foreigners. He's never had to ride the trail, face up to rustlers, work from *can* till *can't* seven days a week rounding up and marking and branding. He thinks I pay the help too much, and treats them like servants when he's around instead of like friends. But I hate to see them taking this route to try to solve their problems, ain't no way they can win -- there's too many nester boys and unemployed cowboys looking for work for them to be able to put much pressure on the syndicates."

"Yes, sir," Ned replied, "Ain't a day goes by that I don't have two or three ride into camp looking for work. Most of them look like they ain't ate a decent meal in a month. I think they'd be willing to work for nothing if I just gave them a place to sleep and a place at Biscuit's dinner table."

Cole and Chief had remained quiet during all of this activity, but they had been listening with interest. Cole asked, "Pa, what do you think's going to happen? You saw what the men said on that petition about anyone violating their demands will suffer the consequences. Seems to me, that could lead to gunfights and killings."

"Seems that way, Cole, but I hope it doesn't go that far. Every one of those cowboys are friends of ours. We've worked roundups with them, fed them and they've fed us. Most of them are good, hard working men -- I just hope there's not any blood shed before this is all settled," Ned answered, with a worried look. "I 'spect we'd best be heading home. I want to get our boys all together and have a talk with them before this news gets spread."

Colonel Goodnight walked with them to the hitching rail, shook their hands and said, "Thanks for coming over, Ned. If you feel like you'd like to try some of these Hereford bulls, just let me know. And if you need any help as a result of this strike, just holler."

"I'll do that, Colonel," Ned said as he turned the buckskin up the trail and headed for Ceebara headquarters. They would make it to Saint's Roost before night.

* * * * * * * *

Three hundred and twenty-five cowboys eventually signed the petition and went on strike. Tom Harris and his boys pulled their wagons into headquarters on the Alamocitas and took their demands to ranch manager McAllister, who tried to compromise and offered the men forty dollars a month. Harris and the LS boys stuck to their demands, it was fifty or nothing. McAllister sent a message to LS owner, W.M.D. Lee in Leavenworth, Kansas, informing him of the trouble. Lee arrived at the ranch headquarters thirty-six hours later.

Lee called Tom into the office and asked, "Tom, when you went to work for me you set your own price and terms and I didn't quibble, ain't that right?"

"Yes, sir," Tom said, "and I ain't complaining for myself, other than I don't agree with the policy of not being able to run a few of my own cattle with the LS herds. It's the boys that I'm looking out for. Twenty-five dollars a month won't hardly keep 'em in smoking tobacco and a visit to the girls in Hog Town. Some of them is good men and want to get ahead in the world. Most of this grass don't belong to nobody and is free grazing. It don't cost the syndicates anything. We need to be allowed to brand a few mavericks and run them with the rest of the LS herds."

"Tom, I want to be fair," Lee said, "We got over a hundred men working the ranch and I suspect there's some of them that ain't worth twenty-five dollars a month -- and probably some that's worth more than they're getting. Would you agree?"

"Yes, sir, I agree," the wagon boss said.

"Alright, I tell you what I'll do. I'll pay fifty dollars to every man you recommend as a top hand, and the others will get twenty-five. What do you think about that?"

"No, sir, Mr. Lee. We agreed that either all the cowboys and cooks get fifty dollars or none of us will work. I'll stick with the boys."

"Then by damn, you're fired!" the old cattleman said,

then walked outside where eighty cowboys were standing a-round waiting for the outcome of the parley. "You're all fired and I'm cutting you off the chuck line. You can get your saddles off LS horses and draw your pay."

The cowboys were dumbfounded, they had never expected an outcome such as this. They walked dejectedly back to the bunk house.

Twenty of the men who had refused to join the strike were put in charge and Lee instructed them to bring the fired cowboys in, one at a time. To each one, he asked if they were willing to return to work at their original pay without any more foolishness. About a third of them agreed, the others joined Tom and they set up a strike headquarters on a creek just a short distance out of Tascosa.

The LIT offered to adjust the pay scale to thirty-five dollars a month for cowboys and cooks and sixty-five dollars for wagon bosses. The offer was refused so the ranch fired them and took away their horses. They were, however, allowed to hang around the chuck wagon and take their meals.

The LE cowboys were fired on the spot but the LX decided to just wait and see before making any rash moves. Jules Gunter, of the T-Anchor, receiving word that the strikers planned to attack his ranch, booby-trapped a building next to his ranch house with dynamite and a keg of nails. Luckily, it proved to be only rumor. Had he been forced to set off the dynamite, several men would have been killed.

The ranks of the strikers swelled next to Tascosa. "Alright, men," Tom ordered, "it may be a long wait before the ranchers give in. We're going to need a grub line. Sandy brought in a chuck wagon from the Turkey Track. We need money to stock it, so I'm asking each one of you to kick in twenty-five dollars."

The chuck wagon was stocked and cooks prepared the meals as the cowboys sat around the campfires waiting to see what would happen. The problem was, the camp was too close to Jess Jenkin's Hogtown saloon and the abundant girls that sold their wares in the Tascosa cribs.

Within six weeks, the cowboys were broke and the strike fell apart. They began to drift back to their old jobs only to find that the managers had already replaced them with new drifters, and they had been black listed at all the ranch headquarters.

* * * * * * * *

"Cole," Ned said, "we need some supplies from Hidetown. I wish you and Chief would take the mules over tomorrow and pack in what we need."

"Alright, Pa," Cole replied, "I'll check with Biscuit and Slim and see what they need."

"Better check with your Ma, too. She said her pantry was getting low."

The next morning the two boys rode out, trailing the two pack mules behind. They covered the thirty miles by mid-afternoon, and rode into Hidetown before dark. After stopping in at Uncle Johnnie Long's mercantile and leaving their list, they ambled down the dirt street to Mark Husleby's hotel and paid for a room. They would spend the night before loading their pack mules and returning to the ranch. Next stop was the Lady Gay saloon.

Ned accepted the fact that they were no longer children, and knew he couldn't control their activities when they were off by themselves in the wild frontier towns. All he could do was advise them and hope they had enough horse sense to stay out of trouble.

"Just remember," he had advised, "don't drink more than you can hold --you get liquored up, someone is apt to start a fight and there'll be a dozen of those hunters or saddle tramps on your back, they're just like a pack of coyotes."

"I know, Pa," Cole replied. "I ain't never seen you take more than one or two drinks, and I don't intend to ever do more'n have a friendly drink with some of the boys."

"Howdy, Cole, howdy Chief," the bartender said, as the two boys elbowed up to the crowded bar. "What'll it be?"

"Just a couple of beers," Cole said. "Trail dust just about turned us into a couple of horny toads."

They took their beers to an empty table and nodded greetings to Temple Houston and Cap Arrington who were seated at a table in the corner, discussing business.

Mobeetie, like Tascosa, was full of unemployed cowboys who had participated in the ill-fated cowboy strike. They sat around, appearing bitter and angry over their failure -- looking for anything or anyone to blame their failure on -- the two Ceebara cowboys made good targets.

Three of the tougher looking cowboys walked by Cole's table and bumped his chair, nearly upsetting him. Cole, holding his temper, smiled and turned back to his beer. The tough looked at him and said, "You're a couple of them damned Ceebara riders that refused to help out in our strike, ain't you?"

Cole could could see that there was no way to placate him. He was itching for a fight, and wouldn't leave it alone until he got one.

"Didn't see as how it was any of our business," he said, "we was already paying more wages than what you was demanding."

The tough glared at him, "You mean that red skin is getting paid more than we was," he asked.

"He's a top hand, and draws top hand wages," Ned replied.

Two of the unemployed cowboys eased behind Cole and Chief, kicking the legs of the chairs from under them while pulling them backwards. The two Ceebara cowboys rolled on the floor and the three toughs began to punch and kick them.

Grabbing their adversaries by the legs, Cole and Chief pulled them to the floor, rolled quickly to the side, and reversed the situation. All five pulled themselves up from the floor -- a quick, short, right jab by Cole to the leaders chin sent him crashing into the table, upsetting it. However, the second unemployed drifter grabbed Cole with an arm lock to the neck and started punching him in the face. Chief, putting the third tough on the floor with a right uppercut, landed a left jab to the nose of the one who had Cole pinned and knocked him to the floor.

Cole and Chief quickly assumed their back to back stance and watched the crowd of angry cowboys as others threatened to get into the fray. Suddenly a gun shot rang out and everyone froze. The authoritative voice of Sheriff Arrington boomed in the silence, "Don't anyone move! Looks to me like these two boys is outnumbered. Now any two of you who would like to take them on, one on one, just step outside. I'm sure they would be glad to oblige you in the middle of the street."

When an inebriated cowboy who was standing behind the sheriff began to draw his revolver, newly elected Senator Temple Houston quickly pulled Old Betsy and stuck it in the gunman's gut, "You break air with that hog leg and you're a dead man," he warned. The gunman let the pistol fall back in its holster and raised his hands to his shoulders.

"I ain't going to do nothing," he slurred as he backed away.

Nobody offered to take the challenge to meet Cole and Chief in the street, and Sheriff Arrington invited the two boys to join him and Senator Houston at their table.

"There's lots of animosity over this strike failure, Cole," he said. "and they're just looking for a place to lay the blame. You just happened to be picked for that honor and there's probably a hundred men in Mobeetie who would put a bullet in your back, if they get the chance."

"I can't understand it, Mr. Arrington," Cole replied. "The Ceebara ranch didn't take sides. We called our men all together and told them that anyone who was dissatisfied was free to join the strike. Not a one of our men pulled up stakes."

"I know that, Cole, but it's hard to convince these boys who are out of work and blacklisted that you wasn't agin them. Me and Temple will walk you back to the hotel and I'll put a deputy on guard until morning, just in case. Ned would never forgive me if I allowed something to happen to you while you was in my town."

"Thanks, sheriff, I 'spect you're right," Cole replied as they all stood and walked out of the saloon.

Cole and Chief were unhappy -- there wouldn't be any socializing with the Hidetown painted ladies tonight.

* * * * * * * *

The next morning they picked up the mules from the livery stable, loaded them with the supplies at Long's Mercantile, and headed out of town. Their way was blocked by the three mounted cowboys who had attacked them in the Lady Gay the evening before.

"How tough do you reckon you are without the sheriff to back you up," the leader asked.

"Ain't no use in this, boys," Cole replied. "We've got no quarrel with you. Someone is fixing to get hurt over nothing."

"Nothing, hell!", the younger one said, "We got no job and can't get one. All the ranches have got us blacklisted and its your fault!"

"No use in arguing the point -- I guess if you want the truth, just ride out to our ranch and talk to some of our cowboys," Cole said.

"We ain't riding nowhere, we're calling you down right here," the leader said, as he grabbed for his gun.

Cole's gun was in his hand and firing as the leader's gun came up. His shot hit the cowboy in the shoulder, knocking him from the saddle. Cole heard Chief's gun blast a heartbeat after his first shot, and knew that the gunman on the right would have received a forty-four slug somewhere in his body. He turned his Colt slightly to the left and fired, striking

193

the third gunman in his gun hand.

The gun spun to the ground as the cowboy screamed in pain and clutched his shattered right hand with his left.

Two of the gunmen lay in the dirt of the street with blood pouring from wounds while the third remained in the saddle looking at his bleeding hand.

Cole and Chief dismounted and walked to the wounded and groaning men. Looking at the wounds, Cole decided they needed a doctor rather than an undertaker. Turning to one of the gathered crowd, Cole said, "Fetch Doc Wilson, these owl-hoots are going to live."

Then, to several cowboys who were looking on, said, "It's time you fellers stopped trying to find someone to blame for your troubles. I'm truly sorry that you've been blacklisted and can't find work, but it's not my fault. I'd be glad to put some of you on my branding crew, but I've got all the help I need. I'd advise you to ride south, I hear there's lots of trail herds being put together to stock this new Capitol Syndicate ranch over on the New Mexico line and I'm sure they could use some experienced trail hands."

Reaching in his pocket, he pulled out three five dollar gold coins and flipped them to the three wounded cowboys. "This'll help pay the Doc for patching up your holes. Come on, Chief, we need to make tracks if we're going to get home before dark."

9

The rumors were correct -- the land deal between the
state and the Capitol Freehold Land and Cattle Company had
been finalized, Barbeque Campbell had been hired as ranch
manager, fencing was taking place at a fast pace, and orders
had been placed for over a hundred thousand head of longhorns from South Texas. The first herd of cattle was already
on the trail.

Ned, anxious to meet the new manager, told Cole to put a
pack on one of the mules with enough supplies to last him,
Chief, Smokey and Cole for ten days. With bedrolls and
slickers tied behind their saddles, they struck out across the
broad and sparsely settled country towards Buffalo Springs,
one hundred fifty miles to the northwest.

Traveling up Red Deer Creek, they crossed the Canadian
River at Adobe Walls, stopped and looked over the old settlement. The Indians had burned all of the buildings after the

ill-fated battle, and there was little left to identify the battle-ground.

Chief was enthralled with Ned's tale of the battle between the Indians and the buffalo hunters on this site, and questioned him as to how it was possible for such a small number of buffalo hunters to hold off a virtual army of Indians.

"I reckon most of the credit can be given to the big fifty caliber buffalo guns, and the accuracy of the hunters. I remember hearing your pa, Chief Quanah, say that the hunter's guns could shoot today and kill tomorrow. One thing for certain, a lot of brave Indians died on this spot, trying to stop the killing of the buffalo."

Pointing to a low butte in the distance, Ned continued. "That's a good way to explain it -- they say that Billy Dixon was standing about where we are standing and pulled down on a mounted Indian on top of that butte -- must be near about a mile -- and knocked him from his pony. I don't doubt it, I've seen him knock down a running buffalo at half a mile."

Continuing their journey, they rode out of the valley of the Canadian River and onto the flat prairies of the north plains. Where once had roamed hundreds of thousands of buffalo, the prairie was filled with longhorn cattle. From the smallest suckling calves to huge cows and bulls, the flat plains were dotted with the multicolored herds. The grass was green and tall and the cattle were fat. It truly was a cattleman's paradise.

Coming to the drift fence which had been erected from the eastern Panhandle border with the Indian Nations to the western border of the Territory of New Mexico, Ned and the boys turned due west and rode along the fence line until they found a gate, opened it and rode through.

"We must still be on Mr. Bugbee's ranch, Pa," Cole said, "these cows have all got the Quarter Circle T brand."

"It's not Tom's anymore, Cole. He sold out to the Hansford Land and Cattle Company. They also bought the Turkey Track from McAnulty which joined Tom on the north."

"That's a British company, ain't it Pa?" Cole asked.

"That's right, son -- most of the country which we'll be riding the next couple of days will be owned by folks either in England or Scotland. We should be close to the Quarter Circle T west line now," Ned answered.

"Look, Mr. Ned," Chief said, pointing to the northwest, "wagons and men up ahead."

Ned looked in the direction indicated by Chief's pointing finger and said, "I don't see anything."

Chief had learned to speak English as good or better than most of the Ceebara cowboys, and he smiled as he responded, "Indian eyes are better. I thought you was a scout for Mackenzie during the Indian wars. I don't know how you kept your scalp if you can see no better than that. It's no wonder you had a hard time whipping us Comanches."

Ned laughed, "You got me there, Chief. Most of the time, all we could find was the tracks of your pa. He would spot us and be gone before we could ever see him. What do you see?"

"Looks like fence builders," Chief replied, as he shaded his eyes with the palm of his hand, "there's a chuck wagon and a supply wagon, and maybe four or five men."

Cole looked hard into the dancing heat waves, then said, "I see them, Pa, over there," and pointed.

"Danged if you ain't right, Chief. I see them now, must be three or four miles over there. Looks like they are going to be right on our way, maybe we can beg a cup of hot coffee."

As they rode closer, Ned could see that they were, indeed, a fence construction crew. "Howdy," he said as they rode into the camp.

"Well, howdy Ned," a tall, raw boned, red-haired cowboy said, leaning the post hole diggers on the wagon bed and wiping the sweat from his brow. "What brings you this way?"

"Well, Randy Pope!" Ned said in recognition as he dismounted and shook the red head's hand. Last time I saw you was in the battle of the Palo Duro. You was wearing corporal stripes then. Cole, you boys step down and shake Randy's hand -- Randy, this is my son, Cole -- you know Smokey -- and this is Jim Bold Eagle, Quanah Parker's son. We call him Chief."

Randy shook Cole's hand, then Smokey's, "Good to see you again, Sarge," he said, "didn't know you had been drummed out of the service."

"Wasn't drummed out, Corporal," Smokey said, smiling as he shook Randy's hand. "I decided that Mr. Ned paid better wages than the army, so I jes didn't sign up again when my tour was done."

Chief shook Randy's hand, and looked mischievously at the long red curls that fell below the cowboys hat. "Maybe so I take one more scalp back to hang on my lodge pole," he said, speaking like an uneducated savage. "Me no got one with red hair."

Ned laughed, "The war's over, Chief. Remember what your pa said, Comanches ride white man's trail. No more scalps."

"O.K.," Chief replied, smiling, "if white cowboy give hungry Indian coffee and steak, he keep scalp."

Everyone laughed as Randy introduced the group to the other fence builders.

As they sat around the campfire that night, Randy explained that he, like Smokey, had tired of the cavalry, and had signed on with the LX . "We're putting up a fence between the LX and the Quarter Circle T, to try to keep these mangy longhorns separated.

"How's it going with the LX, Randy, since the American Pastoral outfit bought out Bates and Beal?" Ned asked.

"I guess as good as could be expected, considering they don't know a damned thing about cattle. It's doing better since you ran Outlaw Bill out of the country, we're not loosing nearly as many cattle to rustlers," the red head said.

The four Ceebara cowboys shared breakfast with the fence builders, then hit the trail for Buffalo Springs. Before sundown, they came upon another fence, stretching north and south.

"Must be the line between the LX and LIT," Ned said, as they looked for a gate. Finding none, they pulled staples from two posts, pushed down the wire and led their horses across, restapling the wire to the posts after crossing. Camp was made on a small, spring-fed creek.

"This must be the Dodge City -- Tascosa trail," Ned said,

the next day, as they crossed a well worn wagon trail, bearing southwest to the northeast. Riding on west, they soon encountered another prominent trail bearing northwest to the southeast.

"I'll bet my hat this is the trail from Tascosa to that new Capitol Syndicate ranch headquarters at Buffalo Springs," Ned said, as he turned the buckskin up the trail.

The sun had set when they finally spotted the ranch house that had been erected next to the springs. "Hello, the house," Ned shouted as they rode in. He didn't want to surprise anybody and have a Winchester sighting down on him and the boys.

A large, round faced, bearded man stepped from the door, a rifle in his hand. "Who's there?" he shouted.

"Ned Armstrong from the C Bar A over on the Canadian," Ned answered.

"Well, come on in and let me have a look at you," the man said.

Ned and the boys rode up, dismounted and tied their horses to the hitching rail in front of the newly constructed ranch house. Ned stepped forward, hand outstretched and introduced himself, Cole, Chief, and Smokey.

"B.Q. Campbell," the cowman said. "Most folks just call me Barbeque. Come on in and tell me what brought you up to this neck of the woods."

A Mexican cook brought a pot of hot coffee from the stove and poured five cups of the steaming brew as they all sat down around a rough hewn table, with a coal oil lamp flickering from the the middle.

"I heard that you was getting your ranch set up and that you had several herds trailing up from South Texas and thought I'd come up and meet you," Ned said, as he took a sip of the coffee.

"C Bar A, you say -- ain't that the ranch that Colonel Jim Cole started back in 1866?" Barbeque asked.

"Yes, sir," Ned answered. "I was his partner, and since his death me and his wife, Belle have been holding things together. Got nigh onto fifty thousand head of cattle running south of the river."

"Well, you come just in time to see our first herd come in," Barbeque said, "Ab Blocker's bringing in a herd from the Fort Concho country and will arrive tomorrow."

"Ab Blocker, the trail driver from Central Texas?" Ned asked.

"That's right," Campbell answered. "You know him?"

"Sure do," Ned replied. "Met him a couple of times in Dodge City when he brought herds in from South Texas -- good cattleman."

They small-talked awhile before the new ranch manager suggested they were welcome to go down to the chuck wagon and join his cowboys for supper. "Just find a place around the fire to roll out your suggin's," he said. "Turn your horses into the corral. I'll have my wrangler throw them a bait of oats."

Ned and the boys led their horses to the corral which was lit up by a huge campfire. Several cowboys were sitting around, finishing their supper. "Plenty left for you boys," the cook said, friendly like. "You'll find plates and spoons in the chuck box.

The cowboys were glad to see the newcomers and were quick to ask them about activities in the country's only two towns, Mobeetie and Tascosa. Most of the questions had to do with the girls and the gambling halls.

* * * * * * * *

Next day, Ab Blocker brought in the first herd from the Fort Concho country, arriving mid-afternoon. The cattle were released next to the springs, took their fill of water and then scattered and began grazing on the lush grass.

Ned joined Barbeque and Ab as they slowly rode through the herd, inspecting them for final settlement.

"Good looking herd, wouldn't you say Ned," Barbeque asked.

"Yes, sir -- mighty good. Looks like they might have put on weight on the trail."

Ab spoke up, "That's right, Ned. I've drove enough herds up to Abilene and Dodge City to know that if you don't push them too hard, they'll arrive in better shape than when they left Central Texas."

They rode back to the newly erected corrals next to the springs, dismounted and tied their horses to the corral fence.

"What brand you want burned into their hides?" Blocker asked.

"Don't have one," Barbeque answered. "All I've been told is that this is Capitol Syndicate range." Owners had failed to give the ranch a brand, and were either ignorant of the fact that cattle had to be branded, or had overlooked this crucial decision.

"Guess it's left up to you and me," he told the trail driver. "I want it simple, one that can be made with a single bar iron -- and which can't be changed with a running iron."

Ab thought about it for a minute while he cut a plug out of a square of Star chewing tobacco. Placing the plug into his mouth, he chewed until it was soft, then spit the first brown saliva into the sand. Wiping the sand smooth with the sole of his boot, he took the toe and carved X I T   in   the   sand. Five strokes with one branding iron would mark the hide as the property of the ranch.

Barbeque looked at the brand, shifted his cud from one jaw to the other, spit a brown stream which landed squarely in the middle of the dirt brand, nodded his head and ordered, "Get to branding, boys, you're now working for the X I T ranch."

Branding over one hundred thousand head of cattle was going to be time consuming with the old South Texas method of heading and heeling each one. Barbeque had built a long chute within his corrals which would hold twenty cows at a time, and was narrow enough that the cows could not turn back. By pushing a bar in front of the first and another to the rear of the last, all twenty head could be branded standing up in a matter of minutes. His cowboys began bringing in two hundred head at a time, ran them through the long chute where they were held immobile while branding irons began burning the first X I T brands into their hides. Cole, Chief and Smokey climbed into the corral and pitched in, keeping the fires going and the irons hot.

Watching from outside the corral, Blocker, Ned and Campbell discussed the plans of the new ranch.

"I've got over a hundred thousand head contracted to be delivered this year, Ned," Barbeque said. "I intend to hold most of them north of the Canadian River the first year while we construct facilities at the Yellow Houses, Spring Lake, on the Tierra Blanca, Alomocitas and Rito Blanco. Then I'll scatter them over the entire ranch."

"I guess you know that we've got an organization of ranchers to try to keep down rustling and to keep the fever from South Texas being spread through our herds, don't you, Barbeque?" Ned asked. "We've got a quarantine line below the caprock and don't allow any cattle from south of that line to cross our pastures."

"I'm aware of it, Ned, and I have it specified in my contracts that no cattle will be purchased from below that line," Campbell answered.

Ned thought for a minute before replying, "A hundred thousand head is a goodly number of cattle, Barbeque. And seems like you're taking the word of the sellers where they may have picked them up. I hope there ain't no fevered cattle in the bunch."

* * * * * * *

The summer was filled with dust clouds as the herds began to trail in from the south. Ned, Cole, Chief and Smokey left the Buffalo Springs headquarters of the X I T, and rode to Tascosa, seventy miles to the south. W.M.D. Lee had introduced the Hereford breed of cattle into the area and Ned was anxious to purchase some of the pure bred bulls which Lee was running on LS ranges in Deaf Smith, Potter and Oldham counties.

Riding west out of Tascosa, up the Canadian River, they crossed the river at the confluence of Alamocitas Creek and the river. Five miles up the creek, they came to the Alomocitas headquarters of the LS ranch. Ranch manager, J.E. McAllister, *Mr. Mac*, welcomed them into the ranch house.

The rock ranch house had been built by Captain Ellsworth Torrey, a former Boston sea captain, when he came into the area in 1879. The house was a mansion, compared to most ranch houses in the area, and was furnished with fine Boston furniture. Shortly before Billy the Kid's death, he and his gang had brought in a herd of stolen horses to sell in the Tascosa country. When Torrey refused to feed the bandits, the Kid threatened to kill him if he did not apologize for the way he had treated his gang.

Captain Torrey, in his seventies, later apologized at gun point on the main street of Tascosa, and was so embarrassed that he put his ranch up for sale. Lee and Scott purchased the ranch and all of the household furnishings and moved their headquarters into the fine rock house.

"What brings you our way, Ned?" Mr. Mac asked, as they sat down at the huge dining table and were served steaming coffee in real porcelain cups and saucers.

"We've been up to Buffalo Springs to meet the new manager of the Capitol Syndicates property," Ned replied. "Got there in time to see their first herd brought in from down south. Ab Blocker was trail boss of the herd."

Mr. Mac poured some of the steaming coffee from his cup into his saucer and began to blow to cool it, a habit that most westerners had formed. Taking a sip, he then asked, "Who did they hire to run the outfit?"

"Barbeque Campbell," Ned replied.

"That old scalawag!" Mr. Mac said. "We'll have to keep a close eye on our herds with him running things. He'll bring in all of the riffraff in the State of Texas to work for him. What you reckon they're going to call this outfit?"

Ned put his cup down and answered, "They're burning X I T on the hides of the Blocker herd, so I guess that's what it'll be called."

"X I T, huh," Mr. Mac said. "Damned good brand -- be hard for rustlers to change that."

"That's the way I figure it, Mr. Mac. Seems like they've found a way to change every brand running on these ranges up to now. It'll be interesting to see what they'll do with X I T," Ned replied, then continued. "Saw some mighty good looking Hereford bulls when we rode in, are those some of the ones I heard you was offering for sale?"

"Not those, Ned, but I've got about fifty head over in the Alamosa Creek pasture just as good. Ten miles over there, if you'd care to take a look."

"Sure would, Mr. Mac. We been cross breeding with some Durham bulls, but I like the looks of these Hereford crosses."

They finished their coffee and walked out the door. One of McAllister's cowboys led his big sorrel gelding from the

barn, they mounted up and headed east, down a well used
wagon road, and had gone no more than five miles when a
couple of riders pulled up on winded horses which were carrying the LS brand.

"You men know better than to ride my horses into the
ground, Bud," Mr. Mac scolded as they pulled up in a cloud of
dust.

"Yes, sir, we know, Mr. Mac, but we thought you ought to
know that a big herd is coming in from the south, moving
right across our grass," the young cowboy replied, pointing
back at a dust cloud that was rising from the herd.

"What brand they carrying," the old cattleman asked.

"Didn't wait to see," Bud Turner answered. "We figured
we'd best let you know quick as possible."

The boys had been looking for strays in the Alamosa pasture when they spotted the huge trail herd. "How many boys
in your crew?" McAllister asked.

"We got Dunk's chuck wagon and crew -- six of us," Bud
answered.

"Ride back and bring all of them and make certain
they're armed," Mr. Mac ordered. "We'll meet you at the
herd."

Bud and the other cowboys arrived at the trail herd the
same time that Ned and Mr. Mac pulled up. The trail boss rode
up and, pushed his hat to the back of his head and wiped the
sweat from his brow. "Howdy," he said, "Name's Boyce, and
this here herd belongs to the Snyder brothers. We're deliv-
ering them to that new ranch at Buffalo Springs."

McAllister looked him in the eye with no sign of welcome. "McAllister, manager of the LS. and this is our range. You know about our quarantine? We don't allow fevered cattle on the LS. You'll have to find another trail."

"My cattle aren't fevered," Boyce replied. "I drive wherever I please, and right now it pleases me to cross the Canadian River with my herd."

Some of Boyce's trail drivers rode up, all well armed.

Mr. Mac whispered to Cole, "Son, you know the way to Tascosa?"

"Yes, sir," Cole replied.

"Ride into town and fetch Sheriff East and tell him I need him to come pronto," the LS boss ordered.

Cole turned Comanche and kicked him into a lope down river.

Cole soon returned with the sheriff and one of the Home Rangers of the Panhandle Stockmens Association. Tempers had flared and it looked as if there was going to be gun play when the sheriff rode up.

Sheriff East introduced himself to the trail boss and tried to explain the association's rule about tick infested cattle. Boyce explained that his cattle had come from north of the quarantine line, and he intended to take the herd up the trail.

"Mr. Boyce, I'll have to arrest you unless you turn back," the sheriff said.

The trail cowboys all placed their hands on the butt of their guns and the LS cowboys did the same. Ned could see that gun play was just a breath away, when Boyce looked at his men and said, "Stand easy, men. I'll go into town with the sheriff and see if we can't work this out. Circle the herd and hold them until I get back."

Mr. Mac instructed his cowboys to return to the chuck wagon and wait for his orders as he joined Ned, the sheriff and the ranger as they rode the three miles back to Tascosa.

Boyce, refusing to bend, spent the night in jail. Next morning, Ned suggested he lead the Snyder herd east to one of the trails which had been designated for northbound herds to use. Mr. Mac and Boyce agreed and bloodshed was averted.

Before the year was out, over 100,000 cattle had been branded and turned loose on the three million acre ranch, seven hundred miles of fence had been strung, one hundred and fifty cowboys had been hired, fifteen wagon crews formed, and seven headquarters established -- Buffalo Springs, Middle Water, *Ojo Bravo, Rito Blanco, Escarbada,* Spring Lake, and *Las Casas Amarillas.*

* * * * * * * *

Fences were also going up on the Ceebara spread. Cole and Chief didn't like it, but they did their share -- from cutting posts along the Canadian River breaks, hauling wire from Dodge City, staking the lines and digging the post holes, then stretching the wire and nailing it to the posts with staples.

The fences were successful in keeping their cattle inside their boundaries and preventing strays from mixing with their herd, but failed to prevent rustling. All cattle thieves carried a pair of wire cutters in their saddle bags, along with a running iron, and the ranchers continued to find wires cut and remains of cow chip fires where irons had been heated and brands changed. Ned suspected Outlaw Bill to be behind most of it -- the trail always led west towards New Mexico territory.

Pat Garrett had been hired by the Panhandle Cattlemen's Association to head up their Home Rangers and try to rid the plains of the rustlers. The governor had commissioned him as a captain in the Texas Rangers. He hadn't been very successful and was looking for help.

"Ned, you've got to come help," he said as he, Ned, Cole and Chief, sat on the veranda of the Ceebara ranch house after a huge meal of steak, biscuits, gravy and beans which Belle and Kate had prepared for them. "About the only help I can find is a few barflies over in Tascosa. Most of the cowboys seem to know that they would probably be going up against some of their friends that were blacklisted during the cowboy strike, and refuse to ride with me."

"I wish I could, Pat," Ned answered, "but we've been having hell with the politicians down in Austin over lease on the school lands. They've scheduled a hearing over in Saint's Roost for next week that I have to attend."

Cole interrupted, "Pa, me and Chief could help Mr. Garrett out. We know the country as well as you do, and you know that Chief is the best tracker in the country."

"I don't know, Cole -- your ma would raise cain if she knew I agreed to let you go looking for rustlers after that run in you had over in Cheyenne Canyon."

Pat spoke, "I'd look out after the boys, Ned. They'd sure be a big help if you would agree to let them come. I have the authority to swear them in as Texas Rangers, and they will be paid Ranger wages."

Kate opened the door and stepped out onto the veranda with coffee and cups. She heard Pat's last statement. "What kind of help you talking about, Pat," she asked.

"Well, Kate, I'm needing some help trying to track down some of that System bunch that seems to be responsible for most of the cattle rustling that's going on, and I was hoping that Ned could help out."

"System bunch, who's that?" Kate asked.

"We think it's a bunch of the blacklisted cowboys that got fired during the strike, but haven't been able to prove it. They're the most likely since they know the ranches and the trails over in New Mexico Territory. Tom Harris is over in the Fort Bascom area putting together a ranch. I've heard it said that he calls it the 'Get Even Ranch' and is offering to run cattle for any of the blacklisted cowboys."

Ned interrupted, "I can't go with him, Kate, because of that hearing over in Saint's Roost. Cole and Chief want to help but I told them they'd have to talk it over with you."

"Well, there's not anything to talk about -- the boys can't go!" Kate said, emphatically.

"Ah, Ma," Cole said, "we know how to take care of ourselves. It's time you stopped worrying about us. Besides, it's our cattle that the rustlers have been stealing -- looks to me like it's our responsibility to help Pat run them down."

Ned took the boy's side, "Cole's right, Kate, we can't expect someone else to be doing our work. Pat needs help, and Cole and Chief are the best we've got. I think they should go."

"It's your decision, Ned Armstrong -- I'm wiping my hands of the whole affair. If these boys get hurt it's going to be your fault," she said and turned angrily back into the house.

Ned looked at Pat and nodded his head in agreement.

"We'll leave at sun up," Pat told Cole. "We may be gone a couple of weeks, so pack an extra change of clothes with your slickers and bedrolls." Turning to Ned, he continued, "We've found wires cut along the Canadian with the trails leading into the rough breaks over towards the New Mexico line. I figure on starting there."

* * * * * * * *

Finding the wire cut on the west line of the Ceebara Ranch, they dismounted and inspected the damage. "Looks like forty head of cattle and four horses crossed here," Chief said as he knelt and examined the tracks.

"How long since they crossed?" Pat asked.

"Hard to tell," Chief answered, "Maybe seven days."

"That means they are probably a hundred miles or more ahead of us, if they didn't stop to spend some time with the girls in Tascosa." Cole calculated.

"I doubt they stopped," Pat said, "probably hightailed it until they crossed into New Mexico Territory."

Following the tracks, they rode until dark, then stopped and made a dry camp on the plains. They hobbled the horses and allowed them to graze, ate a meal of cold biscuits and jerky, and then crawled into their bedrolls. The horses could be heard, nipping the grass from the prairie floor and crunching it between their teeth. Now and then one of them would sneeze and stomp, to be answered by another which had strayed away in the dark. A family of coyotes began to yelp to one another as Cole, Chief and Pat fell into deep sleep.

"Looks to me like they're headed for Endee," Pat said as they mounted their horses the next morning and once again took up the trail to the west.

"Yes, sir," Cole said, "but I'll bet they steer around it. The LS has a line camp there and they ain't going to want to be seen driving cows to New Mexico by some of Mr. Mac's cowboys."

Midday they were surprised to see the tracks joined by another set of tracks. Chief dismounted, examined the tracks and reported that another six cowboys with an additional sixty head of cattle had joined the drive.

"Looks like they've got some LS cattle mixed with our C Bar A cattle now," Cole said.

"With more riders they're going to be able to move faster," Pat said. "If they keep heading west, we may not catch them until they reach Las Vegas."

Dropping off the caprock north of Endee, the trail turned northwest, back towards the Canadian River. Again a newly constructed fence was approached, and the wire had been cut and pulled out of the way for the rustled cattle to cross.

"Must be the state line fence which the X I T is constructing around its perimeter," Pat said.

"More cattle have joined the herd here," Chief said as he

rode up the fence line, north of the cut wire.

Sure enough, upon closer inspection, Pat could see where a large herd had been driven down the fence line from the north by six riders and joined the rustled herd.

"This has been a well planned operation," Pat told the boys. "I don't know who might be in charge of it, but whoever it is, he's got several men on the payroll and it took some planning for the three herds to join together the way they have. By bringing several small herds across the plains, no one is going to notice dust or tracks. And since there is no line camps across that section of the prairie, they've not been discovered by ranch riders."

Cole dismounted and joined Chief as they examined the tracks of the new herd. "Looks like this bunch might have two hundred or more. Probably picked them up along the fence line between here and the river. Wouldn't take more'n three or four riders to herd them down the fence."

"Who you think might be behind this operation, Cole?" Pat asked. "You've been in this country all your life and have worked with most of the local cowboys on roundups."

Cole thought a minute before answering. He remembered what his grandad, the colonel, had cautioned him before he was killed, *Don't ever accuse anyone of some wrong doing unless you've got evidence to prove it.*

"I'd hate to say, Pat. Could be one of the blacklisted cowboys, but that don't seem reasonable to me. Most of them are just cowboys and wouldn't have the influence to get a group like this together in such a slick operation. I know Mister Harris, and I don't believe he would steal cattle, even though he lost his job because of the cowboy strike. He might offer a place for rustled cattle to graze on that Fort Bascom ranch, but I just don't believe he's the one we need to be looking for."

He pulled a square of Brown Mule chewing tobacco out of his chaps pocket, and bit off plug before continuing. Deep in thought, he gazed off to the northwest, his eyes following the well defined trail of the rustled cattle. Turning his eyes back to Captain Garrett, he said, "Captain, if I had to place any money on the owlhoot that's behind this, I'd bet on Outlaw Bill Moore. He was run out of the country with his tail between his legs and everyone speculates he landed somewhere in New Mexico Territory, where he had been putting together a ranch and stocking it with stolen cattle for the past five years. He has the money to bankroll a big operation, he knows the country, and he knows the cowboys who are inclined to be dishonest. I ain't saying he's behind it, but I am saying he's the type person that could put it together."

"Sounds reasonable, Cole. I had my mind set that it had to be Tom Harris and the 'Get Even' bunch, but you are probably right. Mr. Mac sent Tom to ride with me when we was trying to catch the Kid back in eighty-one. He sure didn't impress me as being someone who would steal, no matter how angry he might be."

Remounting, they followed the trail to a point above the Canadian River where the river had cut a deep channel leaving a steep cliff on either side. The trail cut back west, paralleling the cliff to a point where it intersected a small dry creek bed, which wound down to the river bottom.

Reaching the bottom of the creek bed, they followed it

towards the river. Suddenly, Chief, who was riding in the lead, held up his hand and stopped. Turning in the saddle, he placed his finger to his lip for Cole and Pat to make no noise. Listening, they heard the sound of cattle, bawling in the distance.

Tying their horses to a mesquite tree along the creek bank, they slipped slowly towards the sound of the cattle. Rounding a bend in the creek bed, they could see the river and on the far bank, cattle grazing on lush grass along the river's edge. A campsite was erected on a huge sand bar, and several men were lounging around a small campfire where steaks were being roasted over the coals. A boiling coffee pot was sitting in the coals. Five naked men were bathing in the clear water of the river, and the others had removed their gun belts and hung them on their saddles which were piled next to the campsite. They apparently had no idea that they had been followed and were being observed by the three rangers.

Captain Garrett motioned for the boys to move back a-round the bend of the creek where they were hidden from view of the outlaws. Motioning for them to follow, Garrett led them back to where the horses were tied.

"Get your rifles," he instructed, "and fill your pockets with cartridges. Surprise is on our side, and with half the gang naked and in the water, we should be able to take them before they can make a move for their guns."

Looking the situation over, Cole said, "I believe if Chief and I climbed up to those rocks overlooking the river, we could cover them while you make your move down here."

"Good idea, Cole," the captain replied, "I'll give you time to get into position then I'll step into the open and shout for them to keep their hands away from their guns. If any of them go for their weapons, I want you to shoot to kill. Bring one of them down and the others will probably give up."

Cole and Chief climbed carefully up the creek bank and moved to a hidden position behind two small boulders. When they had the entire campsite in view and their rifles sited in on the group, they motioned to Captain Garrett who began to move towards the river.

"We've got you surrounded," he shouted," throw up your hands and don't make a move for your guns!"

The rustlers froze -- then one of them who was nearest to the saddles, jumped to his feet and stepped towards the weapons. Cole, bringing him into his sites, quickly fired, hitting him in the right knee, knocking him to the ground.

At the same time, Chief put two quick shots into the sand next to the feet of the other outlaws. They all threw their hands into the air, shouting "Don't shoot!"

Cole pulled his rifle sites around and fired two quick shots into the water, splashing water into the faces of the five naked bathers. They, too, threw their hands above their heads.

Captain Garrett moved into the open and splashed across the knee deep water of the river. "My men have you covered from the cliff," he said, "and have orders to kill the first one of you who offers resistance."

Cole fired another shot over their head just to let them know that he and Chief were ready to carry out the captain's orders.

Garrett stepped to the saddles and removed the revolvers from the holsters and threw them into the sand behind the campsite.

"You," the ranger captain shouted at the nearest of the bathers, "get out of the water and bring a rope from these saddles and start tying up these hombres -- and tie them tight.

After each had been tied securely, he instructed the naked bathers who were still standing in the water, to come out one at a time and be tied. When they all had been tied, he instructed them to sit down in the sand with their backs to the river.

"O.K., Cole, ya'll can come down now," he shouted.

Soon Cole and Chief climbed down from the cliff, retrieved their horses and splashed across the river.

Cole examined the wounded man's knee and tied his bandana around the wound to stop the bleeding. "I didn't see any need in killing him, Captain. I knew I could stop him with a shot to the knee. We had plenty of time to take them out if they failed to obey your orders."

The captain smiled, "I thought it was just a poor shot, Cole -- I should have known you was a better shot than that. I guess I would have done the same thing if I'd have been in your place."

"What do we do now, Captain?" Chief asked.

"What do you think we should do, Chief," Garrett asked, smiling.

"If we Comanches had caught them stealing our horses, we'd just scalp them and be done with it," Chief answered.

"I've got a sharp Bowie knife if you want me to take care of it."

One of the rustlers shouted, "Keep that redskin away from me, mister!"

"I don't know, sounds like a good idea to me," Pat said, "but I might let you keep your hair if you tell me who's boss of this outfit."

The outlaw replied, "Not any of us -- its Outlaw Bill, and we were to drive the herd to his ranch over by Las Vegas."

"Where's the ranch located," Cole asked.

"About halfway between Las Vegas and Springer, just below the mountains,' the whimpering rustler replied.

"What about Tom Harris and the 'Get Even Ranch' outfit -- are they a part of it?"

"They don't have anything to do with our operation," another one of the rustlers said. "I've heard that they may be taking cattle around Tascosa, but we don't have anything to do with them."

"How many cattle has Outlaw Bill stolen from the ranches along the Canadian River?" Garrett asked.

"I heard him tell a buyer that he could furnish eight thousand head," the rustler replied.

Garrett thought a minute, planning their next move. "Which one of you is boss of this outfit?" he asked.

"I guess that's me," a large, burly cowboy with a prominent scar across his brow which ended just above the right eye, said.

"What's your name?" the captain asked.

"They just call me Scar," he answered.

"O.K.," Captain Garrett said, "here's what we're going to do. Chief, gather up all of these owlhoots weapons -- revolvers, rifles and knives -- and dump them in the river. Cole, you untie them and guard them while they saddle their mounts. They're going to drive this herd back to LS headquarters at Tascosa. This time we're taking the Tascosa - Las Vegas stage road along the river which is much closer than the way they came with the cattle."

Turning to the rustlers who were still sitting in the sand with their hands tied, he said, "Me and Chief are going to be riding behind you with rifles cocked and ready to shoot the first one who tries to slip away. Cole is going to ride point with Scar and if he hears so much as one shot fired, he's going to shoot Scar. Now, let's get started."

The rustlers were untied and saddled their horses while Cole looked on with cocked rifle. They all mounted up, gathered the herd together and pushed them out of the river bottom. When they reached the stage road, they turned the herd east and struck out for Tascosa.

The outlaws gave no trouble, afraid if they made one false move they would receive a bullet in the back. Pushing the herd hard, they were able to make the Alamocitas headquarters of the LS in two days. Mr. Mac had his men cut the herd according to brands and drive the cattle back to their home ranges.

Pat, Cole and Chief took the rustlers into Tascosa and lodged them in the jail to await trial at the next District Court day.

Cole and Chief returned to Ceebara headquarters while

Captain Garrett gathered a posse to ride after Outlaw Bill. He was too late, however, as word reached him that Outlaw Bill had gotten into an argument with two men in a Las Vegas saloon, killed them and had fled the country with a price on his head.

10

"Pa!" Cole shouted as he rode his winded horse into the ranch compound and slid to a stop in a cloud of dust.

Ned rushed from the house to see what had Cole so excited. "What is it, Son," he asked.

"Fire, Pa! We was riding the west pasture just up on top of the caprock when we seen it. Smoke reaching way up in the sky back southwest."

"How far away?" Ned asked.

"Couldn't tell, Pa. Must be a long way. Couldn't see any flames, just smoke."

Prairie fires had become a problem with an influx of sod busters, fence builders and maverick branders. Today would be a bad one because there had been no rain in two months, the temperature had been hovering close to one hundred degrees, and the wind had whipped up from the southwest at forty miles an hour.

Most of the Ceebara cowboys were at the headquarters corrals, shaping up a trail herd to be taken to market. "Fetch the men, Cole," Ned ordered, "and have Biscuit load his chuck wagon. Better get the mules harnessed for the hooligan wagon and load shovels, blankets, water barrels and buckets. Tell the Garcia boys to round up their remuda and bring two extra horses for each hand. I'll tell Belle and Kate that we may be gone for a couple of days."

"We're going, too," Belle said when she heard the news. "We can help drive the wagons and help Biscuit with the meals."

There was never enough help when a prairie fire broke out, especially when the wind was blowing. The grasses, thick and dry this time of year, burned like gasoline, and moved across the prairie ten to twelve miles an hour. Hundreds of thousands of acres could be burned in a matter of a few hours. It didn't matter where the fire was located, it was the law of the plains for everyone who could see the smoke to rush to the location and fight the fire until it was out.

The Ceebara crew was on the trail within an hour and headed to the southwest. Like Cole had reported, the smoke had risen high into the sky and looked like a huge black thunderhead in the distance. It was apparent that the fire was a great distance away, maybe as far as the new X I T ranch on the New Mexico border. That meant that the LS, T-Anchor, LIT, Frying Pan and maybe even the JA were in the line of fire. There was no doubt, this was a big one.

Shortly before sunset, Ned gave orders to stop, eat a cold meal and change horses, then continued the ride without rest.

By sunup the next morning, they were close enough to see the red tongues of flame in the distance.

All kinds of animals, running from the fire, were met -- rabbits, coyotes, antelope, wild mustangs and cattle. Now ashes from the huge smoke cloud began to fall around them as they approached closer. Ned began to search for the leading point of the fire and decided it was at least two miles to the right of their line of travel. To the left, he could see that the flames were not so high, and there was a small playa lake which the fire would have to go around -- this would be their best point to ride through the fire, get on the back side out of the flames and smoke, and begin battling the fire with their shovels, wet blankets and brooms.

Spying a small herd of cattle running from the flames, he pulled his rifle from the saddle boot, stepped to the grass and fired,-- once, then twice, and two of the largest cows fell, their life blood coloring the grass.

"Smokey, get some help and gut those cows," Cole ordered. Four of the men rushed to the carcasses, rolled them on their backs and began to open the bellies with their skinning knives. In short order the entrails had been removed, the heads cut off, and the carcasses rolled back with the opened stomach down, spread-eagled with the legs sticking to the outside. Quickly, lariats were looped around each leg and tied to the saddle horns of four of the horses. Two of the cowboys rode through the flames, while the other two remained in front of the flames and began dragging one carcass down the line of the fire. Most of the flame was snuffed out and the wagons and men crossed to the back side of the fire.

224

The other carcass was dragged down the line of the fire in the opposite direction, snuffing out the flames. Other cowboys dismounted, soaked saddle blankets in the water barrels which were latched on the side of the hooligan wagon and began putting out any flames which re-fired behind the dragged carcasses. Buffalo chips and cow chips which continued to smolder were kicked back into the ashes behind the fire. Belle and Kate, with brooms, followed the blanket brigade, and swept any remaining embers away from the grass.

Like an arrowhead, the fire continued to move to the northeast, but a gap was being formed by the dragged carcasses and the blanket brigade of the Ceebara crew. The problem was that the fire had moved laterally until it was probably more than twenty miles wide. Ned only hoped that other ranch crews were battling the blaze from other points along the line.

The horses which were dragging the carcasses were changed every ten minutes, because of the heat, smoke and lack of oxygen. The carcasses were heavy, and it didn't take but a few minutes for the horses to become totally fatigued, covered with sweat and ashes.

The Garcia boys were kept busy, changing saddles from the winded horses to fresh ones. Cowboys grabbed a quick drink of water from the chuck wagon while the changes were being made.

Cole and Chief were one of the teams of draggers, with their faces and bodies covered with black soot and ashes. Eye lashes and hair below their hat brims were singed, and shirts were full of scorched holes. Chaps and boots protected their legs. After covering about two miles along the burn line, Chief shouted, "Look, Cole! There's another crew fighting the fire down the line, maybe two miles."

Cole looked, "I see," he answered. "When we meet up with them, we'll return to the leading point of the fire and help on that end."

They fought the blaze all day, with little success in holding back the point fire. When it looked as if they were making progress, the wind would change directions slightly and the fire would rush back across the area where they had thought they had won the battle. The heat was so intense they could not get within a quarter mile of the leading edge. Darkness came early because of the smoke, and the scene changed, with the flames reaching high into the sky, lighting up the smoke from a bright orange at the ground level, to a smoky gray a hundred feet into the sky. The light from the flames outlined the forms of the firefighters as they struggled into the night. Ned, stepping away from the fire for a breath of clean air behind the inferno, couldn't help but imagine that this must be what hell looks like.

At times the flames would reach one of the many small playa lakes, slow down and move laterally around the lake, then burst forth with a continued vengeance as the wind was once again to its rear.

They fought the blaze all night without rest, and as the sun rose in the hazy distance, Biscuit pulled his team and chuck wagon up, loaded with a fresh-cooked meal of steak, beans and biscuits. While half of the men ate, the other half tried to hold the flames in check from moving to the side. There could be no rest, however, for the fire was getting closer and closer to the Ceebara pastures.

The fire had started on the X I T range near the New Mexico line, when a cook had let his cook fires get away from him in the high winds. The fire had destroyed most of the grass south of the Canadian River on X I T, LS, T-Anchor and the White Deer pastures of the Franklyn Land and Cattle Company.

The fires were now burning Ceebara grass, and it looked as if it would rush unchecked to the caprock. But just as Ned was ready to concede that they could not win the battle, the winds suddenly ceased. The forward movement of the flames virtually stopped, and the fire-fighters, though totally exhausted after two days of fighting the flames, took on new hope as the carcass draggers were able to snuff out the point of the fire. Now it was only a job of mopping up a few hot spots behind the draggers.

When Ned finally rode along the fire line and announced that the men could take a much needed rest, most of the cowboys curled up on the black ashes where they stood, and fell asleep.

All up and down the twenty mile fire line, cowboys and nesters fell exhausted, and rested for three or four hours before they dragged themselves up, mounted their horses and rode back to their headquarters. Most of them had no eyebrows and little hair left, beards were gone, blisters covered the backs of their hands and the skin around their necks above the protective cover of their shirt collars.

Only Shorty, who had been caught in a backfire, was burned seriously. Belle, Kate and Biscuit had loaded him in the hooligan wagon and had smeared his burns with bacon grease. He would be back in the saddle within two weeks.

* * * * * * * *

The fire had destroyed two million acres of prime grass, burned to death three thousand head of cattle, and had destroyed the homes and barns of several hundred sod busters.

The long term effects were even more drastic. The dry grass, which was absolutely necessary to feed the cattle during the winter, was gone. Winter storms would freeze and starve many more thousands of cattle.

11

Belle hadn't intended to ride down into the Canadian River breaks when she left the ranch house early that morning. It was such a beautiful fall day -- little wind, large fluffy white clouds floating slowly overhead, and fat cows with suckling calves dotted over the prairie. Along the edge of the river, she could see the leaves beginning to turn from the dark green of summer to a dozen different shades of oranges, yellows and reds. Her heart raced with excitement as she took in the view.

Kate and Cole had gone to Hidetown for supplies and intended to spend the night visiting with friends.Ned and the men had been gone for two days, rebuilding burned out fences on the west side of the ranch, and she decided to spend the day riding the north pasture where most of the mama cows with younger calves were held. She gloried in the beauty of the scene, "God certainly knows how to paint a pretty picture, Peg," she said to her roan mare as she stopped on top of the cliff which marked the caprock. Below, she could see the valley floor and the thin blue ribbon of water which was shaded by the huge cottonwood trees .

As she sat in the saddle, basking in the beauty of the moment, she heard a noise behind her. Turning, she was surprised to see Big Red, the two thousand pound longhorn steer which had led the first Ceebara herd to the plains from her ranch on the Brazos River.

Smiling, she greeted the old steer, "Red, you old son-of-a-gun, you startled me. I guess you've come begging again."

Red had been on so many trail drives, that he had become gentle as a dog. On the trail, he would approach the chuck wagon and beg for sugar. Biscuit would usually give him a spoonful then rub his ears and neck and send him back to the herd.

Any time he was kept in the pasture around the ranch house, he would come to Belle's kitchen door and sound his approach with a loud bawl. Belle or Kate would have to acknowledge his presence with a spoonful of sugar and a little petting.

Cole had even taught the old steer some tricks -- by tapping him on his front knees, he could get Red to lie down, then he would crawl onto his back and ride him around the yard.

Belle dismounted and rubbed the old fellow on the head and neck and apologized, "Sorry, Red, I don't have any sweets for you today. I promise to bring some the next time I ride this pasture."

Remounting, she spoke to Peg, "We may as well ride to the river and take our fill of cool water before we start back."

Peg's ears twitched and she nodded her head as if agreeing with Belle's suggestion. She moved down the gentle incline and struck a ground-eating trot. Reaching the river, Belle dismounted and allowed the mare to drink, then kneeled next to a quite pool and dipped several hands full of the cool liquid to her lips.

A doe deer, trailed by a spotted fawn, bounded from a plum thicket and stopped next to the streams edge and looked at Belle with large, dark, unblinking eyes. Belle stood motionless and returned the stare, smiling at the doe. Apparently deciding that the woman and horse offered no danger to her and her fawn, she stepped into the water and began to drink. When she had taken her fill, she nudged the fawn and they bounded back into the protection of the thicket.

Noticing a couple of circling buzzards in the sky to the west, Belle decided to investigate. Riding through the canopy of cottonwood trees along the river's bank, she soon found the remains of a yearling calf which seemed to have recently been killed by animals. The two buzzards took wing as she and Peg approached.

Dismounting, she examined the area around the carcass and discovered several large animal footprints. "Wolves," she said to Peg, "looks like five or six. I'll have to tell Cole and Chief and send them on a hunting trip."

The mare was not comfortable next to the dead yearling, and looked about nervously. "Smell those wolves, don't you, girl," Belle said as she examined the tracks.

Stepping back into the saddle, she again spoke to the mare,"time to head for home, Peg," as she urged the mare up a steep, sandy bank. Soon they had reached the trail which led to the cut in the caprock, and climbed to the prairie on top.

Belle, lost in her thoughts, was relaxed, sitting loosely in the saddle when she heard the sound -- the high pitched rattle of a disturbed rattlesnake. At the sound, Peg jumped to the side and Belle lost her right stirrup. Apparently the snake struck at Peg's leg, missed, and the mare made another leap. Belle lost her balance and fell, striking her head on a rock. Her world went black.

The excited mare bolted into a run away from the scene and struck out for home. Fortunately, the snake crawled back into its den under one of the caprock boulders.

The sun was setting when Belle finally regained consciousness. Lying on her back, she tried to remember what had happened. Her head throbbed and she placed her hand on the knot and discovered dried blood which had flowed from a deep gash in her forehead. Pulling herself to a sitting position, she looked around for the snake, thinking she had probably been bitten since her leg was filled with pain.

The snake was gone -- she tried to stand and realized that the pain was not the result of a snake bite, but a broken bone. Looking at her leg, she could see that it was bent at an odd angle just below the knee.

"This is a fine kettle of fish," she thought, "darkness coming on, a broken leg and no horse." She felt at her side for her Colt -- it was gone. Then she remembered, she had decided she wouldn't need the heavy thing on such a short pleasure ride. She had brought her Winchester and stuffed it into the saddle boot, but now with Peg gone, the rifle was also gone.

She couldn't decide which hurt the most, her head or her broken leg. But even with the pain, she remembered what had caused her troubles in the first place -- the rattle snake! "I must put some distance between me and that snake," she thought as she began to slowly crawl away from the rock strewn caprock and onto the smooth grass of the prairie, watching closely to make certain the snake had not moved in that direction.

After crawling no more than a hundred yards, she was forced to stop -- the pain was too intense to go further. She shuddered, realizing that there was no hope of any one finding her before morning, night was coming on and the wind had shifted to the north. Looking back towards the river, her heart raced. Low clouds in the distance could mean only one thing, an early fall cold front was moving in. And she didn't like the looks of the clouds, they were carrying moisture -- rain or possibly even snow!

Hurting too much to move further, she pulled herself into a ball and began to cry. Whether it was the noise of her crying, or the smell of the blood from her head wound, her situation became even worse when she recognized the dark forms of the wolf pack slowly circling her position.

She sat up, removed her hat and began shaking it at the skulking wolves, screaming at the top of her lungs for the animals to leave her alone. Her actions resulted in the pack moving back into the darkness, but she could still hear them circling her position. She realized it was only a matter of time before the smell of the blood would overcome their fear and the wolves would attack.

She continued to scream as once again she could see their forms as they moved closer. They were now close enough that she could see their eyes glowing with anticipation and their tongues dripping with saliva.

"Ned," she cried, "please help me!"

But Ned was many miles away, sitting around the campfire with the fence building crew, chewing on a steak which had been served up by Biscuit -- and unaware that Belle was in trouble. He was, however, looking closely at the approaching storm front.

Thoughts flashed through her mind of her beloved Colonel Jim -- and the good times they had together riding these prairies before he was gunned down on the streets of Dodge City. As if he was present, she thought she heard him say, "Be calm, dear Belle, I am with you." Her fright left and she began to think rationally.

She had no weapon, not even a tree limb or a rock. If she crawled back to the cliff's edge, she could get rocks to throw at the wolves, but she realized if she made a move to escape, the pack would attack. She must remain where she was and hope the wolves would continue to be frightened of her screams.

Reaching slowly to her good leg, she removed her boot -- it wasn't much, but if the animals attacked she would have something to use as a club.

One of the pack moved closer, almost close enough that she could smell his stinking breath. "This is it," she thought, "dear Jim, we will soon be reunited."

She could not imagine what it would be like to be torn apart by the sharp teeth of the vicious wolves. Determined to defend herself, she brought the boot over her head, ready to strike the brute as he moved in.

Suddenly, a dark shadow appeared behind the circling wolf pack, and with head lowered, Big Red rushed onto the scene! With horns slashing, he caught the wolves by surprise, and a sharp, four foot horn plunged through the body of the first one! The wolf yelped in pain as the huge bovine raised his head with the wolf impaled on his horn, shook his head and threw the wounded animal into the darkness.

Never letting up, he knocked the next wolf to the ground and mauled him with his head and feet. The animal, screaming in pain ran from the angry steer, it too, disappeared into the darkness.

The remainder of the pack, realizing they were no match for this huge apparition which had appeared out of the night, tucked tails between their legs and disappeared towards the river.

Belle couldn't believe her eyes, Big Red stood over her, looking around as if challenging the wolf pack to return. Lying on the grass beneath his front legs, she reached up and rubbed his neck. "Thank you, Red -- oh thank you!" she said. Red stood over her and refused to move until he was certain the wolves would not return, then stepped back and lowered his nose to Belle's wounded head. His big tongue came out and tenderly licked her forehead.

Sitting up, she took his head in her arms and rubbed it gently, and began to laugh uncontrollably. "Red, you just re-paid me for all of that sugar I have given you through the years. But if I live through this, I promise that you will get a larger portion from now on!"

She didn't have much time to be thankful for being saved from the wolf pack, the cold front blew in with a vengeance and the first flakes of snow began to fall. Belle shivered as she realized that she had been saved from the wolf pack only to face the chance of being frozen to death on the prairie.

Then she remembered Cole teaching Red to lie down. It appeared that the steer had no intention of leaving her on the prairie by herself, so she gently tapped his front knees with her palm. Red looked at her in confusion before remember-ing what he had learned several years before. He dropped to his knees, then his hind legs folded below him and he was lying on the grass next to her.

Dragging her broken leg and gritting her teeth to keep from screaming at the pain, Belle curled up between his legs, drawing herself as close to his warm hide as possible. "Please don't move, Red," she asked, as the snow fell softly around them and the huge body protected her from the blow-ing wind.

* * * * * * * *

Ned realized that the weather was in for a drastic change

when he saw the low clouds approaching from the west. After the crew had completed their meal, he gave orders to break camp and return to headquarters. They would have to ride all night, but that would be better than to be caught on the plains if a full-fledged blizzard blew in.

Reaching the barn at daylight, Ned was confused to see Belle's mare, standing at the gate, with saddle and bridle still on. Smokey took Peg's reins and led the mare into the barn out of the wind and snow.

"That's not like Miss Belle to go off and leave her horse saddled, Mr. Ned," he said.

A worried look on his face, Ned nodded and replied, "You're right, Smokey. Tend to my horse, I'm going to the house and see what could be the matter."

"Belle!" he shouted as he entered the house.

No answer -- "Belle, are you O.K.?" he once again shouted as he looked in Belle's bedroom. The bed had not been slept in.

Rushing from the house, he returned to the barn where Pedro was helping Smokey with the horses.

"What about Miss Belle," Ned asked the boy, "do you know where she is?"

"No, Senor Ned," Pedro replied. "She left early yesterday morning to check the cows in the north pasture. I was working on the corrals and didn't see her when she came in."

"Apparently she didn't come in," Ned said. "Her horse must have come in without her."

Turning to Smokey, Ned ordered, "Saddle some fresh

horses and harness a fresh span of mules. I'll tell the men to put on some dry clothes and get ready to ride. Something bad must have happened, and if she has been out all night in this weather, no telling what kind of condition we'll find her in."

Within thirty minutes, twelve mounted cowboys, and Biscuit driving the chuck wagon, climbed the caprock to the north and struck out across the prairie towards the Canadian River. The snow was beginning to let up, but the grass was covered with four inches of the wet powder. The sun was beginning to break through the clouds to the east.

Two hours later, they arrived at the cut in the caprock where Belle had ridden down into the Canadian River valley the previous day. Ned believed that this would have been the route she would have taken, although they had seen no sign of her. The snow had covered any trail she might have left.

"Chief, you take half the crew and ride along the cap down river. Stay on top so you can see into the valley. If you find her, shoot three times and we'll come running. Biscuit, you follow me with the chuck wagon, and I'll take the rest of the crew along the west rim. If you hear me fire my rifle, hustle back to our position. Let's go!"

Ned noticed several cows with calves following, heading towards the valley, but still hadn't found Belle. Then he saw the big steer lying a short distance from the caprock cliff.

"That's strange," he told Smokey. "That looks like old Red but he shouldn't be laying around with all the other cattle up and heading for the river. He must be sick. Ride over and check on him, I'm going to search this canyon up ahead."

Smokey kicked his bay into a lope towards the steer. Big Red continued to lie in the grass chewing his cud and watched as Smokey approached.

"Lord have mercy," Smokey shouted, "It's Miss Belle! Mr. Ned, it's Miss Belle!"

Ned heard his call, pulled his Colt and fired three times into the air as he kicked the buckskin into a run.

Belle was curled between the huge steer's legs, snow had piled on her head and back, but she was breathing. Smokey was brushing away the snow when Ned pulled up and dismounted. Big Red refused to move while they examined her, discovering that her leg was broken.

Biscuit pulled up with the chuck wagon and Ned asked if he had anything in the wagon which could be used for a splint. "Yes, sir," the old cook said, as he dug into the cook box and pulled out two large, long handled spoons which he used to stir his food over the cook fire.

Tearing some strips of cloth from one of his aprons, he held the spoons in place as Ned began to wrap the cloth around the broken leg.

Belle's eyes opened, and through chattering teeth, she asked weakly, "Biscuit, you got any sugar for my friend, Red?"

"Yes, Miss Belle," Biscuit said, wiping a tear from his eye, "I'll get him a whole cupfull!"

After getting the leg splinted securely, Ned and Smokey lifted Belle from between the steer's legs, loaded her on a bed of saddle blankets in the chuck wagon, and covered her with a tarp.

Big Red waited until Belle had been removed, slowly got

up and stretched, licked the cup of sugar which Biscuit set before him, then moved slowly towards the other cattle which were walking down the trail to the river below, satisfied that he had protected his mistress from harm.

12

The early snow which had caught Belle on the prairie was just a harbinger of things to come. The winter of 1886 was one of the worst in history. One norther after the other roared across the plains, dumping several inches of snow. Then, in January, the worst blizzard of the century hit, dumping two feet of snow with fifty mile an hour winds. The snow fell and the north wind blew for three days, while the temperature dropped below zero. Trains in Kansas became snowbound and could not move.

In the blinding snow, cattle started drifting from Kansas into the Oklahoma Panhandle, then into the Texas Panhandle. Many fell exhausted and froze to death as they drifted south. Reaching the drift fence north of the Canadian River, they could go no farther. Unable to continue walking with the wind to their backs, they froze to death, piling one on top of the other until the fence was lined with piles of dead cattle for the entire two hundred miles of the drift fence. A person could walk for miles along the fence, on top of dead cattle without ever stepping on the prairie floor.

Tens of thousands of cattle were found frozen to death after the weather cleared, and many small ranches were completely wiped out. Most of the larger ranches found themselves in financial difficulty when they tallied their herds in the spring roundup and discovered how many cattle had perished.

Ned's policy of keeping the Ceebara herd along the creeks and rivers below the caprock during the winter, offered protection for his cattle and they did not drift any farther than the North Fork of the Red River. His losses during the storm were minimal.

However, the coming of spring found all of the cattle weak, and during heel fly season, bog riders were kept busy along the river pulling the weakened cattle from the clutches of the quicksand. Cole and Chief were assigned the area of the river on the western property line of the Ceebara ranch, riding west along the banks for half a day, then back to their camp by nightfall. The next day was spent eastward along the river bank, then back to camp by night fall.

Ceebara cattle, having wintered better than those of other ranches, were stronger and presented less trouble in the sand, therefore, Cole and Chief rode farther west, up the river, helping bog riders from the LX and LS ranches who had their hands full trying to keep the weak cattle pulled from the quicksand. "Cole, we're much obliged for your help," Ed King, LS bog rider said, as they struggled to pull a emaciated cow from a bog near Tascosa.

"You're welcome," Ed, Cole responded as he kicked Comanche in the ribs and urged him to keep the slack out of the lariat which was looped around the cows horns. Ed was in the water behind the cow, pushing and twisting her tail. The cow bellered, put a little more effort in lifting her front legs and soon was free of the sand. Cole pulled her from the water's edge and Chief threw his rope under her belly and caught her hind legs, pulling them from beneath her. She fell to her side, Cole moved Comanche forward and Ed released his rope from her horns. Chief moved Badger forward two steps, the rope slackened and the cow kicked free, stood and wobbled slowly up the sandy bank.

Fred Chilton, Frank Valley and John Lang struggled with another cow a short distance upstream from Cole. They soon had all of the bogged cattle free, dismounted and sat exhausted in the shade of a huge cottonwood tree.

The LS cowboys pulled cigarette makings from their shirt pockets and began rolling smokes. Cole and Chief refused offerings of the Bull Durham sacks, and instead, cut a plug of tobacco from a square of Brown Mule, placed it in their jaws and began to chew. No one said a word until the cigarettes were lit and the first smoke inhaled.

Ed was the first to break the silence, "Damned if this hasn't been a helluva year," he said. "First the big fire destroyed half of our winter range, then the blizzard hit in January and froze half of our herd, and now the heel flies are the worse I've ever seen. Looks like the river's trying to drown the rest of our herd."

Cole spit a brown liquid stream into the sand and replied, "Yep, it's been a year to remember, Ed. Some folks over in Hidetown are trying to blame everything on the XIT bringing in so many cattle at once."

"How they figure that could cause so much trouble," Frank asked. "Ain't no one could cause a blizzard like we had in January."

Cole nodded, "That's right, but they're saying the fire was started by an XIT wagon crew, and after the fire there just wasn't enough grass left to feed the hundred thousand head of cattle which the XIT owners brought in."

Fred took a drag on his cigarette, then spoke. "That's right. We've even found wire cut between the LS and XIT where their cowboys drove large herds of cattle off of their burned range onto our grass. Mr. Mac is fighting mad about that."

Chief had been listening in silence with a smile on his face.

"What you smiling about, Chief?" Cole asked. "You look like a possum that just swallowed a ripe persimmon."

"I was just thinking," Chief replied, " we Indians never did have this kind of trouble with our buffalo. No fences, no fires, and no bogs. Buffalo are smarter than cattle, they stay away from quicksand, they don't freeze to death in blizzards and if the grass is gone in one area, they just move to where the grass is better. White man kills all the buffalo, builds fences and brings in longhorn cattle that don't have enough sense to stay out of bogs or to find shelter during a blizzard -- so you work like hell to try to keep them alive, then drive them two hundred miles to cattle buyers who steal them from you."

He spit a brown stream onto a grasshopper that had landed three feet from his boot, looked at the other cowboys and smiled mischievously. They thought about what he had said, then all began to laugh

"Leave it to a damned injun to put us in our place," Ed said.

They sat around and rested for half an hour before resuming the work of locating and pulling more bogged cows out of the quicksand. As the sun reached the western horizon, Ed pulled his horse up next to Cole's and said, "Ain't but three miles to Tascosa. Me and the boys are going to ride into town and renew some old acquaintances with the crib ladies. Why don't you and Chief join us?"

Mr. Mac had cautioned his bog riders to stay away from the saloons in Tascosa. Tempers were running high and already there had been clashes between the cowboys who had refused to join in the cowboy strike and those who had been blacklisted by the big ranch owners. Most of the blacklisted cowboys around Tascosa blamed the LS manager for breaking the strike, and Mr. Mac was concerned that his men might be murdered if they showed up in town.

The animosity had increased when the Panhandle Livestock Association hired Pat Garrett to take charge of their home rangers, with orders to track down all cattle rustlers and maverick branders. Mr. Mac had allowed the Home Rangers to establish their base of operations at the Alamocitas

LS headquarters, and the rangers became known as LS men.

The first thing Captain Garrett did to instigate trouble between the two sides, was to issue three edicts -- one, no civilian was to be allowed to wear sixshooters or other firearms -- two, small cattle owners could not participate in the cooperative roundups to 'protect' their brands -- three, many of the small rancher's brands were declared outlaw brands and any cattle carrying those brands were to be considered property of the county.

Tascosa was split down the middle, with the Upper Tascosa saloons taking the side of the big ranchers and the Home Rangers, while the Lower Tascosa (Hogtown) saloons taking the side of the small ranchers and the blacklisted cowboys.

"I don't know, Ed," Cole said. "We had a run in with three of the strikers over in Hidetown. Tempers are running pretty high -- we might should stay out of town until things kinda cool down."

"Hell, Cole, we got just as much right to be in town enjoying a few drinks and carousing with the ladies as the Systems boys. They're not apt to make trouble if there's six of us ride in," Ed argued. "Besides, I know you're a friend of Casimiro Romero and he's throwing a *baile* in his plaza. All the pretty Mexican senoritas will be there."

Cole thought about it for awhile before finally agreeing. "O.K., Ed, but if trouble starts, we're lighting a shuck out of there."

* * * * * * * *

Ed was correct, all of the pretty Mexican senoritas were at the Romero plaza. The six bog riders, after bathing in the Canadian River, joined the revelers at the plaza and danced the evening away. Casimiro welcomed Cole and Chief, inquiring about Ned, Belle and Kate, and joined them in a drink of some of his imported Mexican Tequila.

Piedad, Casimiro's pretty daughter grabbed Cole's arm and pulled him to the dance floor, laughing at his embarrassment. "I don't know how to dance," Cole confessed, but she insisted she would teach him.

Piedad was a good teacher and soon she had him doing about as well as any of the visiting cowboys. When Cole began to sweat from the activity of trying to keep in step with Piedad, she led him to the punch table, and they shared a glass of lemonade.

"How is Manuel?" she asked as they stepped to the shadows of the porch.

"He's fine," Cole answered, smiling. "Except he is always talking about you and pining to come and visit."

She blushed, and told him that she, too, could hardly wait until Manuel would once again pay her a visit.

"I 'spect you two should get married," Cole said, "since it's apparent that you love each other very much."

"Manuel says he wishes to wait until he has more money -- maybe by Christmas," she answered wistfully.

They walked back into the hall and joined the other celebrants. Ed caught Cole's eye and motioned that they were leaving. "Sally Emory sent word that she wants to meet me in Hogtown," he said. "Maybe you and Chief should go with us."

Sally Emory was the queen of Jenkin's saloon, and had been the sweetheart of Lem Woodruff, a former LX cowpuncher and now bartender in the saloon.

"I don't think so," Cole replied. "You're just asking for trouble if you go down there."

Ed had told him that he had taken Sally away from Lem, and he and Lem had a cuss fight the last time he was in town. Lem had taken up with Rocking Chair Emma, which had peeved Sally, and she had been urging Ed to kill Woodruff.

Cole believed that fighting over the affections of one of the painted ladies could spark an all out war between the Systems boys and the Home Ranger crowd.

"Why don't we get our horses and ride back to camp, Ed. There's no sense in taking on the whole town over some gal that will take up with anyone who has two dollars to spend for a frolic in her bed," Cole pleaded.

But Ed had made up his mind -- he had come to town to see Sally, and he wasn't leaving until he had his meeting. "You and Chief go ahead. Me and the boys are going to make a visit to Jenkin's saloon."

"Let's get our horses and head back to camp, Chief," Ned said. "Ain't no use in arguing with a hardheaded jackass like Ed."

Walking to Mickey McCormick's livery stable, Ned and Chief saddled their horses, mounted and rode down Main Street. Seeing Valley and Chilton inside the bar, Cole decided to try one more time to get them to ride back to camp.

"Ed and John have gone after the horses, we'll be coming along directly," Frank said as he placed a bet in the poker game he had joined.

After getting their horses, Ed decided they should see if they could find Sally before leaving. Riding to Hogtown, they stopped in front of Jenkin's saloon and Sally came out. Ed stepped down from his horse and took her in his arms, patted her on the rear and kissed her passionately. She whispered something to him, and they walked towards her crib down Spring Street.

John continued to sit his horse, holding the reins of Ed's sorrel. "Won't be but a minute," Ed shouted to John, laughing.

It was the last words he would ever utter -- a shot rang out from the shadows of Jenkin's saloon and he fell dead with a rifle bullet in the head. Lem Woodruff rushed from the shadows, placed the muzzle of the Winchester to Ed's throat and pulled the trigger.

Sally ran screaming down the street, and John Lang kicked his horse into a run towards the Equity Bar.

Cole had heard the shots and a feeling of dread passed through his mind. Grabbing Chief, he rushed to the door of the Equity as John pulled up in a cloud of dust, screaming -- "They've killed Ed! The've killed Ed!"

Frank Valley and Fred Chilton rushed to the door, grabbed John and shouted, "where!"

"In front of Jenkin's saloon," Lang answered. "I seen it all, they blowed his head clean off!"

Rushing to the scene, the five bog riders were met by

a stream of bullets from the saloon where Woodruff and three of his friends had holed up. Before they could turn around and find shelter from the bullets, Cole was knocked from the saddle with a bullet to the shoulder. Chief quickly dismounted, pulling his saddle gun from its boot and began pumping lead into the saloon as he stood over Cole.

"Get out of here, Chief," Cole said through clenched teeth, "before they kill you too!'

Chief kneeled next to Cole and looked at the wound. Pulling his neckerchief from around his neck, he plugged the hole and stopped the flow of blood. More shots rang out from the saloon and Chief felt a burning in his left arm. Flexing his fingers, he discovered that nothing was broken, and pumped another volley of shots into the door of the saloon. He heard someone scream from behind the door.

Pulling Cole to his feet, Chief helped him onto his horse, mounted Badger, and they quickly disappeared into the night.

Lang, Valley and Chilton continued to stand over the body of Ed King while pumping lead into the saloon. Other men appeared on the scene to back up the LS boys, while the sound of additional guns began firing from the darkness behind the saloon as friends of Woodruff joined the battle.

For five minutes the night was filled with the roaring sound of guns as both sides fired into the darkness. Sheriff Jim East and his deputy, hearing the gun play, quickly dressed and rushed to the scene, too late. The bodies of King, Chilton and Valley lay dead in the street. Further investigation disclosed the body of Jesse Sheets, lying in the doorway of his restaurant across the street. He had been hit in the head when Valley mistook him for one of Woodruff's friends.

Woodruff had been hit twice, once in the stomach and once in the groin. Charley Emory had taken a bullet in the leg which was bleeding profusely.

Chief led Cole's horse to Casimiro Romero's plaza and shouted for help. The old don rushed from the house and helped Chief carry Cole inside. All of the guests had departed and the Romero family was preparing for bed.

Piadad appeared, dressed only in her nightgown, and gasped when she saw Cole, lying on the bed with blood covering his chest. She rushed to the kitchen, grabbed some clean dishtowels and a pan of water and returned to Cole's side. As she began to wash the blood from the wound, she asked her father to bring a bottle of whiskey.

Chief held Cole down while she poured the whiskey liberally over the wound. Cole screamed as the burning liquid filled the hole in his shoulder. Chief turned Cole onto his side where they could see his back and discovered that the rifle bullet had passed through his body, leaving a nasty wound where it had exited. Luckily, however, the shot was high enough that it hit no vital organs and low enough that it broke no bones.

After cleaning the wound and stopping the bleeding, Piadad poured the remaining whiskey into a glass and ordered Cole to drink it. The whiskey soon dulled the pain and Cole smiled.

"Thanks Chief, for getting me out of there. It looked like I was a goner," he said.

Chief smiled, "I couldn't leave you there, you still owe me five dollars for losing that bet that you could ride that black bronc last week. Well as I remember, you only lasted about three jumps before he threw you into the corral fence."

Cole laughed, "I thought you'd forgotten all about that bet," he said.

Piedad noticed that Chief was holding his arm, "What's wrong," she asked, then saw the blood between his fingers.

"Why, you've been shot," she said, "let me see!"

"Just a scratch," Chief said, removing his hand.

The bullet had passed through his shirt and cut a shallow gash in the flesh of his arm. It was more than just a scratch, but not deep enough to cause any concern.

Piedad washed the blood away and poured some whiskey over the wound before wrapping a clean cloth around it.

A servant brought hot coffee and the group sat around and talked about the night's events.

"We were actually just innocent bystanders," Cole told Casimiro. "When we heard that Ed had been shot, we rode in to help get him to a doc, not expecting to be bushwhacked by a bunch of hidden gunmen. I had warned Ed about going into Hogtown tonight, but he wouldn't listen. Now I expect he's dead, and no telling how many more. With all the shooting that was going on, there could be a dozen killed. I'd just as soon you didn't say anything to anybody about us getting caught in the crossfire, Senor Romero, at least not until we find out exactly what happened."

"I've sent Pedro to find out what happened," Casimiro said. "He should be back soon."

* * * * * * * *

Dunk Cage and his brother Hays, LS riders, had been in town before the gun battle, but had mounted their horses and headed for the Alomocitas headquarters, not wishing to get involved in any kind of argument with Ed. They had only gone about a half mile from Tascosa when they heard the first shots being fired. Suspecting that the bog riders had gotten themselves into trouble, they turned their horses and rode hard back to town. Too late, they reached the battle ground and found their three friends lying dead in the street.

"My God, Dunk, this is terrible," Hays said, looking with disbelief on the scene.

Dunk, shaking his head in disgust, said, "I'm riding to the ranch and fetch Mr. Mac. You start notifying all the boys from the camps. Looks like we've got a war on our hands!"

Shortly after two o'clock in the morning, Dunk rode into the Alomocitas headquarters compound on his winded horse and rushed to the ranch house door. "Mr. Mac, Mr. Mac," he shouted as he pounded on the door.

McAllister opened the door, dressed only in his long johns. "Dunk, what's the matter," he shouted, shaking the boy by the shoulders.

"Mr. Mac," Dunk said, breathlessly, "they've killed Ed, Frank and Fred in Tascosa."

The ranch manager couldn't believe what he was hearing, and stood speechless. Mrs. McAllister joined them at the door. "Who killed them, Dunk?' she asked.

"I don't know, ma'am. It's awful -- they were still lying in the street when I left."

McAllister found his voice, and angrily ordered, "Get the boys up, Dunk, we're going to town."

"I'm going with you," Mrs. McAllister said as she rushed into the bedroom to get dressed.

Lon Chambers brought up the buckboard and the McAllisters climbed in. He took one side and Kid Dobbs took the other as armed guards of Mr. Mac and Miss Annie. The rest of the LS men brought up the rear as they headed for Tascosa, not knowing whether they would be bushwhacked on the way in or not.

By the time they reached town, the three LS boys had been moved to the porch on Wright and Farnsworth's store and were covered with a tarpaulin. Mr. Mac immediately had the bodies moved to a vacant room in a nearby adobe house. Next, he sent a telegram to Lee and Scott, informing them what had happened.

The town began to fill with armed cowboys from the surrounding area as the news spread through the country. Every man on the LS payroll rode in, ready to do battle with whoever was responsible for the killings. Systems men also began to show up and take sides and it looked as if Tascosa was about to erupt in an all out war between the two factions.

Mr. Mac called his men together and warned that if any of them started trouble, they would be fired on the spot.

Sheriff East and several local influential men were able to keep the Woodruff supporters in line, and soon peace was established.

The funeral was held the next day with over five hundred people joining the procession up Main Street to the Boot Hill Cemetery. Mr. Mac and Miss Annie, in a buckboard, followed the wagon bearing the three dead LS cowboys, with Chambers and Dobbs, well armed, riding shot gun. Seventy two LS cowboys, riding two by two, followed the buckboard, then Tascosa towns people and cowboy friends joined the funeral cortege.

There was no clergyman in Tascosa, so Mr. Mac asked a young lawyer, H.H. Wallace to conduct the funeral. From an old Anglican version of the Holy Bible, Wallace read the Twenty-third Psalm, then closed with, "Dust-to-dust." C.B. Vivian reached for a handful of the dry West Texas soil and sprinkled it gently on the three homemade caskets. Several of the friends of the three LS cowboys began to shovel dirt over the wooden caskets.

Mrs. Sheets, blaming the cowboys for her husbands death, refused to have him buried near them. When the Sheets funeral cortege arrived, the people moved from the cowboys' graves to the grave of Jesse Sheets, and participated in his burial.

LS cowboys, reluctant to leave the grave side of their friends, remained until every one had left, then mounted their horses, and led the three riderless horses of Ed, Frank, and Fred, two-by-two by the grave, each removing his hat in silent tribute to their friends.

One old cook, as he rode by, doffed his hat and said softly, "adios, compadres."

* * * * * * * *

Ned, Belle and Kate, with several of the Ceebara cowboys attended the funeral, and after determining that Cole was able to travel, took the trail back to Red Deer Creek. On the second day, the sun had set and a bright, full moon had risen on the eastern horizon when the Ceebara family finally arrived on the lip of the caprock, overlooking the valley of the Red Deer Creek.

The valley was bathed in moonlight as they looked with awe on the pristine beauty of the scene -- the small creek, the cottonwood trees, and the outline of the ranch compound far below. A small herd of buffalo, all that remained of the once huge herds, was grazing contentedly along the edge of the caprock on the prairie grass to their left, while to their right could be seen an equal number of longhorn cattle. The moonlight reflected off their magnificent horns and multicolored hides. Overhead, millions of sparkling stars cast their glow across the darkened sky, as a huge meteor sped from one horizon to the other, leaving a trail of fire behind.

The cowboys continued to set their horses, while Ned, Cole, Belle and Kate stepped down from the buckboard and walked to the cliff's edge, looking in silence at the beautiful setting.Suddenly, from among the mounted cowboys came a beautiful tenor voice, one that Ned had heard many times on the trail as the night riders sang to the herd -- *Oh, give me a home, where the buffalo roam, where the deer and the antelope play; where seldom is heard, a discouraging word, and the skies are not cloudy all day.*

How often at night, when the heavens are bright, and the light from the glittering stars; have I stood there amazed, and asked as I gazed, if their glory exceeds that of ours.

Home, home on the range, where the deer and the antelope play; where never is heard, a discouraging word, and the skies are not cloudy all day.

As the words of the song softly echoed from the depths below, the family moved slowly down the steep trail to their wilderness home on the range.

Epilogue

In 1887, the first railroads entered the Texas Panhandle -- and with the sound of the steam engines roaring and the black smoke curling along the tracks, the land of grass and cattle rushed towards civilization.

A blessing to most of the Panhandle, the railroads were a death knell to the first three towns. When the Fort Worth and Denver City Railroad bypassed Clarendon (Saint's Roost) by five and a half miles to the south, the town fathers voted to move the town -- lock, stock and barrel -- to a new town site on the railroad.

When the Santa Fe railroad missed Mobeetie (Hidetown) by two miles to the north, a new town site named New Mobeetie was established with a depot on the railroad.

The Fort Worth and Denver City Railroad, as it crawled slowly to the north, bypassed the town of Tascosa, laying its tracks across the Canadian River to the south, and the old buffalo hunter camp and cowboy center, died a peaceful death.

The large foreign owned cattle ranches, including the XIT, had failed miserably to show a profit during all of their years of operation, and the investors were anxious to find a way out. The railroads offered that exit, for with the railroads came the settlers and sod busters, anxious for cheap land where they could grow their crops. The ranch owners began to sell off small parcels of land to the settlers for $2.50 to $5.00 per acre, and for the first time in their history, began to show a profit for the investors.

Within a very short time, the huge cattle ranches had disappeared, replaced by smaller, family owned ranches and farms. More barbed wire fences were built, windmills were erected, and dugout and sod homes were replaced with wooden structures. The grass was plowed out and wheat, cotton and grain sorghum began to grow where once the buffalo and longhorn cattle had roamed on the flat prairies.

The Goodnight-Adair JA ranch had gown to over a million acres with one hundred thousand head of cattle grazing its pastures by 1887, and Goodnight decided to terminate the partnership, allowing the Adairs to keep his beloved Palo Duro Canyon holdings. He took his share of the holdings to the south of the canyon. He did, however, continue to operate a profitable cattle ranch until his death in 1929.

The Lee and Scott LS ranch, continued to be operated by family members until 1905, when they sold the eastern half of the ranch to Edward Swift of the Swift Packing Company for $2.25 an acre. The western half was sold to the Landergin brothers, who had ranch holdings which joined the LS.

William Bush purchased the Frying Pan and continued to operate it as a family ranch for many years.

Outlaw Bill Moore escaped the clutches of the law and was never tried for cattle rustling, but was finally killed in Alaska by the noted sourdough gunfighter, Soapy Smith.

Much of the Ceebara Ranch was sold, with Ned, Belle, Kate and Cole keeping the best part of the ranch as a family operation. Ned ran for and was elected to the Senate seat which had been held by his friend, Temple Houston, and served in that capacity with honor for several years.

Cole remained on the ranch, becoming a highly respected cattleman in the state, building one of the best herds of Hereford cattle in the west.

Jim Bold Eagle, "Chief", remained on the ranch with Cole until another Oklahoma Cherokee half-breed, Will Rogers, convinced him to join him in performing in Colonel Mulhall's Wild West Show, demonstrating their prowess with a rope in Madison Square Garden and all over the world.

Comanche Chief Quanah Parker became a noted cattleman, ruled the Comanche Nation in Oklahoma for years, hunted wolves on the reservation with President Teddy Roosevelt, leased Indian grasslands to and became friends of Burke Burnett of the 6666 ranch and Dan Waggoner of the reversed triple D ranch. The lease money was prorated out to members of his tribe. He continued to make annual trips to the Red River country in the Texas Panhandle to visit his friends, Charles Goodnight and Ned Armstrong, and hunting in their protected buffalo herds.

Temple Houston moved his family from Mobeetie to Canadian, Texas, and established a private law practice. But when his beloved Texas Panhandle became too civilized, he moved across the line into Oklahoma Indian Territory at Woodward, at the time of the famous land run.

Opening a law office in Woodward, when the town consisted of a jumble of tents and hastily constructed wooden buildings, he became the most noted and respected criminal lawyer in the west. Any time that Lawyer Houston was to be in court to defend a client, the entire community turned out to hear him, knowing that something historic in the annals of law was about to happen. One of the trials in which Lawyer Houston exceeded his courtroom antics, and which is still a topic of conversation in the west, took place in Enid, Oklahoma. Temple was defending a friendless cowboy who was being tried for horse stealing and murder of the animal's owner, a local rancher. The rancher had a reputation of being a quick-triggered, hotheaded gun slinger.

The courthouse was packed as the jury was picked and the trial began. Temple noted that most of the jurors did not seem too friendly towards his client. He pleaded self-defense for the cowboy, even though several witnesses testified that he had shot and killed his victim without giving him an opportunity to draw his pistol.

The crowd was betting that this would be one case that Houston would lose when he offered no rebuttal to the witnesses. The prosecutor summarized his case with an impassioned plea and sat down.

Temple took a stance several paces away, facing the jury. Dressed in his flamboyant way -- long, black frock coat, yellow-beaded vest, Mexican satin-stripped bell-bottomed trousers, and with his pearl handled pistol strapped to his side -- he rose and took a menacing step towards the jury as he brushed his long auburn hair from his eyes.

"Gentlemen," he said, "you have heard my client charged with a crime which was completely out of his realm to commit. He could have no more have stood up to his malefactor than the spark from a lowly firefly could outshine the noonday sun -- could no more have outshot him than the stubborn, plodding jackass could outrun the fleetest race horse. Such things, gentlemen, are utter impossibilities."

The crowded courtroom became quiet as a mouse, as Temple moved forward towards the jury.

"Gentlemen, this malefactor had a gunman's reputation, while my client here is an ordinary, hard-working citizen like yourselves, little experienced in the use of firearms.

"My client was grievously wronged! He approached his malefactor in a spirit of charity and forgiveness, but this hard-hearted gunman spurned his friendly overtures and flew into a rage. When he saw this gunman coming at him, he knew his life was at stake."

The crowd moved forward in their seats, anxious to hear every word as Houston took one more menacing step, which brought him almost under the noses of the men in the box. There he bent over the pine railing, asking in his most confidential tone: "What would any of you worthy gentlemen have done in the face of such a character? Do you have any idea how you would have fared against the lightning draw of a gun-artist -- unless you had drawn first?"

The jurors leaned toward him, their nerves taut. Then, Houston tossed his long hair and roared: "This malefactor was so adept with a six-shooter that he could place a gun in the hands of an inexperienced man, then draw and fire his own weapon before his victim could pull the trigger. Like this!"

And, before the men could blink their eyes, he whipped the white-handled Colt from under his frock coat, pointed the revolver directly at them, and emptied it rapidly as the quiet courtroom was filled with the loud blast of the pistol.

Judge McAtee, forgetting his judicial dignity, made a hurried jump beneath the bench, the defendant dived under the table, and the jurors abandoned the jury box and joined the spectators in a stampede for the doors and windows.

Looking surprised and innocent, Houston holstered his weapon and turned his eyes toward Judge McAtee, who peered cautiously from beneath the rostrum.

"Your Honor," Houston smiled, "you need not have been afraid. My cartridges were all blanks."

Judge McAtee crawled from beneath the bench and ordered the bailiff to reassemble the jury. Then, glowing with anger, he informed the distinguished Houston that he was of a notion to plaster him with a heavy fine.

Houston bowed low and apologized for "any seeming disrespect for the person of this court -- I only wanted to show what speed this dead man possessed." In his most elegant and convincing tones he talked the judge out of citing him for contempt, and the trial proceeded.

He made his point. But the jury obviously felt that he had

made fools of them. They found the cowboy guilty.

Refusing to admit defeat, Temple immediately filed a motion for a new trial on grounds that the jury had "separated during the hearing and mingled with the crowd."

Judge McAtee, while unhappy over the affair, admitted that a strict rule of procedure had been violated. The jury was forbidden by law to leave the box and mingle with the crowd. The new trial was granted.

With a new impartial jury a few months later, the cowboy was acquitted.

Once again, Old Sam's boy, had stood out in a crowd, in both his dress and his knowledge of the law.

It was anticipated that Temple would someday move into Oklahoma politics, governor or senator, but fate prevented this from happening. On August 15, 1905, at the age of forty-five, he died of a massive hemorrhage of a blood vessel in the brain.

* * * * * * * *

Sometimes fact is more unbelievable than fiction.

The state of Texas did trade three million acres of land in exchange for the construction of the capitol building in Austin. The granite and marble structure is larger and taller than the nation's capitol building in Washington, D.C.

As a result of the trade, the three million acre XIT ranch, with over one hundred and fifty thousand head of cattle became the largest cattle ranch in Texas.

Temple Houston made a cattle drive from South Texas to

Montana before he was fifteen, became a lawyer when he was eighteen, was appointed district attorney in the Texas Panhandle when he was twenty, and was elected to the Texas Senate before he was twenty-five. He did participate in and won a fast draw and shooting contest with Billy the Kid and Bat Masterson in Tascosa.

Charles Goodnight parlayed eighteen hundred head of longhorn cattle into a million acre ranch and one hundred thousand head of cattle in ten years.

Deacon Bates, owner of the LX ranch, was involved with his ranch foreman, Outlaw Bill Moore, in stealing cattle from neighboring ranches.

Cap Arrington, former Texas Ranger and Sheriff of Wheeler County, did chase Deacon Bates to Boston, Massachusetts, arrested him for cattle rustling and brought him back to Texas for trial.

There were several grass fires in the Texas Panhandle which raged for days, destroying hundreds of thousands of acres of grass and killing thousands of livestock.

Tens of thousands of cattle were frozen to death when they piled up against the drift fence during the blizzard of 1886.

The cowboy strike and the big gun battle when four cowboys were killed on the streets of Tascosa did happen.

Most of the other events which are listed in Devil's *Rope*, actually happened -- maybe not one hundred percent the way they are described -- but if they didn't, they should have!